Dear Reader,

Bad boys can be fascinating. With this in mind I decided to write about some, and the result is a miniseries of Regencies that commences with *Mr. Trelawney's Proposal*. The novels feature heroes, linked by family or friendship, who are definite rogues—wickedly charming, wryly humorous, dangerously attractive. Good girls can't resist them. But innocence can be as captivating as sophistication: the heroines are more than a match for their jaded suitors.

Gentle widow Victoria Hart succeeds in taming and securing the devotion of cynical rake Viscount Courtenay in *A Kind and Decent Man*. His friend, Sir Richard Du Quesne, is equally predatory and disreputable in *The Silver Squire*, and relentlessly pursues unassuming spinster Emma Worthington...until *she* catches *him* and brings him very willingly to his knees.

As their separate stories unfold, the couples battle through a maelstrom of action and emotion. I hope you enjoy their passionate skirmishing, the laughter and tears that pave the way to harmony and happiness, as much as I have enjoyed writing the novels for you.

Mary Brendan

Mary Brendan was born in north London and lived there for nineteen years before marrying and migrating to Hertfordshire. She was grammar school educated and has been at various times in her working life a personnel secretary for an international oil company, a property developer and a landlady. Presently working part-time at a local library, she dedicates hard-won leisure time to antiques browsing, curries and keeping up with two lively sons.

MR. TRELAWNEY'S PROPOSAL
MARY BRENDAN

HARLEQUIN®

TORONTO • NEW YORK • LONDON
AMSTERDAM • PARIS • SYDNEY • HAMBURG
STOCKHOLM • ATHENS • TOKYO • MILAN • MADRID
PRAGUE • WARSAW • BUDAPEST • AUCKLAND

ISBN 0-373-51136-1

MR. TRELAWNEY'S PROPOSAL

Copyright © 1998 by Mary Brendan.

Visit us at www.eHarlequin.com

Printed in U.S.A.

Chapter One

1814

'So you are travelling back from visiting your sister in London, Miss Nash,' remarked that unpleasantly soft voice for the second time in five minutes.

'Indeed, yes, I am,' Rebecca Nash agreed, struggling to keep impatience from her voice and revulsion from her eyes as she again raised them from her teacup to glance at the slightly built man sitting opposite her. Having redrawn her attention to himself, Rupert Mayhew lounged his wiry frame back into the battered leather wing-chair.

Rebecca forced a polite smile and tried to prevent her eyes from fixing too obviously on the arrangement of lank, greying strands of hair which threaded across the man's balding pate. At one time he must have had a thatch of gingery-fair hair, she guessed, judging by what remained. The colour would have been similar to those beastly yellow eyes that leeched on to her every movement.

During the twenty minutes or so since she had arrived, whenever she had shifted slightly on the ancient hide wing-chair, a pair with the one in which he was ensconced, his feline eyes had stared boldly as though anticipating something interesting might be revealed.

Rupert Mayhew slid his scrawny frame forward on his seat, enquiring solicitiously of the beautiful young woman opposite, 'And how is your dear sister? And the new babe? Well, I trust?'

'Thank you, yes,' Rebecca replied civilly, suppressing the urge to shrink back as he leaned towards her.

'My own dear wife is in the same delicate condition…as I believe I mentioned in my last letter to you,' he reminded her with a sly smirk.

This time Rebecca was unable to prevent a tremor of revulsion, clinking her delicate china cup against its saucer.

'Had she not been indisposed, Caroline would, of course, have been happy to meet with you today,' Rupert Mayhew informed her smoothly. 'But we are about to be blessed with our infant at any time now, so Dr Willis informs me. So my lady wife is staying with her dear sister in Shoreham for her confinement.' Yellow eyes slid from Rebecca's face to craftily linger on the closely buttoned bodice of her sprigged cotton gown.

The ensuing lengthy silence seemed to be metered by the sonorous tick of the heavy oaken grandmother clock positioned behind Rupert Mayhew's chair. Rebecca felt her spine stiffen and her flesh creep. Desperate for casual conversation to distract his hooded, wolfish gaze, she remarked lightly, 'You must be glad of your stepdaughters' company while your wife is away. Lucy is fifteen, is she not, and the younger, Mary…?' She hesitated, expecting him to advise her of the younger girl's age.

His only response was to mutter on a grunting laugh, 'At times they have their uses.' His manner and words heightened her uneasiness.

Rebecca replaced her pretty china cup and saucer on a low table close by. 'I am most grateful for the refreshment, sir, but I really need to be back on the road to Graveley, without delay,' she informed him with a busy, professional tone. 'Perhaps you would discover whether your stepdaughter is now ready to depart. I'm sure you're aware this unseasonable heat makes travelling after noon quite unbearable.'

As though to reinforce her anxieties about the climate, Rebecca dragged her eyes from Rupert Mayhew's sparsely covered head, where they had once again drifted, and stared through the casement window to one side of her.

On this late September morning. the atmosphere glowed bright and lucid, threatening another blazing, sultry afternoon. Her intention to be directly abroad had as much to do with the valid reason voiced as with the desperation to escape this odious man's presence.

Rupert Mayhew's thin visage pinched further. He straightened himself in the chair and leaned stiffly back into it. Bony fingers steepled together and he regarded Rebecca imperiously across them and the hooked bridge of his nose. He obviously had no intention of acceding to her courteous request and wanted her to be aware of it.

It was hard to determine what about him was the most repellent, Rebecca realised: his puny build, his ugly countenance or his objectionable manner. Thank goodness all prior contact had been carried out by letter. Had she previously been subjected to his obnoxious presence, she might well have turned down his application to send his stepdaughter, Lucy, to board at her school. The notion that she could afford to reject custom, however unwelcome, caused a wry smile to escape her.

Misinterpreting this melancholy humour as cordiality, Rupert Mayhew's arrogant bearing relaxed. One blackened tooth was displayed centrally in an otherwise surprisingly clean set as he smiled widely. His eyes narrowed to gleaming yellow dots as he purred insinuatingly, 'You barely look old enough, Miss Nash, to have acquired the teaching experience to which you lay claim.' His unpleasant smile was back as he noticed her reaction.

An attractive blush immediately rimmed Rebecca's high cheekbones, accentuating the sculpted contours of her ivory-skinned oval face. Her youthful looks were a constant source of embarrassment to her. But her chin tilted defensively.

Rupert Mayhew's avid appraisal continued, his beastly eyes targeting full, shapely lips that hinted at a promise of sensuality. A small straight nose was skipped past as he examined a pair of wide, lustrous eyes of the most extraordinary and exquisite colour. He stared into glossy turquoise depths, lushly fringed with lengthy dusky lashes before his voracious interest roved on to her thick dark-gold hair. Loosely wound ringlets dropped to curl like honeyed silk against the crisp sprigged cotton of her serviceable travelling dress.

But for Rupert Mayhew, the most outstanding feature of this delectable young woman was that she chose to earn her living by running a young ladies' academy situated in the backwoods of a small Sussex coastal hamlet. He had travelled widely and visited the fashionable spa towns of Bath and Harrogate, yet he was hard pressed now to recall a face as classically beautiful. Her figure was too slender for his profligate taste. Yet even so, he knew of skinnier wenches who had procured wealthy protectors and opulent lifestyles only dreamed of by most young women in straitened circumstances.

He regretted now not having taken the time to visit her and her poky establishment at Graveley. He knew from the meagre fees she charged that the business she ran must be struggling to survive and had accordingly negotiated even more favourable terms through their correspondence. Rupert Mayhew knew himself for nothing if not an astute businessman.

And he'd imagined her to be some spinsterish blue-stocking! Undoubtedly she kept herself hidden away in that wooded copse, for Graveley was little more than that as he recalled from passing through. Or did she? he reflected with quickening pulse, his tongue flicking out to moisten thin lips. She resided on the Ramsden estate. Robin Ramsden was her landlord. He could have hardly overlooked her.

'Wily Old Ram', as he was nicknamed, was reputed to exercise his *droit de seigneur* at every opportunity. The last laundry maid he had impregnated had been ejected from Ramsden Manor and bundled off into a labourer's cottage as second wife and mother to that widower and his brood. Bawdy jesting had abounded amongst Rupert Mayhew and his cronies, especially when gossip had it that the newly wed girl had been sneaked back into the house for a repeat performance. The labourer now, by all accounts, had two brats undeniably resembling the lord of the manor.

His darting, foxy eyes pounced on a glimpse of ankle as Rebecca shifted on her chair. She seemed a haughty chit, though. Perhaps increasing her prospects by lowering her principles—and certain items of clothing, he inwardly smirked—was beneath her. How he'd like her beneath—

'I am twenty-five years old, Mr Mayhew, as I believe I mentioned to you in our earliest correspondence,' Rebecca cut coldly into his lecherous musings, having conquered her indignation. 'I believe my qualifications also met with your approval at that time.'

'My dear Miss Nash, don't feel you have to be defensive with me,' he smugly dismissed, waving a bloodless hand. 'You come most highly recommended. I contacted Mr Freeman as you suggested I might. He continually regaled me with the successes his daughter has enjoyed since leaving your establishment two summers ago. She has bagged a Viscount as fiancé, no less. Mr Freeman was generous enough to credit your establishment with helping them snare the quarry.'

'I'm pleased to hear—'

Rebecca's mild approval was cut short as Rupert Mayhew interjected bitterly, 'Should you be able to achieve anything similar with the lazy, sullen minx skulking upstairs, I shall be above contentment.'

At the mention of her prospective new pupil, Rebecca stood up with a purposeful finality. A hint of genuine amusement hovered about her full, soft mouth as she was abruptly made aware of two things. Firstly, that her ex-pupil, Alexandra Freeman, a girl of little talent and even less to recommend her in the way of either looks or personality, had done so well for herself. Secondly, that the odious little man, who now rose from his chair to stand over-close to her, had little liking for his eldest stepdaughter. Rebecca sensed an immediate empathy with the fifteen-year-old girl she had yet to meet. Judging by the barely concealed envy in Rupert Mayhew's tone as he recounted Alexandra Freeman's excellent prospects, he was now anticipating some similar good fortune to befall the Mayhews.

'Well, the sooner your stepdaughter and I are able to set upon the road, the nearer we come to achieving your ambitions,' Rebecca announced, striving to banish mockery from her tone.

Rupert Mayhew's ochre eyes were on a level with her own and she was certainly not regarded as tall for her sex. Yet she had misjudged in thinking him perhaps frail. There was a wiry strength about him which was now apparent close up. A squat, corded neck and thick expanse of collar bone were exposed by his open-necked linen shirt. The same sparse greying hair that streaked his scalp poked from the unbuttoned collar.

The weather recently had been uncommonly hot for late September, but even so, she wished he had made some effort to dress in the manner as befitted a wealthy gentlemen farmer in the presence of a lady caller. Perhaps he classed her as just an employee and unworthy of any special considerations. Well, she was just such, she supposed, and the sooner he settled his account for Lucy's board and lessons and the sooner they were on their way to Graveley, the happier she would be.

Rebecca tore her offended gaze away from the coarse hairs sprouting from his throat and distanced herself from him by wandering to the large casement window. She gazed out. Heat was beginning to shimmer across the meadow just glimpsed beyond the formal gardens of Rupert Mayhew's house. A splendid house it was too, she realised, rather forlornly, because its solid graceful character was so at variance with that of its master.

When she had alighted from the London post here in the village of Crosby some forty-five minutes ago, the house's classical porticoed façade set in mellow stonework had seemed welcoming and auspicious. At that time, she had imagined cordial introductions between herself and her new pupil, perhaps an opportunity to discuss with Lucy's fond parents any matters of special interest concerning their daughter's ultimate refinement before she was launched into society. And then they would travel on to the Summer House Lodge, her home for the past five years.

She remembered Rupert Mayhew informing her of his wife's delicate condition. But nothing in any of his correspondence had prepared her for the vile man she had met today. From his letters, she had guessed him to be perhaps a little pompous. And she recalled thinking it a trifle odd that the girl's parents had not taken it upon themselves to visit her establishment to assess its suitability for their daughter. The hamlet of Graveley and the village of Crosby were, after all, barely fourteen miles apart along the coast road. Rupert Mayhew had obviously been content to settle his stepdaughter's future on the strength of his neighbour's success. Rebecca couldn't grumble at that: such recommendations were what kept her small, thriftily run establishment in business. No doubt the low fees she charged had also been a consideration. Rupert Mayhew didn't seem a man generous in spirit or coin.

An abrupt noise from behind splintered Rebecca's musing, jerking her attention from the tranquil garden scene into the spartanly furnished parlour. Rupert Mayhew was overlooked as Rebecca gazed towards the polished mahogany door which now gaped wide on its hinges.

The auburn-haired young lady who slouched in its opening was quite lovely, despite the aggressive glower, the sulky, slanted mouth and the livid purple bruising which shadowed one sapphire eye.

Luke Trelawney's dark head fell forward to momentarily rest in his cupped hands before long, blunt fingers threaded through thick, raven hair, drawing it away from his damp forehead. He jerked himself back against the uncomfortable squabs of the hired travelling coach and swore. An irritated flick of a glance took in the sun-yellowed grassy banks along the road side as a dark hand moved to release yet more mother-of-pearl buttons, hidden among the snowy ruffles of his lawn shirt.

'If you're intending supping at the Red Lion naked to the waist, don't expect me to protect your honour,' Ross Trelawney remarked with a grin from the opposite side of the coach. He nevertheless followed his handsome older brother's lead and loosened his upper torso from the clinging confines of a perspiration-soaked shirt.

'Infernal weather,' Luke Trelawney growled. 'That damned fool of a coachman must have taken a wrong turn. He promised us this Red Lion inn was within spitting distance some ten miles back. If we're not upon it soon, I'm out and walking.' Another black glance took in the arid scenery, scorched by a lengthy summer parched of rain, before he relented and half-smiled at his younger brother. 'I told you we should have used one of my coaches…at least we could have roasted in comfort. The springs in this contraption are more out of the seat than in it.'

Ross grimaced a wry apology at his older sibling, aware of his exasperation and the reason for it.

Luke Trelawney was one of the largest landowners in Cornwall. He owned Melrose, a magnificent house set in parkland. He owned an impressive fleet of traders sailing from the port of Bristol and mining interests closer to home in Cornwall. Today, however, the most piquant irony was derived from the fact that the coach house at Melrose was filled with every type of conveyance any gentleman was ever likely to need. The estate also boasted stables full of thoroughbred horseflesh the equal of any aristocrat's equine collection. And it had been Ross who had persuaded Luke to hire a coach for this journey…just for the hell of it, he had said. And hell it had been…complete with furnace. For himself, though, ever seeking just another untasted experience, he rather enjoyed the beggarly novelty of it all.

He looked across at his brother, scowling at passing scenery again, irritation distorting his narrow yet sensuously curved mouth.

Luke had strived to provide himself with the very best. As the oldest son of Jago and Demelza Trelawney he had, on their father's death, taken that gentleman's sizable bequest and increased it a thousandfold. He now had wealth and reputation that no other Cornish landowner could match. There were other things they would certainly never equal, Ross realised wryly: his astounding dark good looks; his eligibility, which had every hopeful mama, trailing nubile daughters, visiting their mother and sister under any ridiculous pretext they could deviously devise. And all to no avail for, at thirty-two, Luke had resisted all temptations, threats and ludicrously transparent plots to hook him.

Ross dwelt on Wenna Kendall, with some relish and not a little envy. The voluptuous dark-haired mistress Luke had installed in fine style in Penzance obviously satisfied him physically, but emotionally...? He gazed at the side of Luke's lean, tanned face, still idly turned towards the uninspiring passing scenery. Emotions were not something often associated with his older brother. They were kept tightly reined, as controlled as every other aspect of his life. Their father's death some eleven years ago was the last time he could recall witnessing Luke in distress. Apart from that, family problems, business pressures, all were dealt with in the same calm, disciplined way.

But he knew how to enjoy himself...as all Trelawney males did. Roistering bouts of drinking and wenching were a regular part of life, so long as business never suffered. And dependable Luke was always there to ensure it certainly never did. Status and wealth were Luke's motivation and priority.

An urgent solicitor's letter, hand-delivered from Bath, had set Luke on the road, unwillingly and with many a curse, but it had moved him as Ross had known it would. For Luke never shirked his responsibilities, even those that disturbed memories of generation-old family rifts. But that estrangement was of little consequence to the present Trelawney clan.

Ross had decided to go along for the ride and to alleviate the insatiable restlessness that dogged him. Melrose had been left in the capable hands of their imperturbable brother Tristan who, at thirty, happily married and living on the Trelawney estate, was the most sensible choice. Being second eldest also made him natural deputy, Ross always thought, when justifying his need to slope off, courting fresh excitement.

Besides, Luke had made it clear the matter was to be dealt with as expediently as possible with a quick return to Cornwall. Luke had neither the time nor inclination to linger in rural Brighton once business was satisfactorily settled.

Luke relaxed back into the battered squabs. He withdrew a half-sovereign from a pocket and tossed it in his palm a few times. The pair of nags doing their best to convey the ancient coach towards Brighton was increasing pace: a sure sign that, having travelled the route many times, they recognised water and sustenance were soon to be had. 'A half-sovereign says we reach this dive within five minutes,' he challenged his younger brother, stretching long, muscular legs out in front of him and flexing powerful shoulders in an attempt to ease niggling cramps.

'Three minutes,' countered Ross, as aware as Luke of the horses' renewed efforts. They were fairly bowling along now.

Five minutes later the rickety coach swung abruptly left and into the dusty courtyard of the Red Lion inn.

'Order up whatever they've got that's long, cool…' Luke hesitated, noting the direction of Ross's gaze, which had, on alighting, immediately been drawn to a titian-haired tavern wench '…and comes in a tankard,' he finished drily. 'See what sort of food they've got about the place too,' he said but with little enthusiasm, as cynical peat-brown eyes roved the dirty, whitewashed building.

The seedy-looking Jacobean hostelry was nevertheless a hive of activity. Well situated along the coastal road to refresh those travelling from the west country towards the fashionable gathering place of Brighton, it attracted the patronage of both farmer and gentleman alike.

Luke glanced around in cursory fashion. A coach, displaying an Earl's coat of arms, protected its glossy paintwork beneath the shade of a massive spreading oak on the perimeter of the courtyard.

Two young ladies, elegantly and coolly dressed in pastel

muslin, sat, with parasols twirling, beneath the shielding canopy of boughs on a spread tartan travelling rug. Their coy attention was with Ross and himself. Aware of his observation, their daintily coiffured heads collided as they chattered and giggled, parasols whirling faster. He glanced away, feeling unaccountably irritated. The fact that Ross was now torn between giving them or the flame-haired serving girl the benefit of his hazel-eyed silent charm irked him further.

Not that he was unused to female interest: all Trelawney males had the tall, dark good looks women seemed to find hard to resist. He knew without particular conceit or satisfaction that due to his superior height, and the classical set of his features, framed by a mass of thick, jet-black hair, he, more than any, was most sought after. His looks, coupled with his status and wealth, ensured a limitless supply of eager women. Thus the need for charm or seduction was rarely required for amorous conquests. When the mood or need took him, therefore, he seldom bothered with either, exploiting his attractiveness and willing partners to the full. Occasionally, acknowledging this callousness made him uneasy. Why the sight of two simpering debutantes at a strange tavern on a blazing afternoon should induce one of those conscience-ridden moments he had no idea, and it only served to needle him further.

He kicked at the parched, powdery gravel beneath one dusty Hessian boot and looked down the two or more inches at the top of Ross's sun-glossed chestnut head. He smiled slowly, consciously lightening his exasperation which he knew had much to do with the unwanted responsibility that brought him to this neck of the woods. He inwardly cursed all the Ramsdens to perdition as his businessman's brain sorted through all he'd left in abeyance at Melrose and all that awaited him at Brighton. He clicked his fingers in front of Ross's line of vision, redrawing his brother's attention to himself.

'I'll visit the stables and see what sort of horseflesh they've got on offer. I'd sooner ride a farm hack the remaining miles to Westbrook than set foot back in that boneshaking contraption.'

* * *

'If she dunt wanta move then she dunt and she wunt,' the old man announced morosely, nodding sagely, yet eying the horse with what seemed to Rebecca like any amount of satisfaction.

'Can't you coax her a bit?' Rebecca suggested with a wheedling smile at the squint-eyed old groom, as her lacy scrap of handkerchief again found its way to her perspiring brow.

'Just beat the stupid animal,' was Lucy Mayhew's heartless instruction to the granite-faced old retainer, who served as a stablehand for her stepfather now that advancing years had numbered his farm-labouring days. Bert Morris stared straight ahead not deigning to react at all to this outrageous proposal of treatment for his old Bessy. He fished in his shirt pocket, removed a clay pipe and began to stuff the bowl of it with some foul-looking dried grass extracted from the same source.

Rebecca alighted nimbly from the one-axle carriage and immediately flexed her cramped limbs. The worn benchseat was barely wide enough for two people travelling in comfort. For three packed close together in this stifling early afternoon heat, it was unbearable. The fact that Bert Morris smelled as though he not only groomed but slept amongst his treasured horses had largely added to the discomfort.

Rebecca bestowed a sympathetic look on the exhausted elderly mare who refused to travel up the steep wooded incline towards the Summer House Lodge in the hamlet of Graveley. As though aware of observation, the animal swayed her head round. Such solemn, apologetic eyes, Rebecca thought, before she lifted her face towards the breeze, closed her eyes and, momentarily, savoured the wonderfully refreshing sensation. Soft cooling air disturbed honey-gold hair clinging in damp tendrils to her slender, graceful neck. Then she gazed up into the carriage where the old man smoked stoically, apparently undisturbed either by circumstances or the heat. Lucy Mayhew returned her a sullen look, swiping a careless hand across her forehead to remove beading perspiration.

'We can walk from here,' Rebecca encouraged her with a smile. 'It's barely a quarter of a mile and mostly through wood-

land. The shade will be delightfully cool and most welcome.'
She anticipated objection but Lucy had gathered up her cotton
floral gown in eager hands and jumped from the carriage in a
trice.

Rebecca reached up behind the benchseat, grasping her own
and Lucy's travelling carpet bags. Old Bert Morris stirred himself enough then to aid her attempts at unwedging them, dropping them carelessly to the dusty ground.

'You will ensure that the trunks are delivered as soon as
possible?' Rebecca enquired of the old man. He grunted some
unintelligible noise past the pipe clenched in stained teeth
which she took to be an affirmative.

Rupert Mayhew had testily decreed that a carpet bag of es-
sentials must suffice today and the trunks be forwarded later in
the week. Had they travelled in a sturdier carriage pulled by
an energetic pair they could have brought all with them and
would now be alighting at the familiar white-boarded doorway
of her Summer House Lodge.

Without another word, Bert Morris clicked encouragement
at the tired mare to back step along the narrow path. The animal
did so with amazing briskness, considering its previous leth-
argy. Soon the small trap had turned in the clearing and was
making good progress back towards the village of Crosby.

With a smile at her new charge, Rebecca directed brightly,
'Now you take one of the handles to your bag, Lucy, and I
shall take the other. Thus we can share the load as we walk,
for the woodland path is a little on an incline.'

'What of your bag?' Lucy asked doubtfully. 'Will you manage that too?'

'There's little in it,' Rebecca reassured her with a smile,
surprised and heartened by the girl's concern. Lucy had hitherto
on the hour-long journey from Crosby displayed nothing apart
from a scowling profile and a great reluctance to be drawn into
any light conversation. Uncomfortable silence had been the
prevailing feature of the journey: the blistering heat and her
travelling companions equally to blame.

Rebecca stole a quick glance at her new pupil, trying to

ascertain her mood. Lucy's small hand was fastened on the crown of her poke bonnet, shielding her face from the sun's fierce rays as she dragged her bag across shrivelled yellow grass. Rebecca took the same sensible precaution, settling her own straw headgear firmly on her golden head.

With an encouraging smile, Rebecca lead the way towards the cool, inviting wooded pathway.

Rebecca sensed that the girl now might chat, but her attention was sidetracked by the painful-looking bruising shadowing one of Lucy's eyes. An aged yellowing could be glimpsed amongst the fresh purple and Rebecca's heart went out to the young girl.

Lucy informed her abruptly, 'He did it...but you know that, don't you.'

'I guessed...yes, that your stepfather must have chastised you.'

'Chastised me?' Lucy repeated with a sneer coarsening her voice. 'I don't mind it when he hits me,' she muttered vehemently before changing the subject abruptly. 'Do you always collect your new pupils from their homes? I would have imagined you to be too busy. Where are the other pupils? Who's looking after them?' she ran on, barely pausing for breath.

'Well,' Rebecca began, troubled by Lucy's attitude to her stepfather but glad she displayed an interest in her fellow pupils, 'to answer the first part of your question: No, I rarely collect my pupils from their homes. They are usually delivered to the Summer House by their parents. But while my school has been closed for the summer months... There,' she interrupted herself, 'I have answered the second part of your question first. The school has been closed since July and the boarders now gone. I have only a very small school premises and board only one or, at the most, two girls at a time. You will be boarding alone. But there are day pupils too,' Rebecca hastily added, keen to let Lucy know she would have company and perhaps make friends. 'I have spent two months in London, visiting my elder sister. Elizabeth has recently been blessed with her first-born son and invited me to stay with her for company while she was confined.' And a little fetching and carrying, Rebecca could have added but didn't and felt uncharitable for even thinking it. 'Since I was travelling back through Crosby today, I informed your stepfather that it would be no hardship to break my journey and collect you.'

Lucy was gazing around at tangled undergrowth during this explanation. She abruptly threw back her brunette head, scouring the canopy of shivering greenery entwined above them. 'It's very quiet,' she breathed conspiratorially.

'And very refreshing after the heat on the road,' Rebecca commented.

A magpie flew with a raucous cry between treetops, contradicting Lucy's words. Within seconds its colourful mate joined it in the whispering foliage.

'That's an auspicious sign. Sighting a pair of magpies signifies good fortune, Lucy. You shall obviously enjoy great success at the Summer House,' Rebecca said lightly with no thought for her own future. Her aqua eyes fixed on the birds as she recited softly, 'One for sorrow, two for joy…'

Rebecca's vague smile faded as she noticed the poignancy on her young companion's face: a wistful mingling of misery and hope.

Aware of observation, Lucy became petulant. 'I've never been superstitious,' she sneered, pointedly turning her face away from Rebecca. The bag held between them swung savagely before Lucy dropped her side to the ground. She stalked off and started exploring the perimeter of matted undergrowth.

'I'm hot and thirsty,' she flung back over her floral cotton shoulder. Yanking at the ribbons beneath her chin, she carelessly flung her bonnet down on to peaty ground. Plump fingers raked through her thick, auburn hair, lifting it away from her neck. Then she swirled around, holding the skirt of her pretty, summer dress away from her warm legs.

The two bags Rebecca held slid to the ground and she sighed. It was still hot and sticky, even within this shielding woodland, and she had to admit that she too was thirsty.

'We can have a short rest, if you like.' Following Lucy's

example, she undid the ribbons on her own straw hat. Golden tendrils of hair were loosened from her moist neck by a pale hand. 'There's a pretty pond close by, to your left a bit. We could sit there a while.

It was a sizable pond too. Fed from a spring as well as from the tinkling stream that ran through the gully from the hamlet of Graveley, it retained depth and clarity, despite the recent hot, dry weather. 'Not that you can slake your thirst there, of course,' Rebecca cautioned with a smile. 'I've seen all manner of creatures in the water.'

Lucy managed a weak grin at this. She wordlessly demonstrated her agreement by catching hold of the handle of her bag.

'I shall tell you a bit about Lord Ramsden, our landlord, while we rest.' Rebecca offered conversationally. 'He resides at Ramsden Manor in the village of Westbrook, which adjoins Graveley. The Summer House Lodge is part of his estate. A very good and kind landlord he is too,' she praised him unreservedly, as she led the way off the main track.

They threaded their way gingerly through creeping undergrowth. 'Take care your gown doesn't snag. There are some brambles concealed amongst the ferns,' Rebecca cautioned Lucy.

A musical sound of running water became audible. Rebecca pushed aside the last of the pliant branches that barred their way and they stood in a picturesque rough-grassed glade, a large pond situated centrally.

A small sound of delight burst from Lucy. She immediately relinquished her side of the bag again, but before she rushed away Rebecca received an apologetic smile. Reaching the bank of the pond on fleet feet she called back, 'Look, a toad, there on the water lilies.'

Rebecca nodded and smiled, repressing a shudder at the sight of the enormous speckled creature. She knew all manner of wildlife took refuge in this quiet oasis. She had often sought its soothing sanctuary herself in the past when needing privacy and solitude.

Lucy slipped her soft shoes off and Rebecca enjoyed a pleasant, relaxed moment before it dawned on her that the girl was, incredibly, intending to wade out to fetch the creature. No doubt that sort of slimy beast was preferable to the one Lucy was obliged to share a home with, Rebecca surmised with a sigh.

'Lucy…come back at once,' Rebecca admonished, threat and plea mingling in her voice as the girl eagerly hitched up her skirt and inched forward into the still green depths of the pond.

Lucy's high-pitched giggle was all the response Rebecca received. Anxiously watching Lucy's painstaking progress towards the glossy flat-leaved lilies was nerve-racking. Foreboding was taking hold of her with a vengeance. The uneasiness that she had experienced earlier that day with Rupert Mayhew returned to haunt Rebecca. She was becoming certain she would have fared better without this family's patronage. She was an accomplished tutor and took pride in what she achieved with her students, but so far Lucy's moods had been totally unfathomable and unpredictable. At times her conduct and attitude seemed completely inappropriate. Disciplining her might prove impossible.

Sensing danger, the toad dived into the still surface of the pond.

'Come back now, Lucy,' Rebecca ordered firmly, an icy prickling stalking her spine, as she noticed the girl's dress dragging in the water.

In response, Lucy ducked herself down in the water, submerging up to the shoulders. She twirled about, and gaily coaxed, 'Come in…it's so cool.'

'Come back here this minute, Lucy,' Rebecca bit out through clenched teeth, her heart now in her mouth. She knew the pond was quite deep towards the centre. Her worst fears were realised when Lucy suddenly shrieked and slipped backwards, thrashing her arms.

Without further conscious thought, yet inwardly cursing, Rebecca sped to the pond and began wading, skirt gripped high about her thighs, towards the struggling girl. As she approached, Lucy surfaced, giggling. 'See…I told you it was refreshing. It's better than the spa at Bath. It's better than sea bathing at Brighton. Have you swum in the sea at Brighton?' she demanded gaily, splashing water at Rebecca's still relatively dry figure.

Rebecca gathered her skirts into a clenched hand. The other covered her face, clearing pond water and shielding the raging fury and utter disbelief contorting her delicate features. Had Lucy been within reach, she would have shaken her until her teeth rattled and her stupid, selfish head fell off.

'Well, what have we here?' came a sardonic male voice. 'Water sprites? Woodland elves? A welcome diversion?'

Chapter Two

The ironic well-modulated voice had Rebecca swirling unsteadily around.

Two strangers were watching their antics from the pond bank mere yards away. Rebecca felt her heart pumping painfully as she hurriedly smeared filming pond residue from her vision. Then she stared, horrified.

One man sat astride a grey farm horse, the other was lounging comfortably against the bole of a centuries-old oak, and was the most handsome man she had ever before seen in her life. His long, thick hair appeared jet-black beneath the shading oak. His narrow mouth was curved a little with the same mocking humour that had tinged his words, for she knew instinctively that it was he who had spoken. Peat-dark eyes were heavy-lidded and fixed on her with the same intensity that she watched him. In one hand he idly held the reins of a second rather mangy-looking horse, placidly cropping the rough grass. As his lazy gaze lowered to slowly survey her drenched form, her fists abruptly opened, dropping her thigh-high skirts into the water.

Rebecca closed her gritty, stinging eyes momentarily in utter despair. Why did disasters invariably always cluster together? Why would they never spread themselves out a bit in her life? This was too much for one day! Thank heavens five years had lapsed since she had last endured times such as this, crammed with alarm and anxiety.

The stranger astride the horse, who had fairer colouring and looked to be younger by some years, laughed down at his broad-shouldered companion and exchanged a few quiet words. Earthy eyes skimmed to her sodden bodice and aquamarine eyes lowered there too. The thin wet cotton was almost transparent and clung to her bosom like a second skin. As her breasts hardened with shame and her nipples stung she instinctively closed screening arms about herself.

She remembered Lucy, positioned somewhere behind her. Her pupil's safety and well being were now her responsibility. Through the girl's stupid recklessness they now found themselves stranded in soaked clothes that served only to display every feminine contour they were designed to cover. They were in the densest part of the wood, still a good way from home, with two complete strangers witnessing their discomfort.

She had never seen either of them before. She would have remembered if she had. Both were memorably good looking but the powerfully built, darker man was quite ridiculously so. She was acquainted with most people in the small communities of Graveley, Westbrook and the immediate surrounding areas. These two were probably just passing through. They might be miscreants…

The disturbing possibility possessed her abruptly, monopolising every thought. Why were they off the main track and in private woodland? Why were they dressed in finely tailored black breeches and white lawn shirts but, confusingly, in possession of horses that looked little better than tired farm hacks? She had heard fearsome gossip about young village women being mistreated by bored gentlemen out looking for diversion. Even as she thought the word, she recalled him uttering it, and her temples hammered as blood surged through her veins.

The hideous danger in their predicament forced itself mercilessly upon her and she twisted towards Lucy, wanting to reassure the girl. The expression on her young pupil's face was the most daunting aspect of the whole nightmare situation. Excited interest was darkening and widening Lucy's blue eyes as she ignored Rebecca and stared at the strangers on the bank.

'Who are you? Why are you trespassing?' Rebecca demanded tremulously of the man who still relentlessly watched her. Before he could reply she swivelled away, aware of Lucy approaching her through the water. She believed the girl to be seeking her closenesss for safety, but Lucy made to glide straight past. Catching at one of Lucy's wet arms she attempted to detain her in the pond. Should the need arise for physical protection it would be far better to be close together. Lucy impatiently slipped her arm through Rebecca's cold, stiff fingers and swayed herself forward. As she approached dry land, her plump arms raised and the movement caused her precociously curvaceous body to be quite deliberately outlined as she slowly wrung out her dripping dark hair.

Rebecca watched in horrified embarrassment as Lucy brushed closely past the tall, athletic figure leaning against the tree. A slight deepening of the cynical smile curving his mouth was the only reaction. His eyes remained with Rebecca. She watched anxiously as the younger man dismounted, his eyes following Lucy's hip-swinging progress.

Fury and humiliation engulfed her. It made her wrap her arms tighter about herself and snap out, albeit it tremulously, 'I asked you who you are and what you are doing here.'

The raven-haired man shoved himself away from the ancient oak then and walked the few paces to the pond. 'Are you intending to stay in there?' That deep, sardonic voice caused Rebecca to involuntarily shiver and take a step back. She attempted to dart a glance past him, desperate to see Lucy's continuing safety from his companion.

'I asked you who you are.' She challenged in a fierce shaky whisper.

Her simultaneous fear and courage erased his amusement. 'Well, why don't you come here and perhaps I'll tell you,' he cut soothingly into her unsteady speech. He extended a lean, tanned hand towards her. When she still didn't move but merely stared at it, he beckoned peremptorily.

Remaining there like a fool to defy him was, she knew, ridiculous. She forced her boneless legs forward but chose to ignore his offer of aid. She scrambled up the bank, slithering a little as her sodden skirt hampered her, and belatedly, gratefully, sought his hand, preventing herself sliding back.

A warm, firm grip pulled her to within a few inches of his tall, spare body and she could feel the heat of him warming her chilled form. Without meeting his eyes, she quickly disengaged her hand, mumbled her thanks and then felt churlish and cowardly. Besides, she wanted so much to look at him more closely. She drew a silent, steeling breath and forced herself to slowly raise her damp gold head in a semblance of pride and confidence.

Turquoise eyes fused with dark brown for a timeless moment. She wasn't mistaken. He was as exceptionally handsome as she had thought. No warts, moles or pockmarks to mar the lightly bronzed angular planes of his face. His hair was as glossy and pitch black as it had seemed when he lounged beneath the shading oak. A small crescent-shaped scar by one thick dark brow was an imperfection yet it only served to enhance the beautifully piratical air about him.

'Thank you for your aid, sir,' she said, striving to casually modulate her tone. But she knew she had failed miserably when one side of his sculpted, narrow mouth lifted in a vestige of returning amusement.

'Do you often wade fully clothed into woodland ponds? Is it a local custom of sorts?' he teased, the humour in his eyes strengthening as they roved her damp and tousled dark honey hair.

Rebecca raised an impulsive hand to her unruly locks, realising just what a fright she must look. She stepped away from him hurriedly, aware that his outstanding attractiveness made her feel even more bedraggled than she probably was. She averted her crimsoning face from sepia-coloured eyes knowing she could do nothing to conceal her accentuated silhouette from his heavy-lidded scrutiny. She hastened towards Lucy who stood idly sliding bold glances at his companion from beneath moisture-spiky lashes.

Rebecca hastily grabbed up Lucy's carpet bag from the ground and with shaking fingers pulled the clasp apart. She grabbed at the dry garments within and brusquely shook them out. She thrust a plain lemon day dress at Lucy, snapping in a vehement undertone, 'Hold this in front of you.' The undiluted anger in Rebecca's voice and the icy sparks in her turquoise eyes made Lucy wordlessly do as she was bid. Removing a dress in the same way from her own carpet bag, Rebecca finally spun back towards the two men. She gulped another calming breath and even managed a wavering smile.

'Thank you once more for your aid. But if you would now be so kind...my pupil and I need to dry ourselves after our mishap. I'm sure you wouldn't want either of us to take a chill...' Her voice trailed off as she watched a tanned, squarish jaw set as he realised he was being summarily dismissed.

'I thought you were keen to know who I am,' he drily reminded her.

'It matters little,' Rebecca rebuffed him, nevertheless managing a small, conciliatory smile. She was quite astonishing herself, accomplishing this sham composure. It disintegrated with equally astounding ease as he commenced strolling towards them. She spontaneously stepped protectively in front of Lucy, and her dress, gripped in white-knuckled hands, was raised a little.

He hesitated and seemed momentarily undecided before changing direction, gathering the reins of his grazing horse, and mounting the beast in a swift athletic movement. He sat thoughtfully considering her before suggesting soothingly, 'Perhaps you'd care to tell me who you are then, as you appear to have lost interest in my identity...Miss...?'

'Certainly, sir,' Rebecca agreed, compelling herself to sound polite and confident. 'My name is Nash...Rebecca Nash. And this is Miss Mayhew...a pupil from my school at the Summer House Lodge. We are returning there directly. It is barely a few minutes' walk away,' she lied for good measure, 'on Lord Ramsden's estate.'

His eyes narrowed instantly at this information and she caught the younger man darting a swift, searching look at him.

'I should warn you,' Rebecca informed helpfully, when he made no move to depart, 'that Lord Ramsden prosecutes all trespassers. He has a reputation for dealing harshly with all such. You really should leave now before his gamekeeper happens upon you.' She seized upon the idea at once, a relieved breath breaking from between her bloodless, trembling lips. 'The gamekeeper…keepers, for there are several,' she lied again, 'scour these woods ceaselessly for poachers…'

His spontaneous smile at this local news made her blush hotly. She was sure he was about to call her bluff.

'You think I'm a poacher?' he enquired softly. 'Do I look like a poacher?'

'It matters not how you look,' she countered sharply. 'Williams is apt to shoot first and examine you later.'

'Williams?' he mildly queried.

'Lord Ramsden's gamekeeper,' she explained. 'Please, sir. If you and your companion would be so kind…' She snatched a searching glance at Lucy who was shivering and now looking as though one of her dejected moods was taking a grip. 'My pupil needs to dry herself and you should make haste to depart. Believe me when I say if you are discovered you will be prosecuted.'

'And what do you suppose…' he paused '…Lord Ramsden's reaction is to you trespassing in his pond?' he persisted silkily, as he controlled his restless mount with a cursory flick of the hand.

Rebecca gave a short, dismissive laugh. 'Lord Ramsden and I are well acquainted,' she informed him with a deal of satisfaction. 'I have no fears on that score.'

This confident declaration drew an amused snort from the younger man. He appeared about to speak but a swift, silencing gesture from his darker companion made him simply shake his head disbelievingly and examine the leaves that sighed above him.

'Lord Ramsden doesn't frighten you?' the dark man suggested with a half-smile as he nudged the horse slowly forward.

'Not at all,' Rebecca confirmed, shifting slowly to keep him in sight and Lucy positioned behind her, as he approached. She sensed a new, disturbing undercurrent to their exchange.

'Good,' was his brief, dulcet response as he reined in close and looked down at her in the same thoughtfully amused way.

He extended a dark hand towards her in the gesture of one wishing to shake hands before departing. Clutching her shielding garment in front of her in one, she politely offered her other pale, slender hand to him.

'Luke Trelawney and my brother Ross…at your service,' he introduced them both as his warm fingers retained her cool ones in his firm grip. A dark thumb traced the delicate skin of her palm in a careful, camouflaged caress as he reluctantly relinquished it.

'Mr. Trelawney…' Rebecca courteously acknowledged, with a small dip of her head, as his horse passed her. She nodded civilly to Ross also as he followed Luke.

Rebecca's eyes stayed unwaveringly with them until they had disappeared from view, when they closed in utter thankfulness.

As the two cart horses started an ambling trot down the grassy bank towards the track that lead to Westbrook, Ross grunted a low, lascivious laugh. 'I'm most definitely at her service. Servicing that wench would be no hardship—'

Luke pulled his horse up sharp and swung about in the saddle. His perfect features were savage as he ground out, 'Touch her and I'll—' The fierce caution ceased mid-flow. He was as aware as Ross of what he had astonishingly been about to threaten.

'—be most put out,' he remedied, relaxing a little. But a wry grimace was the closest he got to apology…or to analysing his aggression, before he urged his lumbering nag into something approaching a canter.

* * *

Rebecca gently disengaged herself from the grey-haired woman's firm embrace. 'It's good to be home, Martha,' she greeted her with a sweet smile as the woman dabbed at her eyes with her grubby starched apron. 'Hush,' Rebecca soothed. 'I've only been gone just four weeks. I'll wager you've hardly missed me at all,' she teased. She contentedly surveyed the familiar pristine interior of her kitchen at the Summer House. Everything looked as meticulously ordered as it always did when Martha Turner was in attendance.

Martha and her husband Gregory lived in a tiny spartan dwelling, on the perimeter of the woodland Rebecca and Lucy had just traversed. Their cottage was situated barely a stone's throw from the Summer House, easily within walking distance for the elderly couple who made the journey each day.

While Martha prepared meals and cleaned, generally helping Rebecca run the household, her husband coaxed the sizeable vegetable patch situated along the western flank wall into providing Rebecca and her boarding pupils with fresh produce. Gregory Turner also tended the few chickens and geese they kept with the same natural diligence, ensuring his wife always had fresh eggs and poultry available to prepare nourishing fare.

The Turners' property, which had been settled on them by Robin Ramsden on their retirement from his service, had very little tillable land surrounding it. Woodland predominated on three sides, rendering it picturesque but poorly self-sufficient. In a way this unfortunate situation had benefited Rebecca and she often felt ashamed acknowledging it. She was well aware that she would never have been able to pay this dear couple for their aid. But she could offer an arrangement whereby, in return for housekeeping and gardening services, the Turners helped themselves to whatever surplus eggs, poultry and fresh fruit and vegetables the Summer House gardens produced.

Approaching the large floury patch on the scrubbed pine table, Rebecca idly dusted her arms free of pastry traces from Martha's welcoming hands. She peered at the mouthwatering sweet and savoury ingredients assembled for supper. As her stomach gurgled a little, she realised just how hungry she was.

She had eaten nothing since departing from the King's Head hostelry early that morning at Guildford, when setting out on the last leg of her journey home.

Martha's silver-bright eyes were crinkle-cornered as she regarded Lucy, standing subdued and quiet by the open kitchen door. Her smile faltered a little and Rebecca knew Martha was focussing on the bruising about Lucy's eye. As she noted Martha's troubled reaction to the injury, she finally relented and gave Lucy a small smile.

It was the first token of friendship she had felt capable of bestowing on the girl following the fiasco at the woodland pool. She was still in equal parts furious and bewildered by Lucy's behaviour.

Having both changed hastily into dry dresses, their final trek through the woods had passed in strained, chilly silence. Rebecca had decided that until her anger was again under control, it was best to keep quiet and keep walking lest she say or do something she might regret. But every speedy step taken had been filled with an inner wrangling about whether to contact Lucy's stepfather to ask him to fetch her. The fact that her meagre income would be again reduced, leaving her in severe financial difficulties, had been the only consideration in the girl's favour. As she looked at Lucy now and met those injured blue eyes, Rebecca sensed a niggling sympathy. Lucy seemed resigned to being rejected.

'This is Lucy…Lucy Mayhew, who is going to be joining us for a while,' Rebecca introduced her, with a strengthening smile for Lucy. 'Lucy, Martha and her husband Gregory have been giving me invaluable help here at the Summer House over the past five years.' Trying to lighten their moods, she indicated Martha's laden table. 'Martha's cooking is delicious, Lucy, it is very easy to over-indulge.' Lucy gave the cook a shy smile before perching demurely on a kitchen chair and gazing interestedly about.

Such a picture of youthful innocence, Rebecca couldn't help ironically surmising. But she cheered herself with again acknowledging just how fortunate she had been since the double tragedy of her parents' and fiancé's deaths some five years ago. At that time, circumstances had conspired to make a future in harsh employment or marriage to the first man to offer for her seem the only avenues. Instead, she now had a kind and generous landlord, friendship and aid from the Turners and also from dear friends who lived close by. But, most of all, she had this small, pretty Summer House, providing her with home and employment. She sighed her contentment, acknowledging that she would persevere with Lucy's education.

Martha fetched a stone jug from the dark pantry and set about filling two glasses with aromatic lemonade. Rebecca smiled her thanks, determined not to let this afternoon's humiliating episode spoil her pleasure at being home. Consciously recalling the incident allowed raven hair and earthy dark eyes to once more dominate her thoughts, but only momentarily before she determinedly banished them.

Luke Trelawney disturbed her by fascinating her far too much. But he had now gone and she would never again see him or his brother Ross. The strange bittersweet pang tightening her chest at that certainty made her fingers instinctively seek the large silver locket she wore. She could feel its warm, solid shape beneath her cotton dress. Her fingers smoothed its oval silhouette as she held on to the dear memory of David, her mourned fiancé.

'I knew you'd be wanting some lemonade. I made that fresh this morning.' Martha broke into her wistful reverie, arms crossing contentedly as she watched the two young women draining their tumblers. 'I knew you'd be along and hot and thirsty,' she emphasised with a wag of the head. 'Mind you,' she cautioned, rolling her sleeves back to her elbows before expertly pummelling the dough on the table. 'Mind you...' she repeated for good measure '...Gregory reckons that rain is on the way at last and you know he's rarely wrong.' Her head bobbed again as deft hands rolled the pastry into a ball. 'His legs have been playing up bad again...a sure sign o' wet on the way...biscuits are nearly done,' she tacked incongrously on the end. 'I can smell them coming along nicely.' She smiled at Lucy. 'I reckon a healthy young lady like you can polish off quite a few before her dinner.'

Lucy nodded, settling expectantly back into her chair like a biddable child. Watching her, Rebecca wondered how she could veer so rapidly between wanton sophistication and child-like innocence. But if what Gregory predicted was true and rain was on its way, she had pressing matters to attend to. She replaced her tumbler on the table.

'Has John fixed the roof while I've been away, Martha?' she enquired anxiously, remembering Robin Ramsden's promise that he would send his young carpenter to repair some summer storm damage.

'No…we've seen not hide nor hair of that young man. Gregory was going to attempt it hisself…but his affliction in the knees meant he could barely rise up three rungs of the ladder.'

'Is Lord Ramsden returned yet from Bath?' Rebecca quickly interrogated.

'Well, he wasn't at the manor five days ago when Gregory fetched the provisions but Miles was expecting him at any time. I reckon he must be at home now. If you chase that John up he'll be over and fix that roof quick as can be before his lordship finds out he's been idling again while he was away.'

'How many staff remain?' Luke asked the sombrely dressed elderly man standing stiff and quiet behind him, as he idly surveyed the weed-strewn gravel driveway. The chippings were piled high at the perimeter of the circular carriage sweep, testament to how long it had been since it was tended or raked. Numerous coach wheels were quite visibly imprinted in the dusty grit.

Both dark hands were raised, bracing against the framework of the large casement window he stood by. He gazed out, far into the wooded distance, his mind still deep in that quiet sanctuary with a girl with turquoise eyes.

'Eight,' came the terse response from behind.

Luke's eyes narrowed, his jaw setting as he recognised the barely concealed insolence in the elderly butler's tone. He swung away from the large square-paned window and faced him across the mellow yew desk.

Edward Miles must have been seventy if he was a day, and in a way Luke could understand his belligerence. What he could not comprehend was the man's stupidity. Had he any sense at all, he would take great pains to appear pleasant and obliging. His livelihood was now at great risk. For an aged butler of three score years and ten, employment was scarce. Employment without a reference would be impossible, as would keeping a roof over his sparsely covered head in his twilight years.

Luke knew he was tired, he knew he was thirsty but mostly, he knew, today he had been frustrated and that irritated him. Meeting the first woman in an age who had tried to rid herself of his presence at the earliest opportunity was quite a novelty and one he now realised he could have done without. Rejection came hard. And the more he dwelt on it, the more he knew it was ridiculous to allow it to matter. He forced himself to concentrate on Edward Miles. A rheumy-eyed gaze challenged him unwaveringly.

'Is there some brandy about this place?' Luke demanded testily, determining to leave matters for an hour or so whilst Ross and he refreshed themselves. They had been travelling solidly for almost two days with barely an overnight stop.

A slow, satisfied shake of the head met this request.

'Some wine of some sort?' Luke persisted, his patience with the butler's aloof attitude nearly at an end.

'Judith might have made some lemonade,' the old man advised dolefully. 'I can ascertain, if you wish.'

Luke stared at him, wondering if he was being deliberately facetious. But Edward Miles returned his black-eyed stare phlegmatically.

'Fine,' Luke agreed, knowing it wasn't fine at all, and wondering how he was going to break the news to Ross. And where the hell was Ross? Since they had arrived in the village of Westbrook an hour ago he had been off exploring. Luke allowed himself a rueful smile; at times his twenty-five-year-old brother was a fitting playmate for his young nephew of five. Thinking of that little lad brought Tristan to mind. His brother Tristan had his own wife and family to look after and couldn't be left to cope alone for too long, sensible and dependable as he was. He needed to deal speedily with this matter and set on the road home to Cornwall

'I'll meet with the staff in the main hallway in an hour. Assemble them there at three o'clock…and bring some sort of refreshment to this study, if you please,' Luke dictated steadily to Miles. The elderly man gave a creaky, insolent bow and quit the wood-panelled study with Luke close on his heels.

Miles ambled slowly towards the kitchens on stiff joints. He slid a recalcitrant glower up at Luke's handsome face as he passed him with one long, easy pace.

Luke descended the stone steps and strode around the side of the house towards the outbuildings, hoping that Ross's lengthy absence didn't mean he'd found a distracting servant girl to seduce. The notion made the throbbing in his own loins increase, and he cursed as he pushed open the barn door and walked in. He wished to God he'd never seen her. If they'd stayed on the main track instead of seeking shelter from the sun in those woods, he damned well never would have. Since the moment she had spun, dripping, to face him in that pond, he had been uncomfortably aware of the impact she'd had on him.

'Mr Trelawney!' Rebecca breathed out the name in utter astonishment as she shielded her eyes from the dusty sunlight streaming in through the open barn door.

Chapter Three

They stared at each other in stunned silence for a moment before Luke removed his hand from the planked door and it swung shut, obliterating most of the light. He approached Rebecca slowly, cautiously, sure she must be a tormenting figment of his lustful imagination. Sun streaking in through windows set high in the barn wall behind him burnished her honey hair with golden tints and made her squint those beautiful eyes. She stepped back, re-positioning herself close to stacked hay bales, so she had an unimpeded view of him.

'What are you doing here?' she demanded, but with an ingenuous, welcoming smile. It was impossible for her to hide her pleasure at seeing him again. She had believed him to be long gone from the neighbourhood. 'Oh, no! Did Williams catch you trespassing after all?' she softly exclaimed. 'Where is your brother?' The tumbling queries didn't halt his slow, purposeful pursuit. She backed off instinctively, angling away from him, still attempting to keep the fierce sunbeams from impairing her vision.

'Are you in trouble…with Lord Ramsden?' His continuing silence started to unnerve her a little so she offered breathlessly, 'I could speak to him for you…tell him how you assisted…' Warmth suffused her cheeks. She hadn't intended reminding him or herself of the sight she had presented when he had hauled her out of the pond. Her tongue tip came out to moisten her dry lips. The closer he came, the taller and broader he appeared. She felt infinitely small and fragile...and vulnerable. She attempted to peer past him and the piled hay to the exit. Why wouldn't he talk to her? Why wouldn't he say something...anything? Just hello would suffice.

Making to slide past his obstructing body, so near hers now, she announced nervously, 'I'm sure I could persuade him. I'll go and look for him.'

A muscular arm shot out to brace itself against the rough brick wall, blocking her intended flight to the door. 'You've found him,' he said softly. 'How are you going to persuade me?'

Rebecca placed a tentative hand on his linen-clad arm, feeling rock-like sinewed muscle flex at her feeble attempt to move him. She looked up into his dark intense features, struck again by how unbelievably handsome he was.

'That's not funny,' she mildly rebuked him, managing a small, sweet smile even though she didn't understand his sense of humour. 'Robin Ramsden can be very...understanding. I've found him so,' she falteringly explained, as she carefully removed her hand from his lawn shirt-sleeve and unobtrusively retreated, giving herself room to detour to the exit.

Luke watched her back off, his black-pupilled eyes heavy-lidded as they discreetly surveyed her from head to foot. Dried off, wearing a plain cotton dress, she was as beautiful and desirable as she'd been with her clothes plastered to her slender curves and damp tendrils of honey hair clinging to her delicate face. Perhaps not quite so erotic...

His tormenting reminiscence tailed off. Her turquoise eyes were watchful, a blend of caution and courage again coalescing in their glossy depths. He recognised it from their last encounter. Then it had been enough to make him reluctantly leave. She was intending to go this time. He had frightened her again. He could tell from the way her eyes slid furtively past him that she was within a hair's-breadth of making a dash for the door.

He didn't want that. If she ran he would stop her and if he touched her that way... No woman yet had caused him to lose self-control, he wryly reminded himself. Nevertheless, he dropped his arm and walked away a yard or so but still casually blocking any escape route.

'Are you often to be found in Lord Ramsden's barn, Rebecca?' he asked mildly, with a charming, boyish smile. His calculated ploy worked. Rebecca visibly relaxed.

'Only when I'm looking for John,' she said, returning his smile and feeling unaccountably pleased he had remembered her name.

'John?' he echoed with deceptive softness, as his smile thinned and he became furiously certain he had just interrupted a lovers' tryst. She didn't look in the least chagrined at having been thus discovered. Perhaps he should have let her try to escape after all, he thought cynically. If she'd been abandoned by some spineless rustic swain, he was sure he would prove a more than satisfactory substitute.

'Lord Ramsden's carpenter…well, he is an apprentice, really,' Rebecca pleasantly interrupted his savage supposition. 'But he's quite capable of repairing my roof.' She gazed about then as though she might spy the lad lurking somewhere. 'He's usually to be found in here, sleeping away hot afternoons…when he thinks he can get away with it.'

Silence between them lengthened and Rebecca became uneasily aware of dark eyes fixed unwaveringly on her. 'For it is about to rain, you know,' she said distractedly. 'Gregory Turner…oh, he and his wife help me at the Summer House…well, Gregory is quite sure that rain is finally due. He's rarely proved wrong. I wouldn't be at all surprised if…'

She trailed off, aware that Luke had approached her again while she had been nervously chatting. He now rested against a hay bale within a foot of her, a disturbing sleepiness in his velvet-brown eyes. '…it rains tonight,' she breathlessly finished, her aquamarine eyes wide and entrapped by his.

A slow hand moved unthreateningly to her face, cupping her fragile jaw. She remained entranced as a dark thumb traced the curve of her lower lip with featherlight softness. Either he wasn't as tall as she had at first thought or… He was bending to kiss her, she realised wildly as his face neared hers. Their eyes were still inextricably merged and when the leisurely descent of his narrow mouth brought their faces within inches of touching, Rebecca breathed out, 'What are you doing here?' She watched him frown and slowly, frustratedly, close his eyes as she shattered the spell he'd been casting.

'Were you discovered by Williams trespassing?' she asked, reverting to her initial line of questioning, stepping away again.

'No,' was the extent of his terse response and she sensed his irritation. He threw his head back and gazed up at the fanlight windows set high in the barn wall. He sighed, knowing explanations were long overdue. But then, so was easing the tantalising ache in his loins she had provoked hours before, and was now innocently boosting. Tumbling her in a sultry barn in the middle of the afternoon…it was hardly the time or place.

Besides, he knew he wasn't going to be that lucky. He almost laughed at his arrogance. Getting close enough for a kiss was proving one hell of a job. What was it he had mourned earlier today? The lack of necessary charm and seduction in his life? He had an unshakeable notion that he was about to dredge up every skill he had ever mastered in those areas. He gazed back at her, momentarily undecided, then said softly, 'Come.'

Approaching the barn door, he stretched out a hand behind him, beckoning for her to follow. She did so, ducking under his arm to gain the dry heat of the afternoon as he held the door open for her.

'Miss Rebecca!' Rebecca twisted about and then hurried the few paces towards Edward Miles as he hobbled across parched grass towards the barn.

'Miles,' she greeted him, for no one who knew him well ever used his given name. Miles was always just Miles. She gave the elderly man an affectionate peck on the cheek, as always, aware of his pleasure at seeing her. His faint watery eyes peered past her to the tall, dark man who impassively watched the scene.

'So you've met the new master, Miss Rebecca,' Miles bitterly muttered.

Rebecca's welcoming smile faded. She frowned her bemusement. 'What do you mean?'

Miles glared purposefully past her. She turned then to watch as Luke Trelawney approached them, aware, oddly for the first time, of overwhelming authority and power in his manner and bearing. Her mind raced back to his puzzling statement in the barn when she had offered to seek out Lord Ramsden. 'You've found him…' he had said and she had believed him to be joking; had wondered at his odd sense of humour. Her eyes sought Miles quickly, pleading for immediate explanations before Luke reached them. But the butler's attention was with his employer.

'The servants are assembled in the hall as you wished, *my lord,*' he informed with a certain disrespectful emphasis on the title which didn't pass unnoticed either by Luke or Rebecca.

Mingling horror, disbelief and recrimination strained and whitened Rebecca's face. She whispered, 'Why didn't you…?'

'I did,' Luke reminded her curtly. 'You weren't listening.'

'In the woods…you could have told me hours ago in the woods. You let me make a fool of myself. Where is Robin Ramsden? You let me warn you needlessly earlier today…about prosecution…about the gamekeeper…' The disjointed accusations and queries jumbled together in her distress.

'As I recall,' he mentioned silkily, 'you seemed to lose all interest in who I was. You were more concerned with ridding yourself of my presence at the earliest opportunity.' He caught proprietorially at her arm as he made for the oaken entrance to Ramsden Manor, intending to take her with him. Rebecca immediately shook him off, her feverish mind foraging for information.

'Where is Robin Ramsden?' she demanded shakily of her new landlord.

He returned her stare impassively. 'Well, come inside the house and I'll tell you,' he coolly answered. 'The staff are assembled.' He cursed inwardly as he realised he had made it sound as though he classed her amongst them. But Rebecca deliberately shunned him, turning to Miles. As Luke alone walked ahead, a solitary thick tear trickled from the corner of one turquoise eye.

Ross weaved down the steps of the Manor, just as Luke was about to ascend them. Luke swore softly, wondering if the day could yet get worse. He grabbed at his younger brother's arm, turning him and making him mount the steps with him and enter the hallway. Ross waved the bottle he grasped under Luke's nose and slurred conspiratorially, 'Found the wine store, big brother.'

'So I see...' Luke replied drily, at one and the same time relieved and exasperated by knowing the reason for his brother's lengthy absence. He was beginning to wish to God he'd made this trip alone. Ross was becoming just another burden he had to deal with. Heaven only knew what he might get up to next. He supposed he ought to be grateful he hadn't discovered Ross naked with one of the female servants he was about to sack.

Two elderly, and three young, women scrambled to stand in a straight line as Luke entered the dim, cool hallway. They shuffled uneasily until they had the courage to look up. All were then instantly still with riveted attention.

Rebecca entered with Miles, and Gregory who had brought her over to the manor in the small trap. She noted the women's unwavering interest and being female knew the reason for it. As mouths dropped open and heads angled back to gaze at perfect features, she realised dully her estimation of his outstanding looks was being openly endorsed.

Cathy, Joan and Sally, the three young women who worked below stairs at the Manor, stared with unabashed amazement. There then began a chain reaction of clandestine rib digging, Joan forgetting herself enough to actually nudge the middle-aged housekeeper in the same way.

Judith instinctively slapped at her for this insubordination before freezing to attention as her new employer's smouldering dark eyes settled on her. She nervously jangled the keys at her waist and then gripped her hands behind her back.

Ross walked with intoxicated precision to the sweeping ebonized stairway, and leaning on the newel post, allowed himself to swing around and sit on a stair. He smiled amiably at everyone, his eyes lingering on the three homely young servants who, aware of his inspection, all blushed furiously and recommenced discreet elbowing.

Luke collected a black superfine tailcoat from a mahogany hall chair. He shrugged casually into it before strolling to stand centrally in front of them and then turned to look at Rebecca. She and Gregory hovered by the open doorway, although Miles paced resolutely forward on arthritic joints to merge with the paltry line of servants awaiting their new master's oratory. Luke stepped back from the people ranged in front of him so that Rebecca was kept in his line of vision. He shot a penetrating look at the elderly man with her, wondering who he was, wondering too why the whole place didn't seem to have an able-bodied man about it. Remembering Rebecca talk of a carpenter's apprentice, and a gamekeeper, he enquired, 'Is there anyone else?'

'Only young John, and Williams the gamekeeper,' Miles informed him stiffly. 'I can't find them anywhere.'

Luke moved a dismissing hand, signalling he wasn't about to wait longer. He looked at the sorry assortment in front of him. At Melrose he had more staff than this working in the gardens and three times as many working in the house. In fact, he was barely aware any more of just how many servants he did have. His mother and sister dealt with such matters for him.

'I should like to introduce myself to you,' he began in a firm baritone, without preamble, 'and tell you of the circumstances surrounding my inheritance of the Ramsden estate and title. I am Luke Trelawney of Pendrake in Cornwall and this is my brother, Ross. We are here because the fifth baron, your late master, has tragically and unexpectedly died of a heart complaint while away from the estate in Bath. He will be buried, in accordance with his wishes, in Bath, beside his wife in the Granger family crypt.'

He paused as a ripple of dismay from the amassed servants swelled in volume. Sally and Joan raised their white pinafores to dab at damp eyes and shake their heads in disbelief. Luke turned his head and stared at Rebecca, his eyes narrowed as they searched her tense white face. Solemn, sparkling aquamarine eyes unblinkingly returned his gaze. He started to speak again, his head still turned in her direction, which made the others in the hallway dart curious looks at her.

'I am sixth Baron Ramsden,' he stressed quietly, 'and have inherited this house and the entire estate and buildings upon it. The estate and title is remaindered to heirs male which means it has passed to me through my great-grandmother Charlotte Ramsden. She left this area and settled in Cornwall more than a hundred years ago,' was the extent of his terse explanation. 'As you know, Robin Ramsden was a widower and on his late wife's death there were no legitimate heirs of the union.'

Another wave of murmuring and coughing interrupted his speech. All were aware of two estate children who bore striking resemblance to their late master. 'Daughters in any case,' was heard to be whispered in a sibilant female voice.

Luke paced restlessly to where Ross sat, speaking to him while waiting for the muttering to quieten. It did almost immediately. He planted a dusty boot on the first step and addressed them from the foot of the imposing stairway.

'You should know that I have no intention of leaving Cornwall or the estates I have there to settle in Sussex.' A renewed buzzing met this information but now he spoke clearly over it, keen to get matters finalised. 'I therefore propose to sell this estate in its entirety.' This time only stunned silence reverberated about the great hall.

'I will honour all back wages due and furnish each of you with references. I will do whatever is in my power to obtain alternative employment for those who wish it.' Luke's eyes tracked Rebecca as he noticed her gliding back to the open doorway. He started to move forward, passing the line of silent, shocked servants, as he stated quickly, 'There will also be a generous severance payment commensurate with length of service...'

He quit the hall and descended the stone steps two at a time and caught up with her just as she was about to flee towards the waiting trap.

He caught at her arm and she half-turned, but seeing it wasn't old Gregory after all, she swung away again trying to break free. He crowded close to her, forcing her back against the mellow brickwork of the house, an open palm braced either side of her golden head.

'Listen...' he soothed but she jerked her white, tear-streaked face away from his.

'Rebecca...listen,' he ordered, authority abrading his tone this time.

Glossy sea-green eyes met earth-brown eyes then and he slowly moved a hand from the wall towards her stained face. She ducked, trying to evade him, but his open palm was flat against the brick before she'd caught her breath enough to bolt. Her abrupt movement brought her cheek up hard against his black superfine shoulder and he moved closer so that she had nowhere left to go apart from him.

Strong arms closed around her as though it was the most natural thing in the world for him to offer her comfort now he had shattered her world. He could feel the thundering of her heart against his chest and smell the scent of lavender in her golden hair. His head dipped, and a lingering sigh escaped him as his mouth sought its perfumed softness and he knew with utter certainty, and quiet amazement, that he was going nowhere without her. He'd known her not yet a full day but nevertheless would take her with him.

Rebecca closed her hot eyes. They stung with unshed tears but she was determined not to cry any more. She would never cry in front of him. At home...at the Summer House, perhaps. She had no home...that was the whole point. She no longer had a home or a business premises. She had nothing other than the paltry few pounds Rupert Mayhew had paid her for Lucy's board and tuition. And now she would have to return it…and Lucy. For she had nowhere to board her or teach her. She didn't know whether to laugh or wail at the irony that she had been uncertain whether to send Lucy home. The decision had now been made for her and she was desolate.

'I only came here to find John…to repair the roof before the rain comes,' she mentioned in a low, flat tone as though merely talking to herself. 'I no longer have a roof to repair…'

He pushed her back away from him to look at her. She met his gaze quite candidly, aquamarine eyes wide and sheeny. Small white teeth clenched on her unsteady bottom lip, making him aware how poignantly hard she strove for control.

'Come back inside…I want to talk to you,' he stated softly, yet in the tone of voice that brooked no refusal. She swallowed as though about to speak, then gazed past him.

'Here's Gregory,' she announced quietly as the elderly man slowly rounded the corner of the manor on his bowing legs. 'Gregory and his wife Martha have helped me at the Summer House for five years,' she tremulously informed him, while persistently plucking his restraining hands from her arms. At her third attempt he slipped his hands deftly about so that they gripped hers rather than the reverse. But she pulled backwards, twisting her fingers to free them until he finally relinquished her.

Rebecca walked slowly towards Gregory and took the man's arm, partly in affection and partly to aid his progress.

Luke leaned back against the warm mellow brickwork of the Manor and watched her slowly pass him without another glance. He didn't move from the wall until the trap was screened from view by poplars at the end of his drive.

Driving rain streamed in endless rivulets down the wide window pane, capturing Luke's mesmerised attention.

'Brandy?' he offered Victor Willoughby, holding his half-full glass of amber liquid out indicatively, although his dark eyes were still with the wet afternoon. He swivelled the leather chair about, his long fingers purposefully rifling through papers on the leather-topped desk, as he gave Robin Ramsden's man of business a cursory glance.

'Thank you…no,' the fair-haired forty-year-old man declined, but licked his lips a little ruefully, as though reluctantly denying himself. 'We should plough on, I'm afraid, my lord. There are several other matters yet, besides those we have covered.'

Luke nodded and decided not to mention yet again that he had no wish to be addressed so formally. He gave Willoughby his full attention as he replaced his crystal tumbler on the desk and then pushed it away. 'Tea?' he suggested, feeling inhospitable drinking alone.

'Why, yes, thank you,' Willoughby accepted with a smile.

Luke glanced over at his brother, ensconced close to the bookshelves in a comfortable brocade armchair with an open newspaper across him. 'Ross, find Judith and arrange for some tea to be brought to the study. Three cups…' he advised his brother meaningfully. Ross delivered a pained look at the prospect of light refreshment but got up good-naturedly and strolled from the room to find the housekeeper.

Luke knew he could have rung for service but a response was erratic. Not that the servants were hostile now; far from it. They were more likely to be beavering away in some odd corner of this Gothic pile.

In the three days since he had been in residence at Ramsden Manor, having found the household provisions sadly lacking, he had immediately replenished all stock cupboards. The lack of alcohol had been his and Ross's first consideration. Old Edward Miles hadn't been lying when he had denied any knowledge of brandy about the place. And the wine store Ross had found was down to its last dozen dusty bottles. So he had made good in buying in both alcohol and foodstuffs and taken care of various other shortcomings at the Manor. That, together with the promise that back wages and severance bonuses would be paid when the estate was sold, had combined to make him increasingly popular.

'Due to the rather dilapidated state of the property, I

wouldn't like to estimate how long it might take to achieve a sale,' Victor Willoughby mentioned, drawing Luke's thoughts back to business, as he leafed through documents in front of him. 'Perhaps if I were to arrange for minor work to be carried out…neaten the gardens, a little redecorating, for example…'

Luke cut in quietly. 'I haven't the time or inclination to tarry here. I would be willing to accept offers for the freehold which reflect its state of disrepair. Renovation is necessary, I agree. But the building is solid and free from any rot as far as I can detect.'

'Indeed, my lord, I'm sure. I only meant…'

Luke interrupted him mildly. 'I know what you meant and I thank you for your concern. The highest price possible isn't my main consideration. Returning to Cornwall is, at the earliest opportunity.' He gave the slightly disconcerted man a brief, conciliatory smile. 'Shall I leave it to you to arrange for the sale of the freehold? And to deal with staff remuneration?'

'Indeed, my lord,' Victor Willoughby assured the preoccupied man who was again gazing through the rain-spattered glass into the drizzly-grey distance. 'It may mean that several of my clerks will be working on your behalf, my lord.' He coughed delicately. 'Will payment for my firm's services be taken from the proceeds of the estate sale, or will an earlier…?'

A small, cynical smile escaped Luke but he didn't turn away from surveying the sodden landscape as he informed Willoughby levelly, 'You will receive interim payments. I want the estate dealt with as a matter of urgency and will pay for that service accordingly. Your fees will not be dependent upon the actual sale. Should the matter be closed in record time, however, a bonus might…' He allowed the enticement to hang between them for a moment. 'I shall be travelling back to Cornwall next week and would like to leave in the sure knowledge that everything possible is being done to expedite matters. And that it is all in capable hands.'

'Of course, my lord,' Victor Willoughby assured him, but sensing that somehow he had just received a subtle reprimand.

A light tapping at the door heralded the arrival of Judith with a laden tea tray. She smiled at Luke, informing him pleasantly, 'I've brought you some treacle biscuits, my lord. You remember, those you liked yesterday.'

'Thank you, Judith,' Luke said graciously, with a small smile for her. She blushed happily, pouring tea into wafer-thin china cups. Once this was accomplished and tea distributed she loitered, shifting uneasily from one foot to the other.

Luke raised querying brows at her, wordlessly inviting her to speak if something was troubling her.

'It's nothing really, my lord...'

'Mr Trelawney, Judith...I thought we had agreed you would use that,' he reminded mildly, hoping that Victor Willoughby was also taking due note.

'Yes, sir, I mean, Mr Trelawney. Well, sir, it's nothing really, as I said, it's just your brother...' Judith tailed off and shuffled uncomfortably again.

Luke sighed out, 'Yes, what now? Is he sliding down the banisters? Rolling drunk in the drawing room?'

'No, sir. He's...er...rolling dice with Joan and Sally...in the hallway. If you want dinner tonight, Mr Trelawney, he had best leave the girls be so I can get them to the vegetables.' She rubbed appreciative hands together as she expounded, 'It's to be smoked trout and roast guinea fowl with roast potatoes and fruit tarts with cream and...'

'And as you pass him in the hallway, Judith, tell him I want him, would you?' Luke cut into her menu, a slow hand spanning his forehead, soothing his temples.

Judith bobbed a quick curtsy before bustling busily from the study.

Poking professionally about in his cavernous document case, Mr Willoughby seemed deaf to the unusual discourse. But he ruined his nonchalance by admitting with doleful sympathy, 'I have a younger brother...'

Luke nodded acceptance of the man's tacit condolences before getting back to business. 'The Summer House Lodge...where is the lease for that building? I haven't found it among any of the documents in this study. Do you hold it?'

'The Summer House?' Mr Willoughby repeated, a trifle surprised. 'Oh, you won't find any lease for that; there is none.'

Luke frowned enquiry across the desk at him. 'Are you sure? The building is presently used as a small school, by Miss Rebecca Nash. She rents the premises on a lease, I would have thought.'

As Ross sauntered back into the room, Luke glanced up idly, scowling a little at his brother's impenitent smile. Picking up the newspaper he had previously been reading, Ross strolled across to the window by Luke's desk, as though enjoying better light there to study it.

'Well, yes, she does reside there. But there is no lease,' Willoughby confirmed as his pale eyes darted from one brother to the other.

'Why not?' Luke asked a little too quietly.

Willoughby noisily cleared his throat and slid nervous fingers between his stiff collar and his warming neck as he sensed an atmosphere fomenting. 'There was never any need of one,' he quickly advised Luke. 'Robin Ramsden and Miss Nash appeared to have…an agreement. She just resides and works there and he—' He broke off, desperately seeking the right words, aware of two sets of brown eyes watching him now. The silence strained interminably.

'And he…?' Luke finally prompted him, in a voice that was silky with danger, while his eyes relentlessly pinned down the weak blue ones seeking to evade him.

'And he allowed her to,' Mr Willoughby concluded quickly, pleased with his innocuous phrasing. It didn't have the desired effect of diverting Luke Trelawney's piercing gaze.

'Possibly he took pity on her…because of the tragedy which occurred some five years ago,' Willoughby suggested hastily. 'It would have been about the same time she took up residence at the Summer House. Yes, that must have been it.' He nodded, sure he had now satisfactorily managed a delicate situation.

'Tragedy…?'

Just one soft word coupled with a penetrating, fierce stare and Victor Willoughby readily explained. 'Miss Nash lost both her parents in a carriage accident in the winter snows. Within the same week she learned of the death of her fiancé in the Peninsula...er...he was a captain in the Hussars, I believe. Then her brother disappeared, too. That I believe was, financially, the crux of the matter. For her brother held the purse strings on her father's death. He was charged with administering her small inheritance for her but no one could find him. I believe they still can't.' He licked dry lips and glanced warily at Luke Trelawney, noting his narrow-eyed thoughtfulness.

'And Robin Ramsden..?' Luke interrogated him calmly.

'And Robin Ramsden appeared to take her under his protection...er...I mean to say, he looked after her, so to speak,' Mr Willoughby flustered, unwilling to imply too much of what he had never been certain. He had his own theories but he was not going to voice them. Definitely not to this man who had become rather daunting in the past few minutes.

Miss Nash was a lovely woman...he had seen her once or twice and had drawn the only logical conclusion he could for his late client's continuing aid and protection. This new lord of the manor seemed also to have taken an immediate personal interest in her. It was no concern of his...but she was very beautiful...

Luke shoved back in his chair and stood up. He walked to the window and stared out, appearing oblivious to his brother barely a yard away, even though Ross's anxious hazel eyes followed his movements. But Luke was peripherally aware of Willoughby behind him, gathering together his papers and stuffing them abruptly into his case in readiness to depart.

A hard, humourless smile curved Luke's mouth as he finally allowed himself to concentrate fully on Rebecca. It was all beginning to fall into place. What a gullible fool he'd been and that rankled. Everyone knew him for a cynic. No wonder she had been prepared to speak to Robin Ramsden on his behalf when believing he'd been discovered trespassing. Using charm and influence on the lord of this Manor was, by all accounts, nothing new for her. Well, that would suit him damn fine. There was no need for that to change.

Whatever Robin Ramsden had provided for her over the years, he knew he could improve on…a thousandfold. And he'd believed her to be some chaste provincial maid he would need to proposition with utmost care. She'd cried on learning of Robin Ramsden's death. Was it the man or the meal ticket she mourned? he wondered. Perhaps it was the prospect of losing her home…the schoolbuilding. What was she teaching there, in any case? If provocative Miss Mayhew, the young temptress he recalled from the woodland pond, was an untried schoolgirl, then…Ross was teetotal.

What did it matter? Rebecca had obviously fallen on hard times five years ago and had survived in any way she could. It was a commonplace tale.

He had already decided to take her with him and this changed nothing. Logically it made things easier, he acknowledged with a callous smile. He could now proposition her without risking having her outraged or hysterical. Even enthusiastic virgins were damn hard to tutor and sometimes barely worth the trouble. By the time they were adaptable and accomplished he was usually bored and looking elsewhere.

He thought of Wenna, something he hadn't done for a week or more. He was bored and looking elsewhere, he acknowledged sourly, yet she had always been the perfect mistress. Passionate, obliging, skilful, discreet, faithful…the list was endless. One of his large, dark hands curled into a fist. She'd suited him fine until he'd come here.

Chapter Four

'Lucy!' Rebecca's low disciplined voice carried easily in the quiet room and brought the girl's brunette head directly around. Rebecca pointed indicatively at the book in front of her on the pine desk and mouthed, 'Read!'

Once Lucy's attention was once more with her work, Rebecca glared at John. The young carpenter shifted from the open doorway where he had been loitering under the pretext of examining its battered wooden framework.

Rebecca quietly left her own desk and, passing the few younger day girls who were chalking on small blackboards, entered the kitchen. John was kneeling on the floor, replacing tools in a canvas holdall.

'The work must be finished now, John, surely?' she asked the fair-haired youth. He scrambled up then, reddening, and she realised that he hadn't heard her approach. He tugged at a lock of sun-bleached hair hanging low over one eye.

'Yes, m'm...' he mumbled. 'Just a few more rafters to look at under them slates...once rain eases off a bit.'

He had turned up, totally unexpectedly, within hours of Rebecca learning of Robin Ramsden's death. The new master had sent him, John had shyly explained and he had set to work. Rebecca was grateful he had arrived so speedily too, for by dusk the first fat drops of rain were staining the dusty ground around the Summer House.

John had been back each of the three days since, awaiting a break in the showers to carry out repairs. That was the problem. While he innocently surveyed the internal structure of the Summer House for chores to occupy him until he could get back on the roof, Lucy was purposefully surveying him. He was now watching her back, Rebecca realised with alarm. Her small parlour-cum-schoolroom often now found him lurking in its vicinity.

'You still here, young man?' Martha greeted John jovially as she entered the kitchen with a basket of washing beneath one capable arm. 'Just about got this lot dry between showers,' she informed Rebecca in the next breath. 'Waiting for them biscuits to get out the oven, I suppose,' she again addressed the blond youth.

'Well, I wouldn't say no, Martha.' He dodged her playful swipe at him.

'You'd best get yourself up on that roof then and earn some. Rain's eased off a bit now.'

He sauntered from the kitchen, cradling his prized tools beneath one arm.

'Never going to rid ourselves of him now, are we?' Martha mentioned with a shrewd meaningful look towards the parlour door.

Rebecca sighed, approached the open kitchen door, and surveyed the dripping landscape. 'I'll have to speak to Lucy again. She distracts him...'

'Distracts him?' Martha echoed with a derisive snort. 'That young miss is a bundle of trouble, if you ask me. Why, even my old Gregory has had eyes made at him. Not that I'm worried...or he's capable,' she added with a good-natured smile. 'But that young John...now there's a different matter,' she warned with a sage wagging of her grey head.

'I know she tends to flirt,' Rebecca admitted, biting anxiously at her bottom lip.

'You're looking a bit brighter today, if I may say so, Miss Becky,' Martha changed the subject abruptly.

'I do feel a little less anxious, Martha,' she said quietly. 'The shock of hearing of Robin's death made me a little illogical. But since then I have been thinking…perhaps things aren't quite so black. Now I have had time to consider…' She sighed, reflecting that 'consider' hardly began to do justice to the sleepless, fretful nights she had endured since first learning of this tragedy. 'I certainly can't honestly blame Mr Trelawney for wanting to return to Cornwall or to the home and estates he has there. Nor could I have complained had he wanted to take up residence at Ramsden Manor and charge me rent for using this building. It is his property, after all, to do with as he wishes. Because Robin was so good to me I tend to forget that I am just here on sufferance. But Mr Trelawney has sent John to repair the roof, so with all things considered, he has been quite kind…quite nice…'

'Gregory says he thinks the young master be quite taken with you too,' Martha mentioned with an astute narrowed look at Rebecca, as she deftly folded laundry. 'He says last time he laid eyes on his lordship, he were watching you walk away from him as though…'

'He feels sorry for me,' Rebecca cut in quietly. 'He realises that I shall be dispossessed and is good enough to sympathise. But I shall manage. I believe it will be some months yet before the matter of the estate is settled. I must use that time to again search for Simon. And I must now succeed,' she announced vehemently, concentrating on memories of her twenty-four-year-old brother and her inheritance, held within his grasp.

It wasn't a great fortune. But her five thousand pounds was the dividing line between poverty and self-respect. It would have been her dowry on her marriage to David. It was hers by right and she now needed to invest it for her future; to keep her free of soul-destroying drudgery as a provincial governess or companion. For she was aware that very little else awaited her once her rent-free tenancy of the Summer House was terminated. She was a spinster of almost twenty-six now and meeting someone to love and marry was increasingly remote.

She rarely socialised. Even when in London with Elizabeth

they had visited the theatre on only one occasion due to Elizabeth's recent confinement.

There was always the chance that a widower with children might take her on and provide her with a reasonable life. She sighed wistfully, for the notion of a loveless, convenience marriage for respectability and shelter was dispiriting. Since David no one had attracted or excited her... Her meandering thoughts circled back to Luke Trelawney. Her heart rate increased and a spontaneous rush of blood stained her cheeks at what would have been her next thought. She abandoned it immediately.

Her fingers sought automatic comfort from her silver locket, and she thought of dear David. She concentrated on his fine straw-coloured hair, his rounded face and the light freckling that dusted his nose and cheeks. It was so unfair. He had loved her dearly, although his parents had been keen for him to make a match with a young woman of better family. A middle-class merchant's youngest daughter was certainly not what they had in mind. The fact that all the Nash children had been well educated and had good connections mattered little.

David's father, Sir Paul Barton, was a baronet with a certain social standing and he had hoped his eldest son would improve the family's status and finances on marriage. There had been no celebration and only a small announcement in the paper, which David had insisted upon. Her sapphire betrothal ring was safely wrapped in tissue in her bedroom. She hoped she would never be forced to sell it to survive.

But David had been strong and loyal and had firmly declared his intention to marry her as soon as his commission terminated. It would have been three years ago, Rebecca realised. She would have been a happily married woman for three years, perhaps with children of her own. And a neat villa in Brighton. It was what she and David had discussed during their nine-month courtship. He had always treated her with such respect...such affection...

Her poignant memories were interrupted by a gravelly voice. 'You be best off forgetting about that brother of yours, Miss Becky,' Gregory sternly noted as he laid pungent, freshly dug leeks on the scrubbed pine table. Martha shot him a warning frown. 'She be best to know,' Gregory insisted. 'It was just a shame your poor late pa didn't know what his son was getting into. If he hada known, he woulda left you your money in safer hands, I reckon.'

'Gregory!' Rebecca admonished him, shocked by his temerity. He always had tended to speak his mind, but as he aged he was becoming a little too blunt.

'You know I speak truth, Miss Becky,' he placated her softly, seeing the distress in her lovely face. 'But I'm sorry fer upsetting you. Just know this. Jake Blacker's been seen in Brighton again recently, so I heard. And that means only one thing. Contraband is coming ashore again.'

'My brother was never involved in smuggling, Gregory,' Rebecca stated stiffly as she occupied her nervous hands by folding laundry with Martha. She noted the anxious look that passed between the couple. 'I know Simon had dealings with that ruffian,' she admitted, trying to ease the atmosphere. 'I challenged him about Jake Blacker disturbing Mama at home once when Simon and I were in town. He swore Blacker was only looking for him because he lost to him at cards. You know how he was always gambling in taverns. But Simon swore to Papa that he had repaid him and that he would avoid mixing with any of those reprobates in the future.'

'Where's he been all this time, then, Miss Becky?' Martha asked quietly. 'Why hasn't he been by to see how you are coping alone? It's a terrible thing for a brother to leave his sister so alone to fend for herself.'

'He obviously knows very well that Robin assists me....' She broke off, realising then just what worried this dear couple. Robin Ramsden was no longer able to do so. 'Besides,' she hurriedly said, 'he knows that I see Elizabeth also. My sister may be married and in London, but we keep in touch.'

A derisive snort met this information and Rebecca knew the reason for it. In all the six years Elizabeth had been married to James Bartholomew, a London lawyer, Rebecca had never once received an offer of help, financial or otherwise. She gave the Turners a conciliatory smile. They were only concerned for her welfare, she knew that. She also knew that without them she would never have been able to cope with running this small establishment.

She had always known that once Robin Ramsden and his patronage were gone she would be alone and vulnerable. She now felt foolish for not having prepared better for that day.

But she had always believed Simon to be alive. She knew sometimes with quite frightening certainty that her hell-raising brother was ridiculously close to her. Just as she was sure that he had used her inheritance as his own and was striving to replace it before he returned with a plausible tale for his absence. Finding Simon and extracting her money from him was now crucial.

Gazing, preoccupied, through the doorway into the damp afternoon, it was a moment before Rebecca noticed the couple strolling down the pathway towards the Summer House. As her eyes alighted on them, her soft mouth immediately curved into a delighted smile. 'Oh, Kay and Adam are visiting us,' she advised the Turners with a backward flick of a glance.

'Best check them biscuits,' Martha noted briskly. 'Be baking another batch, more'n like, what with the girls, young John and vicar 'n wife on the way.'

As Rebecca greeted the new arrivals, ushering them into the kitchen with cordial complaints about the abrupt change in the weather, Gregory mentioned casually, 'You'd best add his lordship to that list, Martha. I heard from Judith that he's pertickler to a biscuit.'

As Kay and Adam Abbott crowded into the small kitchen, accepting the invitation to be seated and partake of a little light refreshment, the bustle prevented Rebecca clearly understanding Gregory's cryptic remark. Noting his weatherbeaten countenance still turned to the window, she doubtfully approached the doorway.

Ross was standing, hands on hips, chestnut head thrown back, staring assessingly up at her roof. He shouted something up at John and pointed. Rebecca walked immediately out into the humid afternoon to greet him. She had an odd liking for this good-looking man she barely knew.

'He considers himself a bit of a carpenter,' explained a sardonic well-remembered voice that had her twisting immediately about.

Luke Trelawney was behind her and just to one side of the building as though he had walked around it. He held the reins of a magnificent pitch-black stallion in one hand. Rebecca's eyes were drawn immediately to the fine animal, such a contrast to the farm hack she had seen him with by the pond.

'Handsome brute, don't you think?' Luke stated ironically, noting her interest.

Rebecca raised thick-lashed luminous eyes to search his, noting the glitter in their dark depths. The description was as fitting for the rider as the horse and he was well aware of it.

She gave him a small smile, trying to calm that sudden increased pulse that his imposing presence always seemed to raise. She turned quickly on her heel, attempting to hide the colour she could feel staining her cheeks.

'Thank you for sending John so quickly,' she said distractedly, gazing up at the roof where the young carpenter was still receiving advice from Ross below. 'I was right about the rain, you see. Or rather, Gregory was. We've only had a little leaking. I'm very grateful.' Confident she had regained her composure, she faced him again, biting her lip a little at the expression in his eyes. They were narrowed and intent, as always. But the amused assessment had a harder edge that disturbed her. She realised he probably no longer found her rustic gaucheness quite so entertaining.

'You knew I'd send him, didn't you?' he remarked mildly, as his eyes followed John's careful descent from the roof's summit. 'It's what the lord of the Manor does for you, isn't it? Looks after you?'

Rebecca moistened her lips, feeling her agitation increasing as dark eyes swooped back to pitilessly pounce on her.

'I want to talk to you. I told you that last time I saw you,' he said a touch irascibly. 'You disappeared before I had a chance to discuss future arrangements…'

Rebecca managed a smile, a coiling and fluttering in the pit of her stomach at the memory of how he had comforted her that day. His arms had felt so welcome…so strong and protective. She sensed another wave of colour about to suffuse her skin and steeled herself desperately against it.

'Well, come in…please. And Ross,' she pleasantly offered. 'Reverend Abbott and his wife are here, too. We are just having tea. Please do come in,' she urged sincerely, a hand extending towards the Summer House. 'I'm sure they would both like to meet you before you return to Cornwall. Have you any idea how long you intend to remain in Sussex, Mr Trelawney?' she asked conversationally.

'I shall be leaving next week,' he brusquely informed her.

This information had Rebecca's golden head angling immediately up to him. 'Next week?' she breathed, her face whitening now, enhancing aquamarine eyes to jewel richness. 'Have you found a purchaser so soon?' she demanded a little boldly in her agitation. She recalled her brave words with Martha barely fifteen minutes ago…how she would cope with arranging her future and her search for Simon in the time it would take to find a new landlord.

'The matter will be left to a man of business…' he tersely supplied, while inwardly cursing that he had managed to turn up to proposition her at the very same time the damned vicar arrived to take tea. He gazed about impatiently and Rebecca falteringly invited, 'Well…would you like to come in and—?'

'Not really, Rebecca.' He bluntly cut across her words, aware how boorish he must sound. But seeing her again, trying to reconcile the role of paramour to Robin Ramsden with this fawn-like beautiful young woman who hesitated nervously before him, was excrutiating. Robin Ramsden had been fifty-two and a renowned lecher. Luke had since learned Robin had suffered with a heart complaint for some years. Instead of expiring atop some harlot in a Bath brothel it could just as easily have been here at this Summer House. God, he wished he'd never seen her. He could have come and gone from this place within a week, attended to business, spent a pleasant few nights roistering with Ross in Brighton, then returned to his life of luxurious contentment in Cornwall.

As his granite-jawed silence became protracted, comprehension dawned on Rebecca. He had come to tell her to leave. He was returning to Cornwall next week and wanted to evict her before he went. He was irritated because he was unsure how to broach the matter now she had company. She had sensed he had something to say. Her pale face lifted to his, her chin tilting in pride. She wasn't about to beg for time or anything else. She had little in the way of possessions. She could probably be packed and out in less than a week.

'When would you like me to leave, Mr Trelawney?' she asked coolly. 'I should have liked a little more notice, but I realise I have no rights in the matter. I would appreciate it if you would at least allow me to get a message to Miss Mayhew's family, so they can arrange to collect her. Thankfully, she is the only boarder at present…' Feeling a lump thickening in her throat and tears spearing her eyes, she swiftly turned and walked away.

She hastened blindly through the crowded kitchen, noting Ross leaning nonchalantly against a wall, a mug of tea in one hand and a large aromatic biscuit in the other. She managed a quiet cordial response to his greeting, and even to swap a few bright words with Kay as she made her way to the parlour and her pupils. She felt guilty now at having abandoned them for so long.

Lucy and John were standing close, chatting quietly by the girl's desk; as they saw Rebecca, they sprang apart. The three younger girls had abandoned their alphabets to chalk pictures on their blackboards.

'That's all for today. You're a little later leaving than usual so hurry home,' Rebecca emphasised as she dismissed them. 'Martha has made some refreshment. Perhaps you'd care for something before you leave, John,' she offered the loitering youth.

'Thank you, m'm,' John gruffly mumbled as he and Lucy quit the room.

Alone in the parlour, Rebecca momentarily bowed her head in despair before abruptly raising it. She would not be cowed by this. She had survived the loss of her beloved parents and her fiancé five years ago—she would surely survive the loss of this building. She glanced about the small parlour, at the white-washed walls hung with a few pictures from her late parents' home, at the polished pianoforte from their parlour. She sighed. It was an enchanting building, filled with fine memories, and she would miss it dreadfully.

With head held high she walked back to the kitchen and forced a smile as she entered. There was little need; apart from Martha the hot room, redolent of cinnamon, was empty.

'All gone out to look at the horseflesh,' Martha advised, on taking in Rebecca's bewilderment. 'Gregory never did say just how handsome a man he is. Nor did you for that matter,' she added with a sideways look. 'Charming as can be, too. Came in and introduced hisself and his brother…such a pair of good lookers as I never did see.'

Rebecca was aware that Adam Abbott was a keen horseman who owned a particularly fine grey gelding himself. The beautiful black stallion she had seen was sure to interest him. And Kay took an interest in whatever pleased her husband.

As Rebecca peeked discreetly through the kitchen window, she noticed Adam mount the magnificent ebony horse and enthusiastically trot it around in a large circle in front of the Summer House. He called something out to Luke who nodded, while casually surveying the scene. Kay and Ross were chatting idly; Kay petting the neck of a chestnut mare that Rebecca had not seen before, obviously Ross's. Gregory leaned against the house, smilingly watching the pastoral scene, while Lucy and John seemed content to observe each other.

After a moment, Luke stepped back a pace or so and then turned and strode purposefully towards the house. Rebecca felt her stomach knot and sat abruptly down at the kitchen table. She had no intention of hiding from him.

She sensed his presence in the doorway long before he actually spoke to her. Martha started to hum tunelessly, busying herself with tidying every crockery item she could lay her plump hands on.

'I want to talk to you, Rebecca. Will you come for a walk with me?'

'You can say anything you need to in front of Martha,' Rebecca calmly replied without turning towards him.

'I think you'd rather I said this in private,' was his steely, quiet response. 'Now…' he smoothly added when she made no move to obey.

She knew it was senseless to defy him. She needed to know when he expected her to move out.

Strolling in tense silence was unbearable. Rebecca realised she would rather be disappointed straight away. She abruptly halted on the perimeter of the woodland close to the Turners' small cottage, and leaned back against the solid trunk of an elm. She crossed her arms around her middle, holding her warm, black-fringed shawl tight about her. It was nearly dusk now and although the rain was holding off, a light breeze was strengthening. Its cool caress fanned wisps of honey hair softly across her features. She shook her head to clear them, removing the stragglers with slender, white fingers.

'Is this private enough? Can you talk to me now?' she queried with tremulous sarcasm and then felt immediately wretched for stooping to it.

He walked back slowly towards her and stood close, so close that Rebecca sensed his warmth through her chill.

'When I leave here next week I want you to come with me to Cornwall,' he stated with quiet candour. He watched her golden head jerk back and her eyes searched his as though she was unsure she had heard correctly.

His narrow mouth twisted in a hard smile. 'I should perhaps explain my worthy circumstances first. I have a large estate in Cornwall…very large. I have considerable wealth and status. It's one of the reasons I have no use for Ramsden Manor or the title. I have various other properties…not only in Cornwall, but a smaller estate in Bath and a house in Mayfair.' He halted as though bored with the details he was recounting. 'I have a lot to offer you, Rebecca. You will want for nothing. I know moving away from here and people you know will be difficult but I will care for you, protect you...'

Rebecca gazed at him in utter awe, unable to credit what she was hearing and equally startled by the spontaneous warm relief that drenched her. She had heard similar promises before...so long ago...when David had proposed and declared how well he would provide for her.

'Why would you want to marry me?' she queried in a husky whisper. 'If what you say about your circumstances is true, you could make a very successful match. You now have a title...'

Luke stared at her, sure she was jesting. He searched her face for guile but there was nothing; no sarcasm, no humour, just glossy-eyed gravity and a heart-wrenching sweet expression on her face. God, she was going to accept him. She thought he'd proposed marriage and she was going to accept.

'You will want time to consider. Think over what I'm offering you,' he stressed slowly and quietly. 'Think it over carefully, Rebecca. But know this...I want you with me. I want you very much and I promise you will never regret allowing me to take care of you in Cornwall.'

A soft, dewy-eyed smile met this affirmation before turquoise and sepia eyes locked. She couldn't believe this was happening to her. Only an hour or so earlier she had been lamenting the likelihood of remaining a spinster her life through or marrying simply from convenience and now...Luke Trelawney was proposing to wed her and the idea of it was simultaneously terrifying and exhilirating.

Conscious of her submission, her allure, but mostly the insistent pulsing tightening his groin, he leaned slowly towards her. Now was as good a time as any, he realised cynically, to find out just what she could do. If she was compliant, screening woodland was barely a pace away. A dark hand was placed deliberately against the tree trunk at the side of her golden hair while the other leisurely moved to her face.

Rebecca allowed her lids to droop, shielding shining eyes as she raised her face a little to meet his kiss. David had kissed her after he had proposed. The first proper kiss she had ever known.

But not like this, she thought, panic-stricken, as a warm, hard mouth slid against hers and firm fingers at her jaw skilfully manoeuvered her lips apart. Her hands slid immediately up between them, to purchase space and try to weaken his hold. His palm moved abruptly from the tree trunk and curled about her soft nape, urging her forward while controlling her head and keeping her close. Dark fingers laced up into her silky hair, intentionally loosening honey tendrils to drape her neck and face. At the first thrust of his tongue into her mouth, Rebecca jerked back so violently that the knuckles of the hand cradling her head, scraped against tree bark.

Heavy-lidded black eyes merged with skittering turquoise. He gave a small sardonic smile. So she still expected to be wooed, even believing that he had proposed marriage to her. He had been right in estimating that seduction would be a requirement with this one. But he was prepared to indulge coy role-playing up to a point. A modest maiden might be briefly diverting. He dropped his head back to hers abruptly, before she had a chance to properly evade him.

Rebecca reflexively bunched her fists against the solid expanse of his torso. But there was no need this time. A gentle moist caress soothed her bruised lips with subtle art. As her fingers uncurled to lay against his muscled chest she instinctively leaned into him, raising up on tiptoe to protract the contact as she sensed him moving away. She felt the smile against her mouth and he deepened the kiss just enough to startle her before he let her go.

'I have to go back now,' Rebecca stated breathlessly, sliding sideways and away from him. She felt utterly confused. He had proposed marriage to her, promised to care for her, and yet there was something in his eyes…in his manner, that made her uncertain he liked her. There was something in the way he had kissed her, too, that had both excited and repelled her: an odd mix of anger and tenderness. 'The Turners will be waiting to leave. They won't go home until I get back.' She pointed distractedly towards the small cottage close by, attempting to lighten the mood between them with bland chatter. 'That's their home just over there. It has very little land about it, unfortunately...' She glanced at him, leaning back against the tree with his arms folded across his broad chest, watching her with that same thoughtful amusement.

Perhaps he expected her to flirt a little with him. She had very little experience of flirting; could hardly remember any of the coy techniques that she and Elizabeth had employed when in their teens attending local assemblies and balls. She had met David at such a gathering. If she recalled anything, it had most to do with the artful use of eyelashes and a fan. A small inward smile thankfully acknowledged that the fan was definitely out of the question.

A poignant curling tightened the pit of her stomach as she was again struck by how incredibly handsome he was. A thick lock of black hair fell heavily across his forehead, nearly into narrowed eyes. There was something disquieting about him too, she abruptly recognised, apart from the arrogance and authority that privilege and wealth had honed. There was an air of menace, something dangerous dissembling behind his sophisticated manner and quiet speech. Through the mounting dusk, she glimpsed the mockery in the slant of his mouth. He was acknowledging her fixed interest in him, she realised. She shivered a little, wrapping her shawl tightly about her, but returned him a small, sweet smile, before turning in the direction of the Summer House.

It was an opportunity too good to miss. She might not catch him alone again. He and his brother seemed inseparable at times. And there was so much she needed to know...to find out about this man who was to become her husband; for she had quietly accepted they would marry.

She had returned to the Summer House some half an hour ago to find Kay and Adam had left. She felt guilty at having

been so ill-mannered as to have abandoned them when they
had come to visit her. Kay and she were good friends, yet they
had barely exchanged a dozen inconsequential words. She wondered how Martha had explained away her absence and that of
the new Lord Ramsden.

Martha and Gregory had made their slow progress home,
hoping to avoid showers threatening in the lowering sky in the
north. Only John and Ross remained, standing at the foot of
the rough-hewn wooden ladder, inspecting various carpentry
tools with great debate and attention.

Luke had immediately returned to the Manor with barely a
parting word either for her or his brother. His mood as they
walked back to the Summer House had been unusually solemn
and preoccupied. He had merely looked long and hard at her
and told her he would call in a day or two to speak to her
again. Before he did, she needed to speak to someone. And
there was only Ross. She needed to know more.

Lucy was safely in her room, indulging in a quiet hour of
sewing before dinner. Rebecca watched Ross stride towards his
chestnut horse, tethered to a nearby branch. Without conscious
decision she lightly ran over the slippery grass towards him.

Hearing her approach, he swung about and gave her a
friendly smile. 'That young lad knows what he's about. His
father has taught him well. He's spliced a piece of rafter—'

'May I talk to you, Ross, before you leave?' Rebecca breathlessly interrupted his praise. 'Just for a moment. I won't keep
you long.'

'Of course,' Ross agreed but Rebecca noted his slightly be-
mused look. She was sure then that he knew nothing of Luke's
proposal.

A silence developed as Rebecca strived to formulate a way
of extracting information about his brother which didn't seem
prying or audacious.

She blurted quickly, 'Luke wants me to go to Cornwall with
him when he leaves here. I know so very little about him, Ross.
It's such a great step to take. I realise what he's offering is a
great honour but...'

Ross cut in mildly, 'Ah, I see. Well, I can't say I'm surprised he has approached you, Rebecca. He has been…umm…' he laughed and looked at her '…quite enchanted by you since he first saw you floundering about in that pond.' As Rebecca flushed, he added, 'It's natural you should be…er…cautious. But whatever he's told you about his ability to provide for you is no exaggeration.' He glanced at the top of Rebecca's golden head. She was amazingly beautiful and desirable and yet what astounded him most was that she wanted to quiz him like this.

Obviously she was more worldly wise than he had imagined. Old man Ramsden had indeed been lucky in finding such a sophisticate hidden away in this backwater. It took quite a bold and confident paramour to investigate a prospective lover's financial standing through his brother. The usual method, as far as he knew, was to discreetly check on how recent cast-offs fared. Not an option in her case, he had to admit. Cornwall was a long way to go to get a reference. So he could afford to be obliging. After all, she had such an engaging way about her, he understood why Luke was so smitten. If he didn't value his health quite so much, he'd be tempted to show an interest himself.

'Luke is well known for his extreme generosity,' he kindly explained. 'He has a reputation for discretion, too. So if, by chance…er…he found that you didn't suit him, after all…' Noting an odd frown and her face whitening, he hastily added, 'Or you were homesick and wanted to return to Sussex, of course; well, he would, undoubtedly, secure your comfortable future and your reputation…' He tailed off, noting that his reassurances seemed to have had the opposite effect. Her lustrous, unblinking eyes gazed into his and she suddenly bit down hard on her full bottom lip. She still stared at him but those incredible blue-green eyes were vacant, her mind far away. 'What I mean to say, Rebecca,' he expounded helpfully, 'is that with Luke…because of his consideration and generosity…umm…*chères amies* remain *chères amies*…'

'Even when they become less expensive, you mean,' Rebecca said in a strangling whisper.

Ross looked at her and laughed, relieved that she had at last spoken and wittily. 'That's very good…dear friends become less expensive. Very true, too,' he wryly reflected with another chuckle.

Rebecca joined him. A laugh jerked out of her with such force that she moved a shaking hand to shield her face, while twisting away from Ross. She regained composure within a moment and her arms wrapped tightly, comfortingly about her body. Ross watched her, enchanted by the way her golden hair draped in fetching tendrils about her slender neck. She appeared to be cold because her white fingers rubbed ceaselessly against her arms.

'You didn't mind me mentioning…?' Ross posed uneasily, unsure why but sensing something was amiss.

Rebecca slowly faced him. She fussed busily at her hair, attempting to shove golden strands back into pins. 'No, of course not. I'm just so glad I managed to have this talk with you, Ross. Thank you,' she murmured graciously, with a small dip of her head.

'So, what have you decided then?' he persisted.

Rebecca swallowed hard. 'Well, I have definitely decided that we ought to keep this conversation just between ourselves. You won't say anything to Luke, will you, Ross?'

Ross couldn't have been more relieved by the request. He was certain he had been more than complimentary about his brother, yet Rebecca had seemed happier before his praise. And how Luke was going to react to that he didn't dare contemplate. 'I promise not to say a word,' he agreed conspiratorially.

Aware of his steady gaze on her, Rebecca smiled and peered up, through the dusk at her roof. 'You're quite right about John, you know. He is certainly a fine carpenter. I hope the next landlord recognises just what an asset he is…' Words failed her then and she swung away, calling huskily over her shoulder, 'Well, goodnight, Ross. It was nice to see you again today.'

She could wait to see him in a few days when he visited the Summer House or she could go tomorrow to Ramsden Manor and seek him out. She could pretend continuing ignorance of his true intentions or she could immediately challenge him. Perhaps it might be interesting watching him squirm off the hook if she persisted with the belief that he wanted to marry her. Or perhaps it would just be unbearably degrading for her to hear him laugh and say he thought she would by now have had sense enough to interpret his proposition.

He couldn't have made it more plain. 'Think over what I'm offering you,' he had said. Not once but twice and still she had not. It had taken Ross to clear her mind. Ross to bring woundingly home to her just what penniless, unprotected spinsters could expect from life and wealthy men. And once the shock of it had dulled, she had indeed almost considered the benefits of what he was prepared to offer her.

When had he once mentioned marriage? He hadn't mentioned love either, but then she hadn't expected him to. They barely knew each other. But she had recognised the instant mutual attraction. It was something to build on. He had been kind to her…comforting, and she had mistaken disguised lust for respect and affection. She had taken David's honest qualities and applied them to this man. Rebecca closed her eyes and leaned her hot forehead against the cool glass of her bedroom window pane. She couldn't help her inexperience. She couldn't help her naivety. But Heaven knew how she regretted them both now. And how she hated Simon—he had taken her small inheritance and left her so bereft that she was obliged to consider sordid propositions from a stranger.

Whichever way she approached it, whichever course of action she took, she knew she had to steel herself against the utter humiliation which threatened to choke what remained of her confidence and self-respect.

Chapter Five

Rebecca walked briskly, swinging her straw bonnet in one hand, concentrating on the pleasant warmth of the October sun on her head. She could now see the Manor—it was barely another five minutes' walk away—but still she curbed her apprehension, attributing the increased thudding of her heart to the brisk pace she was setting herself.

She already had set in her mind what she would say. She had rehearsed the coming interview countless times through the sleepless night. She would not now give it further thought until the actual encounter.

The weather was fine again she impressed upon herself, as she lifted her wan face to the sun, but without the oppressive sultriness of previous weeks. She was determined to do her utmost to urgently seek out Simon and investigate suitable employment. She had Martha and Gregory as companions. She had Kay and Adam as friends, and although neither couple was in a position to help her financially, she knew they would support her in other ways. She had a lot to be grateful for. She would not allow an arrogant, immoral stranger to blight her future. Once the mortification of the next hour or so was behind her, she would be ready to continue with her life.

She lightly ascended the stone steps of Ramsden Manor and immediately rapped the knocker on the sturdy black-oak door. Her palms were clammy and she automatically dried them on her silver-grey cotton skirts. That edginess apart, she looked quietly about at the sunny scene, noticing how the recent rain had brought a little verdure back into the landscape.

'Miss Rebecca…!' Miles greeted her, a smile creasing his lined countenance.

'Hello, Miles,' Rebecca returned in a cordial but wavering tone. 'Is Mr Trelawney at home? I should like to speak to him.'

'Big or little?' Miles asked with a mischievous grin.

Rebecca looked searchingly at him and then said, 'Oh…I see.' She managed a small laugh. 'I mean Lord Ramsden. Is he at home, Miles?'

'Well, come in…come in,' Miles prompted, realising they stood by the door conversing. He ushered Rebecca into the cool, marble-floored hallway. 'I believe he went to the stables. I'll go and check. You make yourself comfortable,' he said as he hobbled down the stone steps. He called casually back to her, 'Judith is about in the kitchens somewhere. She'll be pleased to see you.'

Rebecca stood alone in the vast hallway. A week ago she would have done as Miles prompted and wandered off to find Judith. She had always felt relaxed and at home in this house. Now she glanced about at familiar ebonized panelling and the elegant sweeping stairwell, feeling unwelcome and intrusive. An unsteady hand went to her hair, checking and tidying stray tendrils, loosened by her brisk walk. She moved to one of the high-backed hall chairs and sat down and waited.

Partial obliteration of the sunbeams streaking the floor was the first indication of his arrival and despite her absolute resolution that she would not panic, her fingers tightened convulsively about the velvet chair seat. As heavy, ringing footsteps neared her, she stood up carefully and then turned towards him.

He was closer than she had imagined and she stepped back from him before raising her eyes to his. He was dressed in plain black breeches and an open-necked white shirt, sleeves rolled back from solid tanned forearms, and his overwhelming virility nearly made her seek the chair again. Instead she greeted him coolly.

'Good morning, Mr Trelawney. I'm sorry to arrive uninvited. Might I have a few minutes of your time? I should like to speak to you.'

Luke's eyes and mouth narrowed assessingly. He had been suspicious as soon as Miles told him she had arrived. He was certain even the keenest fiancée would allow her suitor slightly longer to reappear. It was barely fifteen hours since last he'd seen her. A thin smile touched his lips. But he'd known new mistresses take less time before soliciting. When he had left her yesterday she had been subdued but tranquil. Strangely, so had he.

But there was no such serenity about her now. Probing dark eyes slowly surveyed her alabaster face. She was finding it hard to meet his eyes and to cease chewing at her bottom lip. He waited, allowing a brief silence to develop between them, attempting to gauge her mood and intention. But she had prepared well and merely stood before him with a polite, neutral expression fixed on a spot slightly to his right.

He held out a hand, indicating she should walk in front of him. 'Come along to the study. It's a fine day,' he added conversationally.

'Indeed, yes, it is,' Rebecca agreed, forcing herself to adopt his bland tone as she entered the door he held open for her.

'Sit down, Rebecca,' he ordered quietly as he closed it.

She immediately did so, in the comfortable wing-chair across from the one he used behind the large, leather-topped desk. 'How did you get here? Did Gregory bring you? I didn't see the trap in the drive.'

'I walked,' Rebecca calmly informed him. 'I often walk…I often used to walk between here and the Summer House. It isn't that far.' She halted abruptly. She hadn't come here to chat and the sooner she could get through this, the more likely she was to leave with a vestige of pride intact. She drew a steadying breath, about to speak.

'Would you like some tea? Judith will fetch some,' he said at the same time.

'Thank you, no. I have simply come to apologise and then will be leaving.'

He knew then; she was going to reject him because she'd done as he had stupidly hinted she should and thought too long and hard. He had done the same through an endless night until towards dawn he no longer knew which of them was right. The irony was, now he did. And he wasn't prepared for it. His jaw gritted and his lids drooped as he leaned back into the chair.

Rebecca, noting his disquieting change in attitude, launched immediately into her studied speech. 'I have come to apologise, Mr Trelawney, for misinterpreting your proposition yesterday. I am conscious that in doing so I have embarrassed both you and myself. I can only offer my naïvety in mitigation but can assure you that as far as I am concerned the matter is now finished and will never again be mentioned. Good day to you, sir.' She stood up as she murmured this last, and was halfway to the door when he spoke.

'And I can assure you, Rebecca, that the matter is nowhere near finished,' he informed her remorselessly.

She swung back to him then, but continued stepping backwards towards the door. She breathed deeply, desperate to maintain her icy composure. She had been doing so well. Better than she had dared imagine. 'I can categorically state, sir, that nothing could be further from the truth,' she tremulously declared.

He shoved his chair back then and started towards her, making her speed backwards even faster towards the door. She twisted to open it at the same time as his hand jammed across her shoulder, slamming it shut.

She flung herself round to glare up into his tense, dark face. 'You will allow me to leave this instant. Remove your hand,' she commanded icily, spearmint sparks glittering in her eyes.

'No,' he denied her with equal chill and greater authority. He didn't bother elaborating and merely stared down into her white, strained face.

She was losing control. She knew she was. The protective shell of frigid civility was cracking and she could feel hurt and humiliation welling up, waiting to seep out. She lowered her face immediately and studied the mother-of-pearl buttons in the lawn folds of his shirt. Her eyes were inexorably drawn to the expanse of dark, muscled chest exposed by the gaping material so she closed them and bit down on her lip as she felt its first tremor. It was so unfair. She had so nearly made it. Two more paces…and she would have been out, into the meadow, on her way home.

The injustice of it made a final burst of courage hearten her and she clung desperately to it. She shook back her golden head to meet his eyes squarely. 'If you please, sir, I should like to leave. My pupils are awaiting my return. I told Martha I would be but an hour. It is more than that now,' he was glacially informed.

'I thought about you all through last night, Rebecca,' he said softly, ignoring her plea. 'I've thought about you every night…every day, since the first moment I saw you.'

Rebecca hurriedly dropped her eyes from a burning pitch-dark gaze that slowly roamed her set features.

'Do you know what else I was thinking about, Rebecca?' He moved a hand towards her face as though to make her look at him. But then he changed his mind and merely carried it on to lean that against the door too, so she rested within an un-touching embrace. 'I was thinking of children…daughters with molten-honey hair and eyes the colour of foreign seas.'

A pained, bitter laugh erupted from Rebecca. 'How poetic, Mr Trelawney…and there was I believing you an insensitive barbarian. Fortunately, you will not need to worry further about bastards. Leastways, none that resemble me.'

A swift, dark hand relinquished the door and curled about her nape, forcing her head up to his. 'You believed I wanted to marry you yesterday. What would have been your answer?'

She swallowed and her tongue swiftly moistened her dry lips. 'No,' she answered hoarsely.

'Liar,' he rejected on a satisfied smile. 'So you were pre-pared to be my wife but not my mistress. Which makes me wonder what it was that Robin Ramsden gave you that you think I cannot.' His eyes and tone hardened as he spoke and he abruptly swung her about, walking her backwards with him towards the chair she had vacated.

'Perhaps you would like to tell me, Rebecca,' he suggested quietly. 'Or is it simply that you don't want to leave Sussex?'

She pulled herself out of his grasp and to escape him walked about the desk and stood close to the chair he had sat in. She gripped the leather back of it with white-knuckled fingers. 'What is it Robin Ramsden gave me?' she choked on a small bitter laugh. 'He gave me everything. In the last five years he gave me a roof over my head, food to eat, a way of earning my living…he gave me my self-respect.'

'You think I won't care for you…give you all of that and more?' he asked softly.

'I have no wish to earn my living with you. By profession I am a teacher.'

'I'm not judging you, Rebecca,' he said gently. 'I know you have endured a lot of tragedy in your life. You must have been very young when you lost your parents and your fiancé. How old were you, sixteen…seventeen?'

'I have no need of your pity and it is somewhat misplaced as I was almost twenty-one at that time,' she informed him with a strange mix of triumph and regret at letting him know her age.

Sepia-dark eyes narrowed on her and he queried, 'Twenty-one?' He barely paused before calculating, 'You're nearly twenty-six?'

The unalloyed surprise in his voice was simultaneously wounding and satisfying. 'Yes, Mr Trelawney, I am very nearly twenty-six,' Rebecca confirmed, tilting her chin. 'I'm sorry to disappoint you with my advanced years. Perhaps they will now permit me to leave.'

'You haven't disappointed me, Rebecca,' he said with a smile. 'Just surprised me somewhat.' And she had, he had to admit. She looked a good deal younger but, that apart, it also showed Ramsden in a more ethical light. Bringing a poverty-stricken woman of twenty-one under one's protection was infinitely more acceptable than ruining a child of sixteen.

In the brief silence, words hovering and nudging on the edge of Rebecca's mind surged in. She froze and stared, not daring to believe it true. She concentrated on them as they ran back and forth through her head. *What was it Robin Ramsden gave you that you think I cannot?* She moistened her dry lips, unwilling to countenance his meaning or that she had been so incredibly unworldly again. She had just admitted to being a woman of nearly twenty-six years old, yet what he had naturally assumed had prompted Robin's help and protection had never once occurred to her.

'You believe that Robin…you think that…you believe he would have used me in the disgusting way you wish to?'

Her hands gripped so hard on the chair back that it started to tip backwards and she abruptly let it go. It clattered back, castors skidding against the polished wood floor.

'You are quite despicable. I wish my uncle were alive. I wish so much he were alive. He would kill you for insulting me so…' In her fury and agitation, she rounded the desk to confront him, barely noticing the change in his demeanour.

'What did you say?' he grated, as she approached with violence in her eyes.

'I said he would kill you…he would kill you,' she cried, the sheen in her eyes threatening to spill.

'What else…you said something else,' he uttered hoarsely, catching at her forearms to hold her away from him as he guessed her intention.

Rebecca was instantly still. She swallowed hard and shook straggling honey curls back from her flushed face. 'I said that my uncle would kill you. But he can't and I wish I could.'

Luke slowly relaxed his grip on her but didn't let her go. 'What is this ''uncle'' you term him. Some coy epithet for lover?'

A hand immediately attempted to fly up towards his face. It was as instinctive as the struggle to free herself. She fought him silently and savagely until he swung her about and forced her spine back against his torso. A brown arm banded her tight against him until her thrashing calmed. It did almost immediately. She held herself rigid against his tense, hard body, steeling herself to ignore the heat and mingling male scent of leather and citrus soap enveloping her. He released her tentatively, as though believing she might turn and swing at him. But she didn't. As soon as possible she pulled far away and then faced him.

'No,' she finally answered him, as though there had been no break in their conversation. 'It's more a coy epithet for my father's brother. Half-brother, actually. Not a fact that was well known, for they hated each other. My grandmother, Grace Markham, was mother to them both. She married into the Ramsden family. She married Saul, the fourth baron, I believe he was. On his death she married Granville Nash,' she recounted remotely, as her wobbly fingers attempted to straighten her hair and her dress. 'But Robin liked me.' She gave a shaky laugh. 'I should say he liked us all, for no doubt you will again suspect him of singular depravity. He was fond of Simon, Elizabeth and me. Perhaps because he and his wife had no children of their own they were good to their nephew and nieces. He would let us play in the Summer House as children. For that's what it was then: a children's summer house.'

She continued to neaten her appearance as she neared the door, quite collected now. 'So now you know, Mr Trelawney, a little bit of Ramsden history. Not many people do. But then it was none of their concern. Just as it was none of yours.'

She turned at the door to look at him. 'I'm glad that you have decided you're too grand and sophisticated to join us in Sussex. It's comforting to know that you will be relinquishing this property and title to return elsewhere. The Ramsden estate…the people here…the Summer House…all have been dear to me for five years or more, and knowing you despise them only endorses their worth for me.

'So there is something else you should know, Mr Trelawney. I will not give up any of it lightly. I have no intention of quitting the home my uncle gave to me. If you wish me out of the Summer House, you will have to get the bailiffs to forcibly eject me.' She barely paused for breath. 'Good day to you, sir,' she quietly, politely directed to the expanse of broad back positioned by the large window.

'The nights are getting colder, my lord. I'll stoke this up a bit for you,' Miles offered helpfully, as he poked at the already blazing pile of logs in the grate. Luke murmured something inaudible without looking away from the open newspaper across him. He leaned one side of his face in a broad palm and flicked the page over.

Miles slid him a look from the fireplace. He had again been assigned by the rest of the servants to try and winkle out when this unexpected benefactor might be withdrawing his person and purse from the Manor to return to Cornwall. Severance pay and references were all very well but didn't compare with retaining the present status quo.

This sixth baron had inherited just two weeks ago, yet in Miles's fifty years of service at this noble residence, he had never known such open handedness. There was ample food in the stock cupboards, candles enough to light a ballroom, fuel for every fire. A new groom had been hired to care for the two magnificent horses ensconced in the stables, even though, by all accounts, they would soon be gone. Miles had only mentioned once, in passing, that another kitchen servant would benefit and he had been given notice to hire one.

But each one of the servants dejectedly knew it was not to last. This Baron had told them at the outset that the Ramsden estate and title found no favour with him. Yet the week of departure had come and gone...but the Trelawneys had not...not yet.

Miles creased his already furrowed brow thoughtfully at the darkly handsome man who seemed engrossed in three-day-old newspapers. He glanced at the crystal tumbler at one side of him. It was empty...again. He creaked across on his painful joints, collecting the decanter on the way. He carefully replenished the glass, a stiff bow acknowledging the grunt which he now recognised as gratitude. He replaced the decanter on a mahogany side table. Then picked it up again and moved it to another. He scuffled wearily to the mantelpiece and moved a candlestick…then moved it back again. He girded his courage.

'You'll be soon away back to Cornwall then, my lord?' Miles croaked out.

Luke glanced up at him, then down at the paper. He pushed himself irritably back into the brocade sofa and one black-booted foot came up to rest on the opposite knee. He rustled the paper open again and stared at the print without answering.

Miles crept about the room, tinkering with various pottery, cushions and stray books. Luke looked up impatiently at his furtive ministrations, about to dismiss him, when he heard the gravel crunch outside the window. He turned his dark head towards the black night, seeing the blur of the carriage light as it passed.

Miles saw it, too, and ambled slowly across the Aubusson carpet towards the window. 'Can't be Master Ross, he's gone to Brighton…too early for him,' he mumbled to himself. 'Perhaps it's Gregory come over at last.'

He glanced casually at his master as he passed him, and noted that he had somehow just gained his full, black-eyed attention. So he explained. 'Gregory Turner. I've been expecting him all week. Thought he must have been ailing…'

'Why is that?' Luke questioned evenly.

'Afflicted like me…in the knees,' Miles readily explained.

'Why have you been expecting him all week?' Luke spelled out through lightly gritting teeth.

'Well, no one's come to collect the provisions. I thought if Gregory was poorly perhaps Miss Rebecca would come herself. She can drive that trap good as any man. I've seen her. And they must be low on everything. Shouldn't think they've a pound of flour left. Can't think why they've not been…'

Luke could, and a low oath ground out of him as he sprang up and strode to the window. 'It's not the trap. I thought I told you that the Summer House was to be maintained.'

'Oh, yes. But Gregory always collects the provisions. Miss

Rebecca's uncle…that was Robin Ramsden, you know, because not many people do. Only the old 'uns like me and the Turners…'

A harsh bark of laughter made Miles start and cease his rambling dialogue. Luke glowered, thin-lipped, at the ornate plaster work on the drawing room ceiling before piercingly at the old man. 'Yes, I do know now and I would have been obliged had someone thought to mention it sooner.'

Miles squinted uncertainly at him, wondering what had prompted this abrupt passion to overtake his master's previous apathy. 'Well, Lord Ramsden as was, said how Gregory should collect once a week,' he testily explained.

'Well, Lord Ramsden as is…' Luke informed silkily, '…says make very sure that whatever they are lacking is delivered at first light tomorrow. Do I make myself clear?'

Miles peered myopically at him. 'Indeed, my lord. I'll send John,' he warily agreed, before continuing his lopsided gait to the window.

'It's your brother, my lord. And some of his friends by the look of things.' Miles shuffled away from the window, a smile rejuvenating his ancient features. Young Mister Trelawney always livened the place up a bit. This one tended to stamp about, surly and uncommunicative, especially in the last week or so. A wealthy young man like he should be out, roistering with other young blades, Miles deemed, wagging his head to himself as he hobbled towards the door.

He could only recollect him going to Brighton a half-dozen times with his brother and then he never came back in a better mood than he went. He hardly left the house in the evening…which was a great pity, for the servants could frolic a little themselves with no master in residence.

Luke dropped back into the red brocade sofa. His dark head leaned back against the comfortable cushions. He closed his eyes and allowed himself to think of Rebecca. He'd managed not to think about her for practically the whole day. Now he'd worry the night through that she was hungry. Why the hell hadn't the stupid old fool said she was out of food? He'd made it plain enough that every consideration given to the Summer House by Robin Ramsden was to continue. But he should have realised she would choose to starve rather than accept any aid from him.

A hand went to the paper and he idly flicked the pages before carefully folding it and dropping it back on to the seat beside him. He gazed at the intricate ceiling, he stared at the glowing fire and then out into the moonless night. He looked back at the newspaper for a second before he hurled it viciously across the room. He grabbed at the tumbler by his side, downed the brandy in one swallow, and replaced it heavily. He could seduce her, he could coerce her, he could do anything he damn well pleased. He could make her homeless right now…this minute. He could be back in Cornwall in two days with her permanently in his bed. She couldn't deny or fight him.

But he knew he wouldn't. He wouldn't even go over and see her after eight days.

But she'd had the courage to come to him. And politely apologise with grace and dignity for her lack of sophistication. No tearful recriminations, veiled threats or fits of hysteria. She would have come and gone within five minutes had he let her. What wounded him most was that she now genuinely regretted her innocence. Just as he genuinely regretted causing her such hurt and humiliation. She might be naïve…more innocent than she had any right to be at her age, but her intuition was strong. She had recognised instantly what had taken him fifteen hours longer: that they were each other's destiny. It was the source of the quiet serenity that had radiated from her and enveloped him before they parted.

He had arrived at the Summer House to proposition her in irritation; kissed her in lustful selfishness and still she had believed in him. She would have accepted being his wife. He knew it as surely as he knew she would now do her utmost to reject him. Whether it was a sack of flour or marriage he offered, she would spurn him and he would not accept that he had let something so infinitely precious slip through his fingers.

He jerked himself up out of the chair in self-disgust. God,

he was behaving like some maudlin callow youth, bemoaning the loss of his first maid.

The drawing-room door was flung open with a flourish. 'Brought you a present back from town,' Ross said on a laugh, sending alcoholic fumes towards Luke.

Luke enquiringly raised bored dark brows and reseated himself on the brocade settee. The voice that then reached him actually had him back up and crossing the carpet.

'George!' He clasped the sandy-haired man warmly by the hand and shoulder and ushered him in. 'Have a drink. Have a seat. What are you doing about these parts?' he demanded, in one breath, of George Dellon, his Cornish neighbour.

'John's here and brought some flour by the look of things,' Martha said, the relief in her voice plain.

'Thank God for that,' Gregory muttered beneath his breath with a sliding peek at Rebecca as she sat breakfasting abstemiously at the kitchen table.

Rebecca sipped slowly at her mug of tea, her attention on the hot beverage resting between her palms.

Martha repeated for her benefit, 'John's here, Miss Becky. It looks as though he's brought over the provisions.'

Rebecca stared, then rose and moved quickly to the kitchen window. She watched the fair-haired youth drop a sack of flour to the ground from the cart and turn to haul the next to the edge to drop.

She rushed purposefully to the kitchen door but Martha's low caution made her halt with her hand on the doorknob.

'If you enjoyed that tea you were just supping you'd best leave him be for there's no more. There's no more flour either or sugar or spice or...'

Rebecca looked at Martha with pained apology. She knew she could never provide the Turners with the amount of food that they had received from the Manor. The provisions had always been sent to the Summer House, but the Turners also benefitted. What Rebecca could afford to pay for food would barely cover what she and Lucy would use. But she would reject it and try to deal with the consequences later.

Martha and Gregory exchanged looks of worry and disbelief as Rebecca walked towards the laden cart.

'Good morning, John. What are you doing?'

John bobbed his yellow head in greeting. 'Miles told me to bring you your provisions, Miss Rebecca, as no one has been by to collect them,' he explained with a shy smile, letting another large sack hit the ground.

'Please reload and return it all to the Manor. There has been an unfortunate mistake. I'm sorry you have had your time wasted.'

John squinted against the hazy yellow orb gilding the eastern horizon. 'Are you sure, miss?'

'Quite sure. Please return everything.'

John twisted about and surveyed the laden cart: spices, sugar, tea, dried fruit. Who in their right mind would turn it down, even if it was a duplicate load? He gave Rebecca a conspiratorial wink. 'Perhaps you could store it, miss…'

Rebecca gave him a weak smile but looked away from his amiable features. 'I don't want it.'

John stared at her pale, strained face for no more than a few seconds before jumping lightly from the cart and shouldering a sack of flour. It was tipped back on to the cart, the next speedily following it, but John's perplexed gaze tracked Rebecca as she re-entered the Summer House kitchen.

Aware of both Martha and Gregory watching her, Rebecca reminded them quickly and forcefully, 'I have said I will provide us all with what we need and I will. The Jennings' farm flour is a good price and next time Gregory is in Westbrook he can purchase tea. I have money. I have said I will pay…'

Gregory's derisive snort brought her quiet placation to an end. 'You are willing to pay money you can ill afford for what has always been provided free? And still is?'

'Hush,' Martha advised him, with a pointed look for him to remove himself. He did so, but impatiently muttered beneath his breath as he quit the kitchen for the garden.

Aware that a lecture was imminent, Rebecca tried to distract Martha. 'The children will be here soon. I need to prepare for the lessons.'

'You need to prepare for a lot more than that. This won't be the end of it…you mark my words. Just because he's stayed away for a week, doesn't mean he won't be back. That cartload of victuals was his calling card.'

Rebecca swung around at once, her tense face blanching. 'What do you mean by that, Martha?' she demanded, although she knew very well. She had mentioned nothing to the Turners about what had passed between Luke Trelawney and herself. They knew nothing of his proposition or her naïve misinterpretation of it.

But Martha's canny silver eyes and sharp perception missed very little. Would they want her to acquiesce to their landlord's lechery just to keep bread and tea on their tables? She glanced reproachfully at Martha. Recognising the mix of compassion and comprehension in the woman's eyes, she regretted even thinking it.

'I will provide for us, Martha. Not nearly as much or as often, but we will manage, I promise. Once I find Simon and extract my inheritance from him we will never again have these worries.'

Martha walked slowly towards her and enveloped her in a warm hug. The spontaneous comfort choked an involuntary sob from Rebecca. She buried her face in the woman's fleshy shoulder for a moment before regaining composure.

'There…don't be fretting so,' Martha cooed at her as she laid a plump hand on Rebecca's silky hair. 'It'll all turn out right. You'll see. Lord Ramsden's a fine gentleman…I know he is.'

A bubble of hysterical laughter burst from Rebecca at that. An unsteady hand smeared moisture away from her eyes. 'How much flour and tea have we left?' she asked in a businesslike way.

'There is just about enough flour left for one loaf. None for pastry or biscuits. Enough tea for one brew of the pot.'

Rebecca nodded in mild acceptance of this alarming information and then made for the parlour.

Luke lead the coal-black stallion out of his stall and ran a large dark hand along the animal's sleek flank. He would make a welcome addition to his stables at Melrose. The horse fair at Brighton had been an enjoyable well-spent day. He wished there would be another soon. He needed something interesting to divert him from the monotony of his time here. He liked to think he knew a bit about horseflesh and that he could drive a hard bargain. This beautiful animal and the fine chestnut he had bought for Ross were... His pleasant musing tailed off as his eyes followed the lumbering cart making slow progress back towards Ramsden Manor.

He swung up easily into the saddle and was, within a minute, alongside the loaded vehicle.

'What are you doing with this?' Luke asked evenly.

'I'm sorry, my lord. Miss Rebecca said to bring it back. She says she doesn't want any of it.'

Instead of the ire John had been expecting, his master gave a grunt of resigned laughter. The black stallion pawed restlessly at the ground and he expertly controlled the animal, reining it in as it circled skittishly. 'That's what she said, did she,' he muttered to himself.

To John, he ordered, 'Take it back...and tell Miss Rebecca from me that if it comes back here again I'll burn all of it.'

John stared at him as though he must have taken leave of his senses. There was enough food on the cart he drove to see a family through to the new year. Lost in shock, he sat unresponsive until a steely soft voice queried, 'Do you want me to repeat the message?'

John shook his corn-coloured head. 'No, my lord. No.'

'Good. Do it now.' A flick of a jet-black head indicating west sent John back the way he had come.

'You'd better come and look at this.'

'Continue with your numbers,' Rebecca called out to the

four young girls scribbling on blackboards. She quit the parlour and curiously followed Martha into the kitchen.

Martha indicated outside with a sideways nod of her grey head.

Rebecca walked apprehensively to the window. John was once more unloading sacks of flour from his cart. Swinging furiously away, she sped to the door.

'I believe I told you earlier, John, that I don't want any of this.'

'I know what you said, Miss Rebecca, but Lord Ramsden…' He tailed off as though finding explanations beyond him.

'Take it away, John,' Rebecca ordered quietly, fiercely. 'Take it away this minute, no matter what he threatens.'

'If I take it back again, he says he will set light to it,' John advised dolefully. 'He said to tell you that he's going to burn it all.'

Rebecca stared, horrified, at him. The thought of precious sustenance being so wantonly destroyed was quite obscene. She felt it, John felt it and so would the Turners. So would every peasant family in this village…every village in the land. Yet Luke Trelawney would carelessly do it because he knew nothing of being hungry, nothing of hardship.

All he knew was that he could blackmail, threaten and bribe in order to get his own way… 'The matter is nowhere near finished,' he had assured her. He was obviously smugly confident she would submit to his lust. Rebecca was sure she had never hated anyone more.

'Lord Ramsden said he would burn all this food?' she echoed in a whisper.

John's wretched nodding signalled he could not believe it either.

Without another word Rebecca turned and walked towards the Summer House. She called calmly over her shoulder, 'Just wait a moment, John, if you please.' She entered the kitchen and made for the cooking range. Having selected the longest and sturdiest of the spills from the hearth she went back outside. 'Give this to Lord Ramsden, please, John. Tell him I hope it assists with the blaze.'

John stared at her, open-mouthed. But she thrust the sliver of timber into his hand and immediately turned and walked away.

John examined the clouding sky, the timbered horizon, the sturdy mellow brickwork of Ramsden Manor, anything but his lordship's black expression. Relaying her message this time had not prompted his master to chuckle...or smile...even weakly. As the stony silence lengthened John slid a peek from the corner of a blue eye. His lordship's face could have been hewn from granite, his mouth thrust forward in hard sardonic contemplation of the spill he held between the thumb and forefinger of one dark hand. Black eyes regarded it thoughtfully, then just those two digits abruptly snapped and discarded it.

John glanced at him, spontaneously rubbing nervously at the bridge of his nose. Trouble was brewing, he could tell.

'You must be excited at the prospect of seeing your new baby brother,' Rebecca remarked conversationally as she turned the pages of the music.

Lucy looked up at her with a scowling grimace, immediately lost her place and plinked to a discordant halt on the piano. 'I don't want to see any of them,' she rejected in a low voice. 'Only Mary. I'd like to see my sister Mary. I do miss her.'

'I'm sorry, Lucy, I shouldn't have interrupted you. You've lost concentration now and you were doing so well. Start again.' Rebecca flicked the pages back to the start of the piece. Lucy obediently alternatively squinted at the music and at her fingers.

The instrument had a good tone but Lucy was never going to be an accomplished musician, although her singing voice was quite sweet. A lingering sallowness about Lucy's eyebrow drew Rebecca's eyes.

The girl never mentioned her stepfather or her mother or the new baby, although she had received a letter from her mother advising her of the birth. No one had yet visited Lucy at the school and she seemed untroubled by her parents' lack of concern.

Rebecca's slender fingers turned the page and as Lucy faltered, she pointed to the sheet to indicate her place. Lucy wasn't keen on her music lessons and Rebecca knew that her obedience and attention would soon waver and probably give rise to an irritable tantrum. She still found it difficult to control her moods and would sometimes sulk or cry or giggle helplessly with the slightest provocation. She could also be spiteful with the younger girls who came as day pupils and would think nothing of delivering a sly pinch here or a light cuff there when she thought Rebecca was not watching.

Lucy abruptly sighed and shrugged in exasperation. She flung herself around on the piano stool, began to complain and then gawped, straight past her tutor.

Rebecca murmured, her eyes with the music, 'Come along...you were doing so well. Just finish it. There is barely half a page to go.' Lucy's continuing silence made the hair at the back of Rebecca's neck prickle and she instinctively touched the turquoise ribbon, loosely confining her honey hair in a thick, flowing wave that reached to the middle of her back. The disturbing sensation intensified and she pivoted slowly, holding her breath.

'I did knock...the kitchen door was open so I let myself in.' Luke Trelawney excused himself quietly from the doorway.

Rebecca stared, facing him fully, feeling her colour fading and her pulse strengthening. 'Mr Trelawney...' she murmured weakly, partly greeting and partly identifying him.

Chapter Six

He moved slowly away from the door like a large, drifting black shadow in the small, dim parlour. It was barely six o'clock yet the cloudy sky had darkened the day to dusk. The small brass candelabra burning atop the piano was scant flame enough to read the music Lucy had been playing, let alone brighten the room.

Aware of Lucy watching her with a small, knowing smile, Rebecca hastily dismissed her. 'That will do now, Lucy. You can have your quiet hour sewing in your room and then we will dine.'

Lucy approached Luke with a bold, upturned face and an arch smile. 'Lord Ramsden,' she greeted him with an exaggerated, dipping curtsy and a flick of her floral skirt.

He returned her a brief nod and watched her leave before his black eyes returned to the piano and Rebecca.

'Why is the kitchen door not locked?' This unexpected interrogation left her momentarily speechless. 'You should keep it locked…you never know who may be about, up to no good in the neighbourhood.'

'Indeed…' Rebecca breathed with studied irony.

A thin, acerbic smile acknowledged the subtle insult. 'I mean someone who might really intend you harm, Rebecca. Keep the door locked at all times.'

'I do usually,' she returned quickly, compelled to defend her routine vigilance. 'Martha and Gregory have only just left for home. I usually lock and bolt directly they have gone.'

He nodded acceptance of this explanation.

A silence between them lengthened and tautened. Merely to occupy herself, Rebecca turned to the piano to close the lid. The highly polished wood slipped straight through her nervous fingers, crashing shut. She suppressed a small scream at the abrupt vibrating din and closed her eyes, crossing her arms about her waist to still their trembling.

'What do you want, Mr Trelawney?' she demanded in a low voice, aware she could hardly order him from the house. It was his. The land was his, the building was his.

'A mug of tea and a biscuit,' he informed her softly as he approached. He halted just a foot away, steeling himself not to touch her. But a hooded look caressed her fragile, ivory cheek-bones curtained by thick swathes of honey hair.

Rebecca shook clinging tendrils back from her face and forced herself to look up at him. The candle behind her was reflected in his eyes, firing them to onyx stars.

'I'm afraid...I have no tea and I believe the biscuits are finished too,' she stated proudly, understanding exactly why he wanted them.

'I know,' he said with a slow smile. 'That's why I brought my own.'

'Are they charcoal biscuits?' she taunted with sweet sarcasm. The immediate humour in his eyes as he impenitently acknowledged his threats of arson, made her blurt out, 'You can take them away with you.' Gathering her skirts in shaking fingers, she made to walk quickly around him.

Two dark hands fastened on her arms, keeping her in front of him. She instantly attempted to pull back but muscular, black-sleeved arms folded her tightly against him.

'Don't fight me, Rebecca,' he pleaded hoarsely.

She held herself rigid in his embrace, her heart tattooing crazily, while her eyelids drooped languidly as she indeed did fight...but against her own need to lean her head against him and slip her arms about him.

She felt his long fingers spanning her back, sliding up to stroke the sides of her neck and spear into thick golden tresses. The turquoise ribbon slid from her satin hair as firm, dark fingers tilted her head back to look at him. She averted her face, unable to meet his eyes but he was relentless. Tanned thumbs brushed enticingly against ivory skin as he insisted, 'Look at me, Rebecca.' She did so then, sepia and aquamarine eyes fusing.

'This is no way for a fiancée to behave. The servants are beginning to talk,' he gently rebuked her.

Rebecca stared at him, feeling a painful lump thickening in her throat. She forced herself to speak huskily through it. 'I should be obliged if you would leave now, I find your sense of humour distasteful.'

'I'm not joking, Rebecca. The servants *are* beginning to talk and I expect my betrothed to support and respect my decision to provide for her.'

'I am not your betrothed…I am not your fiancée…I am not your *chère amie* or any other fancy name you care to put on it. Now go away and leave me,' Rebecca choked, desperately trying to free herself from his grip.

He twisted her rejecting hands behind her, bringing her closer to his hard body. His mouth lowered to her hair and a sighing warm breath stirred its lavender-scented silkiness.

'You agreed to marry me, Rebecca. You're my future wife…my one choice. And I intend to hold you to that and make public our engagement. A notice needs to be put in *The Times*.'

'I did not agree… When did I?' Rebecca breathed, looking up at him in wonder. He appeared sane and serious.

'After I asked you to share my life. You told me when you looked at me…when you kissed me back…when you put up with my vile mood and still accepted me as your husband. All that was lacking was the word.' He suddenly gave a low grunt of unamused laughter. 'You've been talking to Ross, haven't you? *Chère amie*,' he scathingly sneered. He moved her back a little from him and studied her evasive face. 'You wouldn't

Mr Trelawney's Proposal

have known, would you?' A dark hand relinquished one of hers and moved to her face, cupping it tenderly. 'You would never have realised. Ross told you, didn't he?'

Rebecca felt blood flood her face as she remembered her promise to his brother. 'Ross and I haven't spoken,' she denied quickly, lowering her eyes.

'Don't lie to me, Rebecca,' he said quietly. 'Only Ross uses that ridiculous term for a harlot...apart from the harlots themselves.'

'Would I have used it, do you think?' Rebecca challenged bitterly, unwittingly acknowledging just how susceptible she had always been to his coercion.

Luke lifted her so that her face was level with his and then placed her gently back to sit on top of the piano. He braced an arm either side of her and leaned close. 'You were never going to be anyone's harlot, Rebecca. Least of all mine.' His mouth moved slowly towards hers and she watched it come. Her lips parted before they touched, her eyes closed and her head tilted. He paused to survey her serene beauty; an innate sensuality increasing her breathing to a shallow pant, straining her small rounded breasts enticingly against her bodice.

He recalled the spirited water nymph in the pond who had first enchanted him, her dress tantalisingly stuck to her body, and found her mouth rather too fiercely. A sturdy palm supported her head to prevent her jerking away, but this time she didn't. She accepted his ardour with a yielding sweetness that made him check and pull her forward to the very edge of the piano top and hold her reassuringly close against him.

His mouth slid hot and moist back and forth against hers with slow, calculated eroticism, tasting and caressing every inch of sensitive skin, until she was mindlessly gasping and her thighs intuitively parted to accommodate his body between them. His tongue-tip flicked against her lower lip, making her mouth reflexively widen and her back arch. Biting kisses trailed along the satin-skinned pearly column of the throat curving provocatively to meet him.

'Rebecca,' he murmured her name reverently; then with anguished humour, on hearing her low whimper of dismay as he moved away. Large hands gently enclosed her face to make her look at him.

'Rebecca,' he huskily repeated with strengthening authority.

She raised weighty lids, her dilated turquoise gaze engulfed by smouldering coal-black eyes. He touched his mouth tentatively to her swollen lips, pulling reluctantly back as they spontaneously clung and parted. 'I think I'd better put the notice in *The Times* this week,' he said on a gruff laugh. 'We'll be married at the end of next week, here in Sussex, so you can be amongst friends. Then we'll travel to Cornwall. We'll honeymoon there. For as long as you like,' he said with a slow, sensuous smile as his eyes travelled her beautiful flushed face and lingered on her slick mouth. Long blunt fingers threaded into her silken hair.

'What do you say?' he demanded on a soft, satisfied laugh, noting the sensual torpor that still drugged her. God, how easy it would have been to seduce her. One captivating kiss... And the knowledge made him simultaneously arrogant and ashamed; predatory and protective.

'Will you marry me, Rebecca?' he asked in an aching whisper against her unbearably sensitive mouth.

'Yes.'

One word, it was all the energy she could summon but her lips curved in a smile against his, deliberately tempting. He kissed her gently, lifted her from the piano and placed her close beside him.

'Make me a cup of tea,' he requested with a tenderly amused smile as she immediately swayed against him. 'I can wait for the biscuit until tomorrow, when Martha does her baking.'

Rebecca knew she mustn't panic. Girls liked to wander. She had been the same at that age. It was part of growing up, she remembered, to have quiet times to oneself. Nevertheless, she ran the remaining yards to the Turners' cottage and her rap on the door was loud and urgent.

It was opened cautiously within a few seconds and Martha's rotund face appeared at the crack.

'Why, Miss Becky. What on earth are you doing here at this time of the night?'

'Have you seen Lucy, Martha? I can't find her anywhere about the Summer House. She's not in the coach house or in with the chickens. I don't know where else to look.'

Martha opened the door fully as Rebecca was speaking and ushered her in. She plonked her hands on ample hips and said plainly, 'Have you thought to look at the Manor?'

Rebecca whitened. Martha's initial thought had been the first horrifying possibility that had occurred to her too on discovering her pupil missing. 'You think she may have gone to find John?'

'I'm saying nothing, Miss Becky. But you and I both knows how smitten she is. If she's nowhere to be seen, she's probably up to no good in the hay somewhere.' She nodded her head in emphasis. 'I'd get Gregory to drive you over there, but he and Jeremy Watson have gone to the White Horse supping tonight. He had a bit of luck on cards.' She muttered about her husband's wastrel ways as she stalked off to sit back down by her small fire. The spotless room was spartan but cosy: a kettle hissed steam over the flickering glow and there was a redolence of chicken stew.

'You think she will be at the Manor?'

'I lay a pound to a penny that if young carpenter is there, that is definitely where she is. And doing what she shouldn't. Leave her be. Get yourself home and safe and leave her be. She's a woman grown…however old she is,' Martha advised sagely.

Rebecca put a shaking hand to her forehead. 'Whatever will her stepfather think? She's in my care and I've let her—'

'You've let her nothing. You can't watch that one every minute of the day. If you did, she'd still slope off. It's her way.' She looked at Rebecca sympathetically.. 'You get yourself home. John will look after her…bring her back. He's a good lad.'

Rebecca shoved a shaking hand through her loose, golden hair. After a moment's indecision, she simply bade quietly, 'Goodnight, Martha,' and closed the ill-fitting cottage door behind her.

She stepped hurriedly away, back into the moonless night. She wrapped her shawl tight about her shivering body and hugged the perimeter of the woodland to avoid the worst of the stiffening breeze.

She had felt so joyous barely an hour ago. Luke had been with her then. He had sat with her in the kitchen and taken tea…eventually. Her fingers instinctively sought her tender, swollen mouth and an ache stirred deep within her as she concentrated on him. His kisses had been brief and gentle, lengthy and passionate and every delectable nuance in between. It had been the aroma of her dinner, bubbling slowly away to nothing on the cooking range, that had finally brought her to her senses.

She and Lucy had still not eaten and the hour by then was getting late. Aware just how unbelievably shameless her behaviour had been, especially believing Lucy to be sewing upstairs in her room, she had finally jumped, mortified, off Luke's lap, and begun attending belatedly to saving their stew while Luke drank his cold tea. He had then unloaded the cart of its provisions while she set about tidying her appearance and setting the dinner table.

She should have looked for Lucy earlier, she realised, while Luke was still with her. She had been too bewitched by him and the untasted, glorious feelings he aroused to relinquish him for a minute. Yet she recognised the peril in this wonderful new emotion, for it greatly undermined her logic and self-control.

Rebecca felt her face ice, then burn with embarrassment. She had behaved appallingly. She had allowed Luke too many liberties. One kiss would have been enough to seal their betrothal. Earlier today she had felt she hated him. Now he meant so much, it was as though she possessed no will when he touched her. She wouldn't allow it to happen again. She would show more composure.

Did he think her wanton? He did, she groaned to herself. It
was the source of that warm amusement in his eyes when he
looked at her. Well, it was his fault if she was. She knew he
deliberately made her feel that way. It empowered him and
made her weak. But he wanted to marry her.

He had said so and she believed and trusted him now. He
had no reason to lie; he was well aware just how defenceless
and beholden to him she was. If only he had said...but he
hadn't said the words...nor had she. But they sang mantra-like
through her head now as she sped back towards the Summer
House.

The glow of light from the lamp she had left burning in her
pantry window became visible and she lightly ran across the
grass towards the kitchen door.

Deliberately hiding to frighten her was the sort of antic Lucy
would find vastly amusing. There were only five rooms in all,
including the kitchen and she again searched each. A gust of
tepid wind slammed the kitchen door back on its hinges. Rebecca ran through the dusk to the rickety small coach house
where the trap was kept, although she knew it was fruitless
double-checking. Dorcas, Gregory's old cart horse, whinnied
softly at this second intrusion in one evening before dipping
her head back to her feed.

'Lucy!' Rebecca called, fear and panic making her voice
high and strident. There was nothing. No sound apart from the
soughing of the wind in the trees and the dry swirling of early
fallen leaves.

She would have to go the Manor. She would have to go to
find Luke and ask him to help her look for Lucy. She didn't
like to dwell on it...but she wouldn't be at all surprised if, in
the barn she knew John favoured for lazy afternoons, she also
found Lucy reclining there this evening.

The first sound had her frozen to the spot and she backed
against the closest tree, her hands gripping behind her at scrap-
ing bark. She held her breath, straining to listen but could hear
nothing apart from the increased pumping of her own blood.

She threw her head back and looked at the rustling canopy of leaves swaying above her. An owl called somewhere nearby, making her start and then a white blur broke cover, swooping low and close.

Rebecca closed her eyes, unsure whether to laugh or cry at her terror. An owl! She pushed herself away from the sturdy bole of the tree and had skirted another few yards of woodland when she saw the light. It bobbed intermittent yellow flashes into the pitch of the night. When it was joined by another and then another and three pinprick lamps undulated through woodland, she stepped back rigidly, her hands frantically exploring behind again for another shielding tree.

Voices were audible now too, although actual words were indistinct. She heard a gruff masculine laugh, then another, higher-pitched, in response and heavy twig-cracking footsteps.

Rebecca froze, petrified, to the spot. She glanced quickly down at her clothing. Trembling fingers swiftly gathered her black silk shawl up high about her throat, obliterating any sight of her white lawn bodice. She heard the men pass within yards of her, their laughter and conversation so muted, it was obviously intentionally muffled.

She twisted silently against the tree trunk as they made their way out of the wood towards Westbrook village. She watched them go. There were four of them, walking fast...or as fast as they were able with the hampering barrels hoisted about their shoulders. Each man carried two over each of his shoulders. Their identity was now obvious and chilled her to the marrow.

They were smugglers...the tub men, probably carrying spirits or tea. She remembered Simon telling her how tea was smuggled ashore in kegs. Tea! She might have sent Gregory to Westbrook to unwittingly purchase some. The irony almost made a hysterical giggle escape. She stuffed a shaking fist to her mouth.

Simon had also told her terrifying tales of bodies found on the beaches of people who had been in the wrong place at the wrong time when contraband came ashore. People murdered because they could identify the miscreants who brought illegal goods into the country past the Revenue men. Revenue men too were often found lifeless on the shore.

Rebecca closed her eyes tight, waiting, barely breathing, in case another party of free-traders was trekking up from the coast through this wood. She hardly dared consider just how lucky she had been. Had she left the Summer House a few minutes earlier in her dash to the Manor, their paths would undoubtedly have crossed.

She recalled what Gregory had told her just a week ago: that Jake Blacker had been seen locally, and a sob stifled in her throat. That blackguard was renowned throughout the area for his cruelty and corruption. But he had managed to evade detection and arrest. He had moved away, so they had heard, because there were richer pickings to be had in Kent for he and his cronies.

That had been years previously but now he was back. And Rebecca had missed confronting him or his associates by minutes. Where was Simon? Please don't let Simon be involved with them, she prayed to the whispering leaves above her head.

Gathering her shawl tightly about her, she slipped silently forward, keeping within the screening woodland and fled towards Ramsden Manor, her heart and mind calling out to Luke Trelawney for love and protection.

'Evening, Miles,' Luke amiably greeted his butler as he entered the Manor and strode towards his study. He changed his mind and started towards the stairs instead, realising he was ravenous.

'What's for dinner?' he called over his shoulder to the old retainer who was doing his uneven best to keep up with his master's speedy pace across the wide hall.

'Stew?' Luke suggested. 'I feel quite partial to a nice stew,' he informed the butler, savouring the memory of the rich aroma of the Summer House kitchen.

'Stew?' Miles mouthed at his back, wrinkle-nosed and pinched-mouthed. '*Stew?*' he repeated aloud in a disparaging tone. He wore the expression of someone recently assaulted with a dead fish as he related, 'I believe Judith has done a *nice* roast leg of lamb with roast vegetables and a redcurrant jelly, my lord, with a *nice* crème brulée to follow.'

Luke shrugged and continued towards the carved black-oak stairway. 'Oh, sounds good,' he said, but lacking enthusiasm. He started to hum, then whistle as he disappeared up the stairs two at a time. 'Arrange hot water for a bath, Miles,' he called back, just before he rounded the corner of the landing which lead towards his rooms.

Luke seated himself at the glossed mahogany table and picked up the paper which lay, neatly folded, for his attention. He absently ruffled his damp dark hair to aid its drying, before casually sleeking it back.

Miles eyed him warily. Something was amiss. He was far too cheerful, the elderly man deemed. Something of moment had happened. He must have been out till late arranging his travel back to Cornwall, he guessed. That was it. He was finally leaving Sussex, Miles was sure, and his slack, ancient features drooped further.

'Has my brother been back from town?' Luke gregariously enquired as he set about his evening meal with gusto.

'No, my lord. I haven't seen anything of that young man since five of the clock. Perhaps he won't be back to dine,' Miles suggested dolefully. He watched gloomily as his master cheerfully polished off his dinner then turned his attention to the brandy decanter.

Luke relaxed back in his chair and smiled. He felt content. He felt elated. He felt in… He hastily checked what he had been about to give conscious thought to and straightened in the Chippendale dining chair. He threw the remaining inch of amber liquid to the back of his throat, then stood up and wandered to the square-paned window. He immediately stared off to the west, just making out the fringe of woodland that shielded the Summer House.

He would leave it half an hour and then go back and see

her. He didn't like the idea of her being out there on her own in any case. She was his now. It was official between them and he had an obligation to look after her. He should go back and see her. Make sure she was comfortable. Not in need of anything....like a goodnight kiss.

His narrow mouth curved in sheer satisfaction even though he was aware that these kissing sessions were torturing his highly sensitive body. The straining, bulging discomfort that had tormented him since he had first seen her was still inadequately relieved. And without conscious thought he flexed and rotated his hand. What he desperately needed was a lot more than another tantalising kiss.

He walked back and refilled his glass from the decanter, smiling reflectively into space. His features softened and his dark eyes glazed as he realised that the ache that consumed him when he thought of her now wasn't just confined to his loins. Within a fortnight she would be his bride...in his bed...that beautiful hair spread across snowy sheets...limpid turquoise eyes fiery with passion...

'Young Mr Trelawney's back, my lord.' Miles finally broke into Luke's fevered imaginings with a dry cough to gain his attention. Rheumy eyes now squinted anxiously at his handsome young master. Something was without doubt seriously awry. He had spoken twice. Once from the window, when gazing out at the new arrivals, and then again on approaching the dining table. Yet still glittering black eyes gazed off into space as though the man were in the presence of angels.

Perhaps he'd got religion, Miles brooded. Then proceeded to shake his head to himself. No, it couldn't be. He was from Cornwall, and Miles had it on good authority that the Cornish were heathen reprobates, every one. As long as they were as generous as these two appeared to be, Miles was happy to mingle amongst friends.

He shambled to the dining-room door, peered out, and then turned back to address Luke before disappearing.

'Your brother's brought some of his nice friends to visit again, my lord.'

Luke grunted a non-committal response to this and, collecting his paper from the table, sat down in a comfortable chair to read for ten minutes.

'Brought you a present from town,' Ross bestowed on his brother a tipsy grin.

Luke returned an indulgent smile, wondering which neighbour or old acquaintance he had managed to find in Brighton this time. He had been quite amazed by the varied assortment of people who had turned up at Ramsden Manor over the past fortnight. 'Well, bring him in. You're probably just in time for dinner.'

Ross laughed and swung the door wider. 'George is here, too. Met him again at the Bull and Mouth. He hadn't yet left for Cornwall.'

Luke gave a brief blow of annoyance. He had been under the impression that George Dellon was on his way back to his wife and sons in Cornwall. He had accordingly entrusted him with a letter to deliver to Tristan with important business instructions concerning the mines. He had managed to deal with his shipping interests at Bristol quite easily from here and sent hand-delivered messages to the port every other day.

But he would allow nothing to dampen his good humour. He dropped the paper to the floor wondering why Ross had left the visitors out in the hall. Deciding to investigate, he strolled into the hallway and immediately stopped dead. He looked at Miles placing gloves neatly on the hall table, before his eyes returned to the three young women, two brunettes and one silver-blonde and none of them much older than twenty.

A puzzled look was aimed at George Dellon, lounging by the stairs. The man gave him an uncertain smile and shifted uneasily before his lascivious eyes again assaulted the dazzling women. Luke pivoted slowly on his heel to stare disbelievingly at Ross.

'You've brought three whores to my house?' he enquired quietly. 'You've actually brought them *here*…to this house?'

Ross's smile faltered a little. 'Well, it won't be yours much longer. We'll be leaving soon…returning to Cornwall. Anyway—' he gave a backward nod of his head to indicate Miles '—I told him they're George's sisters, and the servants can have the night off.' He snorted an infectious laugh and George joined him after a second, trying to camouflage his amusement with a coughing fit. Ross continued in a choke, 'The poor old cove must be practically blind…'

'He's not blind,' Luke informed with exceeding calm. 'He's unsuspecting. If you said they're George's sisters, then that's what he believes them to be.'

Ross approached his older brother and placed an arm about his shoulders. 'The blonde is for you,' he whispered magnanimously.

The young blonde woman must have been straining to listen because she launched a triumphant, territorial gloat at her colleagues, then provocatively swayed herself forward. She shimmered beneath the hall candles like a silver and lilac moth and with her movement Luke caught a waft of the cloying perfume Wenna used. They were costly whores, then.

As the woman undulated closer he could tell that the quality of her dress was fine, her coiffure elaborate and her face artfully rouged. Nothing too dramatic that would immediately brand her a courtesan. He wondered abstractedly if Ross was expecting him to pay for them all.

Aware of Luke's impassive attention as she glided forward, Molly Parker wet her reddened mouth with a sly pink tongue. 'Struth, but he was handsome. She had thought the other dark one, that cheeky Ross, a looker and more than welcome, but this one… She gave him a dimpling smile, archly lowering sooty lashes, desperate to please and anticipate what he would want from her: brash doxy or shy flirt. Professional technique or passive obedience.

Luke stood stock still; enraged yet stunned and unwilling to give up his joy and contentment of ten minutes ago. So he was unsure whether to laugh dementedly or swing around and punch his brother straight in the mouth.

'I know you've been hankering after a blonde…' Ross said and the gruff concern in his voice did it for Luke. He laughed, just as Molly reached him and slid possessive, perfumed arms about his neck.

And just as Miles attended the door again, muttering cheerfully about a busy evening, and greeted Rebecca.

Chapter Seven

She stared and actually glided into the hallway a bit as she uncertainly murmured, 'Luke?'

His name was little more than a doubtful sigh yet he heard it.

The shock of finding harlots littering Ramsden Manor was nothing to the devastation which now ripped into him. The one that cluttered his person was shoved ungently back from him and straight at Ross.

Rebecca momentarily froze. She hadn't been mistaken. She understood perfectly this time. What she was witnessing was exactly what it seemed: three men being entertained at home by three harlots.

She was physically exhausted from her run through the woods; she was mentally fatigued from her fears about Lucy and the smugglers she had evaded by yards, yet she turned and fled down the steps of Ramsden Manor as though the hounds of hell snapped at her heels.

She flew into the dark night and instinctively towards the barn, the duty to find Lucy still fast in her mind, even as a hand covered her mouth to stifle her heartbroken sobs. The night was so pitch black and her eyes so awash that she could barely see a yard in front of her but she knew the direction of the barn from the house and sped towards it.

Luke hadn't the vaguest idea which way she had headed.

Guessing she might have instinctively sought home, he ran the wrong way. Within a vain minute he halted and re-tracked to the Manor where the only light was to be had.

'Rebecca!' He thundered her name with such command and pain in his voice that she actually stopped dead and swung about.

It was enough. Her trailing shawl revealed the white flag of her bodice and he walked slowly, purposefully towards her. Rebecca stood shaking on the spot, watching him advance with the amber glow of light from the Manor outlining his silhouette. By sheer willpower he was holding her unmoving, unresisting. She knew it, but acknowledging that he could made her jerk about again and run.

She reached the barn, knowing he was within a second of catching her, so she swirled to face him, warding him off with unsteady, outstretched hands. 'Don't touch me. Please, don't touch me,' she begged and threatened in one tone.

He slowed his relentless progress towards her until he walked the final steps and towered over her shivering form.

'I'm sorry,' she blurted on a sharp, hysterical laugh. 'I arrived unexpectedly…uninvited again. But I had to come. It…I…' She trailed off, unable to force any further words past the aching blockage in her throat.

One black-sleeved arm slowly raised to lean against the barn wall. His head lowered to meet it and rested there. 'Tell me what you think you just saw, Rebecca,' he demanded hoarsely.

'Nothing…' she whispered.

'You saw nothing?' A grunt of mirthless laughter issued from the crook of his arm. He wearily raised his head to gaze down at her. 'You didn't see three whores loitering in my hallway?'

Rebecca swallowed painfully. She looked feverishly about her, anywhere but at him.

Luke moved a testing hand towards her and she reflexively slapped it away. 'I said don't touch me,' she immediately hissed at him.

'Ah...so you did see something. Tell me what you think you saw,' he insisted in a raw voice.

Rebecca slid surreptitiously along the brick barn, the opposite way from the barrier of rock-like arm, striving for composure. She rested her head back, feeling her soft, thick hair catch against the gritty brickwork. A trembling hand went to her face, clearing tearstains and honey tendrils wisping about her neck with every gusting breeze. She concentrated on finding Lucy. She allowed no other thought.

'I'm sorry to intrude,' she said quietly. 'But I must find Lucy. I've searched everywhere for her. This was the last place to look. I think she may be with John. I suppose you haven't seen them?' Had that really been her remote voice? she dully wondered.

He was denied the need to reply. The barn door opened not three yards from where they stood and John's bright head became quite visible through the dusk. Lucy's muted giggling and then whispering was just audible. The intimate way their heads angled towards each other made it clear they were oblivious to anyone but each other.

Luke twisted on the hand braced against the brickwork and glared over his arm at the young couple. He thrust himself in a deliberate, savage jerk away from the barn wall and approached them. Sensing the latent exasperation in him, yet to be vented, Rebecca hastened past him.

'Lucy!' she exclaimed in a voice mingling relief and chastisement. 'I've hunted everywhere for you. What in heaven's name have you been doing here?' The simple query was the first ingenuous phrase that formed in her numb brain.

The young couple jumped apart and Lucy muttered an involuntary exclamation of dismay. Within a few seconds she had regained confidence and her full mouth took on its customary sullen droop. Her eyes scanned from Rebecca to Luke and then back to Rebecca.

'What have I been doing here?' she repeated nastily. 'Why don't you ask his lordship what I've been doing here? He knows. It's something he'd just love to be doing here with you.'

Intolerable humiliation prompted a rash and spontaneous reaction; Rebecca's hand arced up to slap the girl's coarsely smiling face. But it was arrested in mid-air and gripped hard as Luke pulled her close to his side. The silence that followed was broken only by the wind catching the barn door and creaking it back and forth.

'You will apologise, Lucy,' Rebecca eventually breathed in a trembling rush. 'Apologise to Lord Ramsden this minute for that disgraceful outburst.'

'Why? It's true!' Lucy spat back, but warily, her eyes hovering on his lordship's inscrutable dark features.

Luke stepped towards the couple then and they, as one, stepped back against the barn wall. 'Take Lucy back to the Manor,' he ordered John in a voice of silken steel. Then, as he remembered that the place already housed three trollops and another might crowd the place enough to give even credulous old Miles pause for thought, a dry grunt of a laugh escaped. 'No, forget that. Get the carriage out and put her in it…alone. But wait with her until you have my further instructions.'

'Yes, my lord,' John mumbled in a strange croak, rubbing furiously at the bridge of his nose. But neither John nor Lucy made a move or uttered another word. They appeared entranced and rooted to the spot.

Luke stared off back towards the Manor, waiting. A muscle started to jerk in his jaw. He looked down at his booted feet. He kicked the toe of one into damp earth. He roared, *'Go!'*

Rebecca started violently, making the hand that still grasped hers tighten and a slow thumb soothe her chilled skin. Lucy began noisily blubbing, her outrageous impertinence totally expired. John grabbed at the girl's arm and started solicitiously steering her towards the house.

'Don't ever again tell me not to touch you,' Luke ground out, as his hands fastened on the tops of Rebecca's arms and she was pulled close.

The strength in the movement knocked the breath out of

Rebecca. But she was determined this time not to yield to the immediate lure and rest against his solid body for warmth and comfort. He could beguile her so easily. He had done so scarcely two hours ago; her mouth still pulsed from that subtle assault. Yet he must surely have already had business arranged with these women when he was kissing her. This wounding conclusion broke a small sob of denial from her aching throat and her forehead ground involuntarily against him, back and forth. He immediately folded her closer, soothing and restricting her feeble attempts to break free, as he groaned her name.

But her hurt and fury were no longer containable. 'You must surely hold the Ramsden name and all of our small community in such contempt to bring those...' she strived for the vulgarity to flail him with the word but failed '...women...here to my uncle's home. It is a despicable thing to do.'

Luke moved her back and his glittering eyes scanned her face. 'Your memory is improving, is it, Rebecca? You remember something now, do you?'

Her turquoise eyes were as icy as her voice. 'Yes, I remember. I remember you asked me to marry you earlier today. I remember agreeing to do so. But I have forgotten why. I have forgotten why I would do such a ridiculous thing when I know what sort of degenerate you are.' She shook herself to try and escape him but his fingers tightened to painful vices on her arms.

'Go on,' he urged, deceptively softly. 'What else do you remember about my proposal earlier? Or perhaps I should remind you why you agreed to marry me, Rebecca.' He moved her closer. When she resisted, digging into the rain-wet earth, he lifted her a few inches away from it and slammed her hard against him.

'Shall I remind you, Rebecca?' he taunted softly, as black-fire eyes roved her face, lingering on her soft mouth. She turned her head swiftly away, her heartbeat so fast and strong it seemed to knock her yet closer to him. His warmth and familiar verbena scent enveloped her and her eyelids drooped. Recognising at once the sweet ache which coaxed capitulation, she cleaved to the vision that tormented her.

'I remember you embracing a harlot and laughing with her why you did so. That's what I remember. She was wearing a lilac dress…she was blonde and pretty…' Her voice cracked as she was about to add that she looked very young. Instead she whispered, 'Let me go now. I have to take Lucy home. It is getting very late.'

'Well, now you've admitted what you saw, perhaps I should tell you how it came about,' he stated, ignoring her request to leave. 'If I say that what I recount is the truth, will you believe me?' Her answering silence made him bitterly mutter, 'Well, I shall tell you anyway.'

'Ross brought me a present home from Brighton today. He got one for himself and a friend, too…but that's Ross's way. He's ever generous with my money. But he did it with good intentions, thinking he was being helpful…considerate. He's watched me pining over a blonde for two weeks or more and daily becoming more frustrated and miserable. So he tried to ease my discomfort in the only way he knew how: by buying one for me. I didn't know about it. I hadn't arranged it and I wasn't laughing from pleasure. I was laughing because I couldn't credit that he'd actually brought that bawdy trio to my home. I was laughing because of the irony of wanting to speak to him about acting as my groomsman when I knew I was within an ace of hitting him. But mostly I was laughing in sheer disbelief that Ross imagined an expensive whore might be a substitute for even one tormenting thought of you. And I wasn't embracing her or any other damn thing. She had hold of me, but for no more than a few seconds. And she wasn't pretty… Well, she might have been, I suppose. I don't know. I hardly looked at her.' His eyes hungrily roamed Rebecca's perfect features. 'She certainly wasn't incredibly beautiful,' he said huskily. After a brief pause he demanded, 'Do you believe me?'

'I'm not sure,' Rebecca achingly whispered.

'Why aren't you sure?' he persisted, his tone hardening.

'Because I don't know you. I know so little about you... and you about me. All I'm certain of is that we have lived in different worlds. But I'm not so ignorant of polite society that I'm unaware how wealthy men behave.' She slowly slipped away from him and leaned back against the barn, her arms wrapping her shawl tightly about her chilled form.

'I know my uncle had other... relationships. I heard gossip about village children. I believe it was after my aunt had died. But I know it is not always just then... when men live a bachelor existence. I understand that sometimes... men with power and status... can afford to also have a wife and two or more households.' She paused, sadly remembering him detailing his affluence and the properties he owned throughout the country, when first propositioning her. How many homes did he own? She could not now remember the list.

She moistened her lips, feeling a racking pain clenching her insides. She wanted to wail, to lash out at him for so soon ripping away her golden happiness. Instead she quietly stammered, 'I... I know it is deemed to be quite acceptable by some to live that way. But it's not my way.'

She stole a quick glance at his expressionless profile. His head was thrown back a little as he listened to her but she wasn't fooled by his apparent calm. That dormant menace she had already sensed beneath his urbane exterior was strengthening. And it frightened her.

'I'm not very sophisticated, I know that,' she admitted on a weak, shaky laugh, attempting to ease the unbearable suspense between them. 'At times I have wished I were, especially recently...' She trailed into silence and he turned his head to look at her.

'Well, that's easily remedied, Rebecca, and right now,' he softly promised. 'Young Lucy quite accurately predicted my needs. Perhaps yours, too. Ten minutes in that barn would help sophisticate you... and definitely make me feel a damned sight better.'

Rebecca started quickly back towards the relative safety of Ramsden Manor. She had hastened no more than three paces when he dragged her in front of him. 'What are you implying? That you now intend to reject my proposal because you believe I will be an inveterate adulterer?'

'I don't know you well enough. I need time to think…' she quietly prevaricated, desperate to placate him so he would allow her to get home to the Summer House.

He walked into her, forcing her backwards against the barn wall. Her anxious eyes darted up to merge and plead with his. But there was no reassurance or tenderness in his hard, glittering eyes and thin compressed mouth.

'I would say that you've got no more to worry over now than you had this afternoon. You believed in me then, trusted in me, and I in you. I've told you exactly how that farcical tableau you witnessed came about. I will not beg forgiveness for misdemeanours I've not committed, Rebecca.' As her furtive evasion was thwarted by two fists planted either side of her head, she sensed the rigid pulsing of his touching body heating her.

'So, perhaps you need something genuine to fret over for a day or two while I settle scores with my meddling brother.'

His speciously controlled tone made her anticipate anger and cruelty. Both her quaking hands shoved instantly against the broad expanse of his chest, curling against the reflexive leap of muscle beneath her palms. But when his hand manoeuvred her face and his mouth touched hers, it was with no more force than she recalled from earlier that day.

She yielded immediately to the artful skill in his kiss, but the knowledge that he had once again easily manipulated her made a humiliated sob jerk out of her and mingle with his warm breath. Still her mouth clung to his, greedily following every mercurial movement. Firm fingers skimmed her silhouette, lingered tantalisingly at the sides of her engorging breasts, thumbs catching almost unintentionally against taut nipples.

The current of untasted sensation jolted her and even as she arched towards those tormenting fingers, she grasped them in hers and pulled them away. But she couldn't relinquish the kiss and as he took their clasped hands behind her to ease her closer she moved willingly between his spaced feet.

But when he eventually lifted his head there was no triumph or mockery and he breathed as hard and fast as she. He jerked her away from the barn and wordlessly started striding towards the house.

As they approached the carriage, stopped in the warm orange glow of light by the portico, Ross careered down the steps, glass in hand.

'I was just coming to find you,' he carefully enunciated, squinting at his grim-faced brother. 'You've been gone a while. I was worried.'

'Ah, Ross,' Luke greeted, far too cordially. 'Just the man I wanted to see. Come, tell Rebecca who those women are and how they come to be infesting my home,' he drily invited him.

Hazel eyes flicked from one to the other of them, detecting the proprietorial grip his brother had on the lovely young woman and the slick, swollen redness of her mouth. 'Oh, they're George's sisters,' he shrewdly explained, turning to George for confirmation, as that man joined him on the steps of Ramsden Manor. The conspirators faced each other to share a covert wink.

'George's sisters are harlots?' Rebecca couldn't help but acidly comment.

Ross glanced warily at Luke's forbidding countenance. 'So, you've heard that too. I'm sure it's just a rumour,' he dismissed, deadpan. He turned a clandestine grin on George who, in turn, glared, unsure whether to be outraged or entertained by this family slight. He reflected on his pair of vinegary spinster siblings, at home in Cornwall and was unable to prevent a lusty chortle erupting, before he hastily swigged his drink.

Ross swivelled back to his brother with a smug smile just as Luke's fist caught him on the chin and he collapsed like a rag doll.

George Dellon sobered immediately and stuck out both hands in front of him in a gesture of appeal. 'Sorry...sorry, Luke. We just thought it might help. Ross thought...'

Luke ignored him completely, his attention with his younger brother. 'Get those bawds out of my house right now. Get yourself out, too, and don't come back for at least two days. Stay away...I don't care where. Stay with George...stay with those damned sisters of his if you like. Just don't venture back here if you value your life...understand?'

Ross held on to his brandy balloon with one hand and his jaw with the other. His glass got the most attention as he examined the step to ascertain how much had been spilled. He nodded as he drained the glass.

'Can't you just abduct her?' he suggested with drunken forthrightness and then cowered back as Luke twisted menacingly back towards him.

'All right...just a thought,' he squeaked, but winked at George.

The perfume from the rose garden was enticing. As Lucy accompanied herself heavily on the piano but sang quite sweetly, Rebecca rose from the stool beside her with a sigh and quit the parlour. She walked out into the balmy air and threw her golden head back to survey the sky: cobalt blue and with just a hint of thin cotton cloud stretched high. It was mid-October now, yet the Indian summer continued.

The rose garden was situated at the back of the Summer House and an open-windowed parlour benefitted from the sight and scent of it.

She collected the trug from Gregory's potting shed, and the sturdy knife he used in the garden. She selected two dark red blooms, not fully opened, and stripped away some of the superfluous greenery. Her fingertips slipped along the velvet petals of a pale pink bud and she cut that and another to match, inclining to breathe in their fragrance.

'Miss Nash?' Rebecca swirled about, pricking her finger on a thorn as she bumped into a rose bush. She hadn't even heard the horse and rider approach over Lucy's unharmonious trilling and plinking. She lifted a sap-stained hand to shield her eyes from the sun and squinted up at the man.

'I am Miss Nash. Can I help you?' she asked him pleasantly, as she sucked at her injured finger.

She had never seen him before. She guessed him to be a farmer or merchant of some description from his attire of sturdy, serviceable clothes. He was certainly no peasant. The horse he was riding looked a healthy thoroughbred. His pale blue eyes were regarding her with rather too fixed interest and Rebecca glanced about a little uncomfortably.

'I am looking for Simon Nash. Your brother?' the man questioned her as his eyes continued a raking assessment of Rebecca's slender figure.

His bold gaze was starting to unnerve her and she answered coolly, 'I'm afraid I can't help you. I have been desperate to find him myself for some years.'

The man laughed. 'My apologies for troubling you then, miss. I believed you must have been in touch with him since June when last I saw him. I thought he had possibly been lying low with a relative in some out-of-the-way spot. And this is out of the way...' he remarked as he gazed about him and then contemplatively at Rebecca.

The brooding look he turned on her this time passed unnoticed as Rebecca breathed out, 'You've seen Simon as recently as that? In the summer of this year? Where? Please tell me, sir, I am quite desperate to find him.' When he made no attempt to respond to her entreaty, she urged, 'There are important family matters that need to be resolved.'

'Your brother and I had some business dealings, Miss Nash. The matter was never finalised,' he advised in a hardening tone, ignoring her request for information. 'Should he come by visiting, perhaps you would tell him I am urgently seeking him. He will know why and that it is better to settle with me sooner rather than later. Just tell him that's what Jake Blacker said.' He reined in his horse then as though about to turn its head and leave. Rebecca spontaneously stepped forward to arrest his departure.

'*You* are Jake Blacker?' she whispered, astonished. The infamy of the man had conjured up a coarse-mannered, evil-looking lout in her vivid imagination. Certainly not this clean-shaven individual with brown hair and the weakest blue eyes imaginable. He seemed quite inoffensive. Apart from that unsettling way he had of eyeing her.

'Indeed, I am,' he confirmed with a pleased smirk that his reputation had preceded him, even to a beautiful provincial miss living in this backwater. 'You've heard of me, Miss Nash?'

Rebecca moistened her parched lips, unsure how to reply. Admitting to knowledge of his criminal activities was hardly wise. Yet why else would she know him? His penetrating gaze shifted. She watched him frown towards the parlour window as Lucy struck up a new, discordant tune.

'I believe I recall Simon mentioning you once,' she blurted before those icy eyes could pin back on her. 'Would you tell me, sir, where last you saw my brother? Was it locally?'

'It was in Hastings, Miss Nash, where we dealt a little together. No doubt he has just omitted to conclude matters with me,' he informed her, but in a way that made Rebecca certain he believed no such thing. Her stomach plummetted and frosty fingers gripped her heart. It was true then, Simon *was* involved with these blackguards. And Jake Blacker was the worst of the bunch, if what she had heard was correct, however harmless he may look and sound. From his veiled threats, she could only conclude that Simon owed him money.

'Have you any idea where I might start searching for my brother?' Rebecca pleaded.

Jake Blacker regarded the lovely young woman gazing earnestly up at him with those astonishing sea-green eyes. He judged her the prettiest woman he had seen in many a long day. Certainly easier on the eye than his carrot-headed wife who was again beginning to thicken around the middle with her third child. He stroked his chin, scheming slyly that if he couldn't extract money from Simon Nash, he would now give him two choices: his life or his sister.

'Well, last I heard, miss, he was seen at the Bull and Mouth Tavern in Brighton,' he informed her clearly. 'When I looked for him there, I was told I'd missed him by mere minutes. I've heard it's a haunt of his in the evenings.'

'The Bull and Mouth Tavern,' Rebecca repeated in a low breath. 'Well, thank you, sir. And rest assured, if I do happen upon Simon, I shall relay your message.'

He dipped his head in acknowledgement and after another lengthy assessing stare, he turned his horse and trotted away towards Westbrook.

'Who was that?' Martha called inquisitively out of the open kitchen window.

Some innate caution made Rebecca casually dismiss the visitor as, 'Oh, just someone looking for Simon. An old acquaintance, I believe.'

Martha withdrew her head, muttering inaudibly, but Rebecca knew the grumbled comments concerned Simon and Martha's disparaging opinion of him and his friends. The woman poked her iron-grey head back through the window and called, 'Jam tarts are done and so is the brew.'

She would have to go into Brighton and find this Bull and Mouth Inn, Rebecca mused as she bit into a raspberry jam tart and sipped at her tea. She desperately needed to find Simon. She wanted the money her father had bequeathed her before he handed it over to the likes of Jake Blacker...if he hadn't already done so. It was hers. It was her self-respect. It was her dowry. It was also her thinking time. Without it she might be prey to penury and unscrupulous people. And then she thought of Luke Trelawney.

She sipped at her tea again quickly. She had expected to see him by now. It was three days since she had searched for Lucy at the Manor. He had sent she and Lucy home in the carriage, with John driving them. A swift, hard kiss out of sight of Lucy, sulking in the carriage, and a cool parting statement that he would be in touch, was all the farewell she had received before he strode away and into the Manor. Why hadn't he been by? She had been so sure he wouldn't stay away more than a day.

No doubt he was also reconsidering the wisdom of his marriage proposal and was ready to withdraw it. The notion made an icy shiver race through her, even though she recognised the reason in it. He was wonderfully handsome; he was by his own admission extremely wealthy. So wealthy he could afford to disregard the entirety of his inheritance that brought with it a title. He was the sixth Baron Ramsden, a peer of the realm, and could pick a society debutante to marry if he wished. Perhaps he did now wish it, Rebecca reflected, chilled. Perhaps all she could now expect was a reinstatement of his original proposition.

Rebecca stared sightlessly into the steamy teacup. She was without money or status. But she had been gently reared; well-educated by Miss Arden, her governess until she was sixteen. Her grandmother, Grace, had been a Ramsden through marriage, but when Saul Ramsden died and Grace married Granville Nash, her grandfather had been the wealthiest businessman in the Brighton area.

She had heard tell that one of the reasons her father and Robin Ramsden had disliked each other so much was that the illustrious Ramsdens, who could trace their noble lineage back to 1630, had considerably less money at one time than the Nashes who had gained affluence and influence through common trade.

On his mother's remarriage to Granville Nash when he was eleven, her uncle Robin had chosen to stay with his paternal grandmother in straitened circumstances at the Manor, rather than move in with his stepfather and enjoy an easier life.

Her grandfather Granville had owned a terrace of houses in one of Brighton's most fashionable squares. He had bought them just as the Prince of Wales began transforming the farmhouse he had acquired into that most vaunted and elegant palace: Brighton Pavilion. As Brighton's reputation as a fashionable resort and gathering place grew, so did grandfather Granville's profit from renting out his Palladian terrace to the *haute ton* during the season.

Rebecca sighed a little wistfully. Although her father had inherited it all on Granville Nash's death, he had unfortunately not been blessed with that man's inherent business acumen. He was too gentle and trusting, her fiercely loyal mother had once told Rebecca, when they were packing up to leave the large house they could no longer afford to run. How she wished now he had not been so trusting with her money, and left it to someone other than Simon to administer.

Her father had not owned a home of his own for several years before his death. But the leased property which was their last, on the outskirts of Westbrook, had been comfortable and spacious and was, on her father's insistence, one of the few which didn't belong to the Ramsden estate. She missed her parents dreadfully. Despite declining fortune, they had stayed a happy family.

Her father had provided Elizabeth with a very reasonable dowry on her marriage to James Bartholomew. Simon had inherited the bulk of the estate, and it simply wasn't fair that he had never released her money when he had received so much more. Had David been alive she would have had his love and protection, and no doubt her inheritance. She was certain Simon would never have attempted to gull her future husband.

Her fingers went to her locket and she unclasped it and laid it on the table in front of her. She ran a finger along its warm, silver surface. She had barely thought of David, she realised with a wrench. For the past five years she had recalled memories of him daily and yet… Now she dwelt on another man throughout each day, and long night. And he stirred in her something that dear David never had, something new that both disturbed and subdued her, something that had been with her from the moment he had taken her, dripping wet, from the pond.

She yearned desperately for him. She longed for the touch of his fingers on her face…in her hair. She craved the moist heat of his mouth on hers. She ached for that bitter-sweet knotting deep inside her at the sight of him or the sound of his voice…yet knew it was foolish, all of it. Everything she had said to him that night at the Manor was the truth. She didn't know enough about him…his life or background.

But she did know with utter certainty that the thought of

enduring a faithless marriage was anathema. She would rather countenance a marriage of convenience to an elderly widower than discover that Luke Trelawney sought the company of other women while she was his wife. Sharing him would destroy her.

She needed to find Simon. Her five thousand pounds bought her thinking time. Time to perhaps discover if Luke Trelawney was the sincere gentleman she desperately wanted to believe him. Or whether he was an unprincipled rogue without an honourable intention in his handsome head, who might just carelessly crush her spirit before he returned to Cornwall.

Her time at the Summer House was coming to an end. She looked wistfully about the kitchen. She had had five good years but she knew with a quiet certainty there were to be no more.

'The Bull and Mouth'…the name ran through her mind. She hadn't been to Brighton since the summer. She rarely went because of her duty to her pupils. But she would go tomorrow afternoon and leave Lucy in Martha's care. Martha wouldn't mind: she was always trying to persuade her to get to town more. She would beg a lift with Kay and Adam Abbott. They made the trip to Brighton every Wednesday afternoon; Kay to visit her widowed mother while Adam attended to ecclesiastical duties. Kay had often previously tried to coax Rebecca to join her simply for the outing. And that's all Rebecca would explain it as, either to Kay or Martha, just an outing. For she knew they were sure to fret over the wisdom of it all…just as she was bound to herself.

Chapter Eight

Miles wasn't sure what worried him the most: the agony or the ecstacy. Choleric temper was certainly more common, he realised. That fit of euphoria three days ago had been unique and barely lasted the evening out. The following morning had seen a black mood once again settled over the man and therefore the household.

Miles had heard worrying tales of such behaviour: people with brain afflictions laughing and happy one minute and ranting in evil humour the next. He would have to take stock…keep a careful watch. He had no experience of the Cornish, but what he'd heard was not to the good. Even as he thought it he lifted his head a little and peered sideways into the enormous gilt-scrolled mirror at his master's handsome reflection.

Luke Trelawney stood just behind him adjusting his neck-cloth with a steady, dark hand. As he noticed Miles squinting furtively at him in the glass, he gave the man a ghost of a smile.

Miles hastily blinked rheumy eyes and busied himself laying calf leather gloves on the hall table he stood by. He couldn't fool him with a smile. Oh, no. Not even that half a one he was fond of employing to dupe folk as to his humour. He knew the sixth Baron was in no better a mood this Wednesday evening than he had been this morning or yesterday morning or the one before that.

He scuffled away from the tall, dark figure that dwarfed him and ambled towards the kitchens, passing the snoozing figure of Ross, slumped in a hall chair.

Miles threw him a glance as he creaked on. It must be spreading. Even jolly young Mr Trelawney seemed affected now. He had been morose for three days or more and constantly lounging about the place. Very unlike him. Perhaps it was a family affliction. He had heard of that, too. Whole families addled in the wits.

Talking to oneself was a sign, so he recalled. And without a doubt he had heard Lord Ramsden cursing beneath his breath with no soul about. Sometimes several times a day. Laughing manically, that was another. Well, he didn't laugh much but he'd seen him grin off away at something on the ceiling and gaze through the window towards the woods, always the same spot too, as though someone stood there. Sometimes happy, sometimes as though he'd go out and rip every one of those trees up with his bare hands. Teeth grinding...pulling out hair...well, that didn't signify, Miles had to allow, as he shuffled on. He'd never seen two men with such perfect teeth and luxuriant manes. He gave a sour scowl as his tongue probed his lonely gums and an instinctive hand went to smooth down his own sparse, grey locks.

Absent-mindedness was a sign. They were still here. Perhaps they had forgotten to go home to Cornwall. So long as they didn't forget to pay the myriad merchants' bills that arrived daily, Miles was content keep his own counsel...and watch... and wait.

Luke critically surveyed his cravat in the mirror. He glanced past the perfect silver-grey folds at his neck and at Ross, crumpled in the chair, allowing a small, hard smile. It was time to forgive him a little. Ross had been as well behaved as a five-year-old earning a treat for the past few days. He'd been wearing a pathetic, martyred look, reading books studiously in the library or wandering about as if lost. He'd hardly ventured from the house, which was a pity in a way, because whilst here he tended to get under everyone's feet.

Luke turned from the mirror, picked up his gloves and mildly called, 'Ross?' The lack of response made him whistle through his teeth at his brother. Ross shot up in the chair and rubbed his eyes.

'Come on. I'll take you into town for a drink and a game of cards before Miles sends for the physician. He's beginning to look at both of us as though we're mad.'

'What do you think of it now?' Kay asked wrinkling her pert nose.

Rebecca frowned consideringly, head tilted to one side. 'More ostentatious than when last I saw it,' she finally judged as she critically regarded the newest additions to the architecture at Brighton Pavilion. 'I dread to think what it has cost.'

Kay linked her arm through Rebecca's and they walked on. 'Will you come with me today to see my mama? She would adore seeing you.'

'I can't, Kay,' Rebecca hastily demurred. 'But thank you for the invitation and please convey my kind regards to your mother.'

'So how are you intending to spend your afternoon in Brighton? Shopping? Sea bathing?' Kay teased her.

'No. Actually, when last I saw Elizabeth in London, several weeks ago now, she bade me look up an old friend of hers who lives here,' Rebecca told her quite truthfully. It was precisely what Elizabeth had asked her to do. Katherine Bates lived in Baker Street and Rebecca had, indeed, promised to visit at some time. It wouldn't be today but neither Elizabeth nor Kay need know that.

'We shall meet you in Ship Street then at seven of the clock,' Kay said with a smile as she unlinked arms with Rebecca to enter the quiet square where her mother lived. 'Adam will be finished with his meeting with the Bishop then and we can be back in Graveley by eight.'

This was the part that Rebecca didn't relish. She had no idea how long she would need to loiter at the Bull and Mouth. She had decided to remain in the vicinity for some while and watch for Simon. There was no point in just leaving a message with the landlord. She was well aware that if Simon did receive it, he would probably summarily dismiss any request to contact her, knowing exactly why she wanted him. She needed to confront him face to face.

'Actually, Kay, I'm not too sure when I shall be leaving. If I manage to get away by seven I shall be only too pleased to ride home with you and Adam. But please don't wait for me. If I'm not there at the appointed hour, then leave without me. I shall hire a conveyance of some sort to get me home.'

She held up a silencing hand as Kay looked horrified at the very idea. 'No, please. I get out so very little that I want to make the most of my day.' She gave Kay a hasty peck on the cheek. 'Please give my regards to your dear mama and spend a pleasant afternoon.'

She drew her warm cloak about her as a gusting sea breeze assaulted them. While Kay wrapped herself into her own coat, Rebecca briefly waved, then walked briskly away.

Rebecca knew she looked quite attractive today. She had worn her best clothes, as she always did when taking a trip to town, and although five years old, they were little worn and still quite chic. But she wished people wouldn't stare quite so much. Her beryl-blue velvet cloak nearly matched her eyes and the hood had loosened wisps of honey hair to fall in silky-soft ringlets that framed her face. It wasn't just the dandies eyeing her either. Several fashionably dressed women turned as she passed to give a hard-eyed scrutiny to her lone progress through the narrow streets.

She hastened on, hoping she was now on the right track for the Bull and Mouth Inn. She had twice asked the way: from a lamp lighter just beginning his rounds whom she barely understood and from a woman with a cart load of hot pies. The savoury aroma of mutton and onions had made her stomach grumble but she had kept her money safe, knowing that hiring a carriage home later would take all of her coins.

It had all taken much more time than she had anticipated and the breeze off the ocean was stiffening and the light was fading. She couldn't guess the time as cloud was prematurely shortening the day. She walked slowly the length of Brewer Street and hesitated on the cobbles by the wharf. With one hand firm on her velvet hood she threw back her head and looked at the sign: a garish smiling mouth was topped by a painted black bull and it oscillated whiningly in the wind. As she tarried there two gentlemen turned the corner. They ogled her boldly as they approached. Feeling her face heating at their scrutiny, Rebecca purposely peered over the harbour wall, apparently fascinated by the small craft bobbing on the oily swell.

The men disappeared inside the tavern. Once the promenade was again relatively quiet, Rebecca twisted about, wondering what was best to do. Believing she would be able to loiter unobserved and seek Simon had been hopelessly misguided. Obviously the worst possible interpretation would be put on her dawdling presence outside a men's gathering place.

She kept her head down and her hood forward as she discreetly but carefully surveyed another couple of gentlemen who made their jovial way into the inn. They gave her very little of their attention and she relaxed. Feeling reassured, she firmly decided she would have to venture inside. She had some extra money with her, in case the landlord hinted payment might jog his memory about this one particular customer. She would seek him out directly and ask him if he knew of Simon. She might find the landlord helpful and obliging, she encouraged herself.

Thus heartened, she drew her blue velvet cloak about her, settled the hood and walked confidently into the Bull and Mouth tavern.

The interior was danker and darker than she had imagined. It was noisy too and filled with narrow corridors; she stood now at a turnoff, wondering which way to venture.

She backed carefully away from an open doorway, having gleaned from a speedy peek that the room was filled with cigar smoke and gentlemen throwing dice or playing cards, and straight on to a foot.

'Oi, watch out,' a female voice declared none too amiably.

'I'm so sorry,' Rebecca murmured, staring down at the obese woman's slippered feet. She looked up into a red-veined, bulbous face topped by greying brown hair which was in turn crowned by a lacy mob cap.

The woman raised heavy blackened brows at her and pinched a rouged mouth together in her heavy jowls. 'Oh, yes… And what are you about, then?' Queenie Spencer demanded of the beautiful young woman hesitating nervously in front of her.

'I'm looking for the landlord,' Rebecca informed politely. 'I need to speak to him urgently.

'Oh, do you?' Queenie mocked her. 'And why is that, pray? Come along, you can tell me, girl. I'm his wife.'

'Well, perhaps you could help me, then,' Rebecca quietly ventured, hating to feel so intimidated by this florid-faced, rotund woman with reeking breath.

Rebecca moistened her parched lips, flattening herself against the powdery dank wall as two women clad in little more than gauze petticoats pressed past them in the corridor. They assessed her from velvet hood to daintily shod feet with open curiosity and Rebecca dropped her eyes away at once from their painted faces.

'I am looking for my brother. I have been advised to look for him here,' Rebecca said in little more than a whisper. Panic was beginning to curdle her stomach, and she realized with belated wisdom that it might after all have been safer to remain outside this establishment to search for Simon.

Queenie Spencer examined the beautiful young woman in front of her with commercial expertise. She raised a plump hand then and summarily flicked Rebecca's velvet hood back from her face. Tendrils of honey hair trailed her alabaster forehead and neck as the turquoise cowl draped her shoulders.

'Looking for a brother, eh? Well, we get 'em all in here, my dearie. Fathers looking for daughters, sons looking for mothers, brothers looking for sisters. We don't mind. You're looking for a brother, we'll find him for you, sure enough.' She stared transfixed at the classical beauty she knew she would only come in contact with once or twice in her working lifetime. 'How many brothers is it you want me to find you, my lovie?' she enquired hoarsely as she calculated the clientele likely tonight. 'Struth, but she could provide this one with enough custom to keep her on her back for the next fortnight.

'His name is Simon Nash,' Rebecca hastily informed the landlady, her tongue quickly slipping about her mouth to try to ease the croak in her voice. 'Do you know him? If not I'll apologise now for taking your time and be gone,' she courteously rattled off, gliding subtly along the distempered wall towards the exit.

Sensing her agitation and imminent flight, Queenie grabbed hard at Rebecca's slender arm. Soothing fat fingers rubbed back and forth against the soft blue velvet. 'There, there, my duckie,' she cooed. 'You come along with me to the snug. It's nice and quiet in there and we'll talk about this a bit more. You'll be so worried about your brother, then, I reckon...' Queenie solicitiously purred.

'Yes, yes, I am. I need to find him urgently,' Rebecca agreed, relaxing a little as the woman led her into a small, empty room.

'Well, sit ye down,' Queenie offered, still unable to drag her greedy eyes away from the vision of loveliness that tentatively perched on a crude wooden taproom chair. Her furtive gaze darted over Rebecca's body, trying to ascertain what was beneath the enveloping velvet cloak. If body and face matched...

'So, you've been told you might find him here...' Queenie said with a sugary, uneven smile, as her cunning brain started to work. If she was an apprentice bawd seeking work, she was a little too old to be getting started and a little too refined. Still, what a looker, and no mistake. She could still end up as top dog in this establishment within a very short time. Gentlemen looked for freshness and variety in a place like this and Queenie had just struck gold...no exaggeration, she reckoned, gloating over that thick hair spilling ringlets about the shoulders of the blue velvet.

Her mercenary musing was abruptly curtailed as a bloated

man of middle years, with a greasy apron knotted about his distended girth, crashed into the room.

'What are you about, woman?' he growled at Queenie. 'I've a bar full of gents, a gaming room with nary a girl in sight and nor are you....'

He gawked at Rebecca. 'What's this? What's this?' he interrogated, glowering suspiciously at her. The only ladies of quality who ventured beyond his doors were those preaching charity or godliness and he could do without either.

Queenie licked her thick, rouged lips. 'This young lady's here a-looking for a brother. I thought as we would be sure to help her find the young gent she's after. Don't you think?'

Bertram Spencer looked at his wife for a long moment and then consideringly at the beautiful young woman, perched on the edge of the hard wooden chair. An inkling of something important stirred in his busy brain. 'Who is she looking for, did you say? What is his name…this brother?'

'Simon Nash, sir,' Rebecca supplied quickly, wondering desperately how she could extricate herself from this awful place and silently flailing herself for ever being idiotic enough to venture within it.

Bertram approached his wife surprisingly quickly, considering his swollen size, and whispered hoarsely in her ear. Rebecca watched the woman's pink tongue twice poke out and wet her lips.

Queenie pulled irritably away from her sibilantly hissing husband and scuffled towards Rebecca on her slippered feet. 'Well, seems you're going to be a lucky young lady. My good husband here has some idea of your young man you're a-seeking and thinks he can fetch him direct like.' She coughed raucously. 'You'll be wanting to speak in private with him o'course and need a quiet room. I've just the place.'

'Simon's here?' Rebecca breathed, a smile of gratitude and relief softening the strain in her face.

'Er…not quite…but he will be soon,' Queenie assured her, nodding her head and wobbling several jowls. 'Bertram will fetch him. You come with me and we'll find you that nice quiet room.' She grabbed at Rebecca's arms and yanked her off the chair and towards the door.

She propelled her towards some narrow, steep stairs at the end of the corridor and began urging her up them. Rebecca attempted to swing about but the woman's bulk was mere inches behind her and her husband directly behind that.

'Come along now,' Queenie jovially encouraged. 'Let's get you off these stairs and safe out of trouble,' and Rebecca felt a none-too-friendly shove in the small of her back.

On reaching the landing, she immediately twisted around, desperately uneasy. But the Spencers were both still there, narrowed eyes in fleshy faces eyeing her with mercenary purpose.

Queenie scraped the key in a lock nearby and pushed open the door to a low-beamed room. With Bertram close behind her and Queenie at her side, pudgy fingers digging into her arm, she had no choice but to enter. Rebecca took in the daunting aspect in one horrified glance: the large bed, the lack of any other furnishing. She swung instantly about.

'There has been some mistake. I must leave this place right now,' she announced with an authority she was far from feeling.

'No mistake, dearie,' Queenie denied her, smiling smugly, as Bertram withdrew his gross bulk from the room.

'My husband is just off to find your young man for you. Then you can have…a nice long chat with him. For as long as you like,' she slyly chuckled.

Stabbing pinpricks of fear began frosting Rebecca's face and body. Her cynicism and suspicion had been honed lately and both were relentlessly cutting her to the quick.

'Let me pass,' she demanded of Queenie in a strident, wavering tone. But the woman simply roared with amusement and leaned her quivering weight back against the wooden door.

'There's five hundred and I'll raise five hundred,' Luke said impassively as he dropped the notes from dark fingers and they joined the untidy pile nestling in the middle of the table. This hand of brag was drawing onlookers and several inquisitive men gathered about the perimeter of the large circular table where he sat.

Sepia-coloured eyes raised to lock on to the golden gaze of his brother sitting opposite. Ross blew softly through his grimacing mouth, shook his head and folded his hand of cards. Several other men did the same, one or two throwing them forcefully and resentfully on to the baize.

Luke allowed a small smile to curl his mouth. He had nothing. His fingers tapped idly against the cards face down on the table. He couldn't remember ever drawing a hand quite as useless as this one, yet he'd just staked a substantial sum on it, bluffed, and could well take the pot. His eyes met those of the only opponent left and held them steadily. The man was young, perhaps twenty-one, and green. Luke could tell he was getting in up to his ears for a good reason. He most definitely held the winning hand but had empty pockets.

He watched him slip a nervous tongue about his lips and glance around, obviously flustered by the attention the high stakes were attracting.

'Will you take my marker?' he asked Luke with a gruff hint of plea.

'Certainly.' Luke coolly qualified his generosity. 'For payment tomorrow noon.'

The man slid jittery fingers beneath his neckcloth and swivelled his head.

It was as Luke glanced away, bored by the delay, that the silver-blonde curls caught his restless gaze. They seemed familiar and redrew his attention. He frowned reflectively at Molly Parker and then, as his memory finally served him, he scowled.

Even irritated attention was welcome, Molly deemed, and she dimpled at him and weaved through the men thronging around the table now, making proprietorially for his chair. She had recognised him as soon as he had ducked through the low door of the Bull and Mouth with his cheeky younger brother. She had been about to accost them straight away, but Ross had noticed her and manically shooed her away behind his back.

Well, the handsome devil had noticed her himself this time and she was going to make sure that she stayed noticed.

Tentative fingertips rested daintily, questioningly, on the black superfine cloth of his shoulders. When he didn't immediately throw her off, she became bolder. Her hands slid further around his neck and the sheer pink gauze of her gown grazed his cheek as she settled her hips close to his face.

Her musky scent was in his nostrils, her lust for him mingled with that expensive French perfume that reminded him of Cornwall and Wenna. He felt the tightening in his groin and knew it wouldn't wait too much longer. He'd come here tonight to play cards but had accepted subconsciously that three weeks' celibacy was all his starved, tormented body could stand. He hadn't been without a woman this long since…he couldn't remember when.

He wasn't married, he wasn't even officially engaged. It didn't make him unfaithful or any other damn thing. It just made him human. He needed the release every man did. He was also in need of some flattering female attention. He had grown used to admiring glances and willing bodies and unequivocal encouragement. He needed reassurance that he wasn't Attila the Hun but just the same attractive, successful philanderer he had always been.

He felt a soft finger slide possessively along the lean, abrasive side of his jaw and flicked his head impatiently away from it. He had a game of cards to finish first if the youth opposite ever decided what he was going to do about financing this last hand. His eyes slid past the young man with bored indolence. He frowned, grimaced, then swore aloud with such violence that every man seated around the table stared curiously at him, and Molly and her fondling fingers abruptly sprang away.

Ross anxiously studied his brother's face. Noting the direction of Luke's black-eyed stare, Ross swivelled his head. There was nothing…nothing apart from drifting smoke and an empty doorway.

Luke's fingers tightened on the cards he held and he glowered, rigid-faced, down at them.

This was lunacy…sheer idiocy. If Miles was beginning to suppose him addled in the wits he was well on the way to joining him in that worrying assumption. He was most definitely losing his mind. He couldn't sleep, he couldn't eat, he couldn't venture out for the evening to play a game of cards…he certainly couldn't contemplate taking a woman to bed, without Rebecca ethereally materialising in his mind. God, but she'd looked real.

He grunted a low laugh to himself, unaware of Ross's anxious narrowed gaze on him. She'd looked like a blue-clad angel. Why he'd imagined her dressed like that, he couldn't conceive. He'd never seen her wear that colour. The most extraordinary thing was that the gross pair who ran this establishment had been escorting her, walking into his delusion too. He shoved himself back in the chair, transforming Molly's wary return into hasty retreat.

Luke stared sightlessly and thin-lipped at the vacant doorway. Then Bertram Spencer nudged his bulk through it. Luke frowned. He was dressed as he'd just imagined him. But then he probably always dressed like that, he reasoned to himself. He watched the fat innkeeper sidle up close to one of the spectators at his table and mutter in his ear.

Luke watched the man's ice-blue eyes reduce to little more than slits and a smile of sheer satisfaction curl his mouth as he nodded slowly. The man turned away immediately, walking fast to the door with Bertram Spencer hard on his heels.

Luke's mouth thrust out in consideration as, just before they exited the room, money changed hands. The younger man turned right towards the stairs and Bertram Spencer hurried in the opposite direction, stuffing notes into his cavernous apron pocket.

Something heavy and stone-cold settled in Luke. It hadn't been a vision. It had definitely been someone. A regular, jaded customer, eager to be ahead of the pack, would be instantly drawn by a fresh new recruit. And would pay up handsomely for the exquisite harlot he'd just glimpsed.

How many women had hair that particular shade of honey?

Had that cool beauty…pale skin…and were exactly that height? He felt a tic start its intermittent pulsing by his mouth and his back teeth ground together as the chill in him spread. The cards in his hands dropped from nerveless fingers to the baize. Just as the young man finished writing out his marker, Luke said hoarsely, 'Fold.' He pushed his chair back abruptly, sending a cautiously confident Molly crashing backwards again into the welcoming arms of an elderly gentleman behind her.

He was being ridiculous. It sang through his head as he passed where Ross sat. She was at home…at the Summer House. Probably retired for the evening already.

'Where are you going?' Ross hissed at him.

'Find a girl,' Luke told him huskily without losing pace.

Ross laughed then with sheer relief and several other men joined him. 'About time, too…' Ross muttered beneath his breath, relaxing into the sure knowledge that he was about to get his old, familiar Luke back very soon.

Good-natured bantering amongst the men followed his departure. That was some high instepper, the consensus of opinion went, who could lay a thousand pounds down on nothing at all, then walk off to find a girl without bothering to bluff the hand out.

Ross turned his laughing face from the man sitting next to him and caught sight of Molly. Christ, she looked as though she was about to cry. He got up and walked around the table to her. He hadn't had a blonde himself in a while.

'Mr Blacker!' Rebecca cried in a voice mingling astonishment and relief. 'Do you know if Simon is here this evening?' she asked quickly as the brown-haired man walked steadily into the room. At one time the thought and sight of this man would have filled her with revulsion. Now he seemed ridiculously welcome compared to the odious Spencers.

He gave Queenie an expressive look and jerked his head indicatively at the door.

'Well, I'll leave you to your gent then, dearie,' the obese woman smirked as she squashed backwards out of the room.

Jake Blacker proceeded into the room, his pale eyes never leaving Rebecca's face. Rebecca stepped forward to meet him and then hesitated, something in his silent attitude unnerving her.

'Have you seen Simon here tonight?' she repeated urgently. 'I'm sure the landlord and his wife hadn't the vaguest notion who I meant when I mentioned my brother.' She smiled at him appealingly, hoping for reciprocal friendliness.

'But I know who you mean, don't I,' he smoothly insinuated as he continued with his steady advance. 'Show me a little…gratitude on account, Miss Nash, and I'm sure I might find that brother of yours for you.' His tongue flicked to wet his lips. God, but she was beautiful. Dressed now in finery instead of those modest clothes he'd seen her in last, she was every man's fantasy: an angel in a whorehouse. His fingers itched at his sides. He longed to divest her of the garments he so admired. The blue velvet was handsome and set off her pale beauty and incredible eyes, but heaven only knew he'd love to see her out of it.

Rebecca swallowed quickly and then stood her ground. She had been imprisoned by Queenie Spencer in this spartan bedchamber for no more than ten uneasy minutes, yet it had dragged like sixty. She was, now, heartily sick of feeling frightened and intimidated.

'Where is my brother?' she demanded icily. 'Is he here at this establishment or not? If not, I shall…'

Further words were cut off as Jake Blacker unceremoniously grabbed at her arm and hauled her close to him. The thick, frantic fingers of one hand were at her cloak, shoving it from her shoulders, while he thrust his other hand impatiently beneath it and grabbed at a breast. She simultaneously slapped at him, trying to evade him, but a spiteful hand sank into her hair and yanked her head around to his. A hard wet mouth pounced on hers, making Rebecca gasp in outrage and fight him in earnest.

'I think this must be where I say…unhand my betrothed, or suffer the consequences…' said a deadly quiet voice from the doorway.

Chapter Nine

'What the hell do you think you're about?' Jake Blacker growled furiously. He still had vicious hold of Rebecca and she was wrenched violently about with him. 'Get out of here and wait your turn. I suppose that grasping lard barrel of a landlord sent you up…'

'Luke…' Rebecca breathed in wonder and relief, fighting desperately to free herself to fly to him. Jake Blacker stared at her then more purposefully at Luke, standing with his back to the closed door, his eyes fiery coals in his tense, whitening face.

As though just recalling how this intruder had termed Rebecca, Blacker grunted a contemptuous laugh. 'What did you say just then? Betrothed…?' he sneered.

'I said…let her go…now,' Luke silkily advised in a lethally controlled voice, while pacing so lightly into the room, it was as though his feet skimmed the floor.

Jake Blacker easily recognised the danger signals. He faced him fully, abruptly releasing Rebecca. The instinct to protect himself was far sharper than his lust. He backed away, circling, assessing the small room's vantage points in flicking glances interspersed with challenging stares at the tall, athletic figure stalking him.

'Luke…' Rebecca murmured again as she rubbed at her bruised arm and rushed to him.

She wound her arms about him and held on tight, trying to still the shake in her body with his solid, familiar strength. But there was no expected comfort, no soothing words and he jerked her away and towards the wall without once looking at her.

Jake Blacker wet his lips. Everyone around these parts knew him and nobody dared cross him. Which meant that this man was a stranger and didn't know the rules. By the time he did, Jake worriedly reckoned it might be too late. He preferred teamwork…the unquestioning backing of the thugs who ran contraband for him. On his own in a fair fight, and weaponless, he wasn't nearly so cocksure. Especially not with a man like this.

The fellow wasn't that much taller or broader than himself, Blacker arrogantly decided, mentally enhancing his height and shoulders by inches, but his confidence and leashed rage were perilous. He'd been watching him downstairs playing cards and thought him a cool, callous customer and definitely well-heeled. Blacker found his mercenary mind veering off at a tangent, as he remembered that game of brag. He surmised whether this man had in his pocket the stack of bank notes he'd covetously watched mounting on the baize.

As Luke came within arm's length of him, Jake hastily evaded him. Fight or flight. He lived by that code and tonight the latter beckoned. He spread his hands in a brash, conciliatory gesture while sliding Rebecca a disparaging glance.

'If you're that desperate…you have her first. I can wait. There are plenty more downstairs.'

Luke continued his advance. His fists were balled so tightly his fingers were in spasm, yet through the red mist of his pain and fury he recognised the sense in letting him go. He wanted him out of the way so he could deal with Rebecca. And deal with her he would. He halted and one arm indicated the door, wordlessly inviting him to use it.

Jake Blacker sidled, back to the wall, towards it. He had been bested and this maddening outcome, together with the fact that he had vainly been parted from his money by Bertram

Spencer, needled him mercilessly. Someone had to pay for this humiliation. It looked as though it would be the fat innkeeper.

'You're not from around here, are you, friend? If you were, you'd know not to cross me. Perhaps you'd care to tell me who you are so I can look you up at some time,' he blustered.

'Luke Trelawney, from Cornwall,' Luke introduced himself immediately and quietly. 'Find me there any time,' he added, as his narrowed, black gaze followed every movement of the man shifting towards the door.

'Luke Trelawney…?' Jake Blacker burst into genuine laughter. So the fellow did know who he was, and his profession, and was trying to be mocking and clever. *'Luke Trelawney?'* Blacker jeered again, as his ice-blue eyes derisively swept the elegantly dressed man in front of him from handsome ebony head to expensive, black-shod feet. He dressed and sounded like a member of the aristocracy. But at least he had a sense of humour. 'Well, if you're Luke Trelawney from Cornwall, I'm the Prince of Wales…from Brighton Pavilion.'

'I'd get back there, then,' Luke advised him with treacherous quiet. 'I believe you've guests waiting.'

'And you'd know, of course,' sniggered Blacker.

'I should do. I was one of the invited guests.'

'Luke…' Rebecca called his name again on a trembling sigh. She felt icy cold and was desperate to be home and away from this foul place and this vile man.

Jake Blacker glanced uneasily at Rebecca. No, it couldn't be true…but it was the third time she'd used that name. But it was a common enough name. 'Who is he? Do you know of him?' he imperiously demanded.

'Luke Trelawney,' she managed to force out through frozen lips, as she numbly wondered why the name should make a criminal like Jake Blacker blanch and stare and then speed up towards the door. Why did it matter to him so much who he was?

'I'll settle with you another time,' Jake Blacker muttered but with little conviction in the guttural warning. He jerked the door open and immediately crashed it shut behind him.

'Luke…' Rebecca pleaded again as she wrapped her arms tightly about herself. She felt so cold and so tired. She just wanted to go home and sleep and sleep.

'Rebecca…' Luke parodied in a voice mingling steel and sarcasm. He walked to the door and locked it, removing the key which he dropped into his pocket. He slowly turned to face her and leaned back against the door, much in the same way he had done on first entering the room.

Rebecca took a tentative step towards him and then hesitated. She so much wanted him to hold and comfort her. But the wrath in his face was no longer hidden beneath that expressionless mask he employed, it was intentionally in evidence. She stepped back immediately against the wall, her cold palms hugging the damp distemper.

'Perhaps you'd care to tell me what you're doing in a gambling whorehouse?' he remarked in a voice so mild and pleasant it terrified her. But menace was nothing new to her tonight and she sensed a devilish anger of her own starting to burn. The memory of semi-naked women in the hallway downstairs was stoking it furiously.

'And perhaps you'd care to tell me what *you* are doing here?' she insolently returned in a tremulous voice.

'Gambling,' came his curt, chill response. 'And you…?' he silkily inquired.

Rebecca moistened her parched lips. She had felt so utterly relieved to see him. So immensely glad and fortunate and now… She walked wearily to the bed and collected her blue velvet cloak from where Jake Blacker had thrown it. 'I want to go home,' she defeatedly declared. She approached the door, halting just out of his reach and looked up into his handsome face. Rage was etched into each feature. Every harsh, lean plane was darkly, satanically set and so tense that a muscle pulled constantly at one side of his mouth.

'Are you going to imprison me, too?' Rebecca asked on a fatigued, shaky laugh. 'That will be the third time this evening I've been held in this accursed room.' His hand went to his pocket. He withdrew the door key and held it out to her, but didn't budge an inch. Rebecca looked longingly at it but didn't move closer to take it.

'Move!' she demanded, trying to ignore the traitorous blockage forming in her throat and the stinging heat at the back of her eyes. He thought the worst of her for being here and she couldn't blame him. She recalled the lascivious, disrespectful stares of the men she had seen outside this sordid establishment. They had believed the same of her.

However she explained it, it would appear ridiculous. She could barely credit that she'd taken such an appalling stupid risk herself. She had never so acutely or humiliatingly suffered for her naïvety. Jake Blacker had tricked her…baited her with the promise of Simon and she had suspected nothing, even knowing the man for a villain. She had simply gone like a lamb to the slaughter.

Luke pushed away from the door and walked towards her. Rebecca immediately side-stepped to pass him, but he followed her circumvention, forcing her back into the room with him, although he never once touched her. She felt the edge of the bed against her legs and as he kept coming and there was nowhere else to go, she abruptly sat down. Belatedly realising the folly in that move, she immediately attempted to spring up again but he was leaning over her, an arm braced either side of her on the bed, forcing her to angle backwards away from him.

'Tell me what you are doing here, Rebecca,' he requested in that deceptively mild voice.

To avoid him, she turned her head, presenting him with a view of artlessly draped golden coils of hair. She was determined to ignore him and his questions, and yet even as she garnered that courage, she complied unsteadily. 'I came here to find Simon. That evil man told me to look here for him.'

'Your brother Simon?' he asked quietly. Rebecca simply nodded without turning her head.

'When did he tell you to look here for him? When have you seen him before?' he rapidly interrogated her.

'He came to the Summer House yesterday. He was searching

for Simon and asked if I knew his whereabouts. I told him that I also needed to find my brother and he appeared to want to help me. I foolishly believed him sincere when he stressed this place was a regular haunt of Simon's.'

'And why is he looking for this elusive brother of yours, Rebecca?'

'I believe Simon must owe him money. I think my brother has become involved with a fearsome band of criminals. I…I think he has joined a smuggling ring. That man, Jake Blacker, is their leader, so I've heard.'

She looked at Luke then as she recounted the full horror of her tale, and Simon's likely involvement, sure he would be disgusted by it.

She watched an odd smile alter the hard, thin line of his sculpted mouth and he repeated softly, 'Smugglers?'

'Yes,' she murmured, scanning his face, wondering why he found that amusing.

'So you needed to find your brother so urgently that you risked entering a place such as this?'

'Yes,' Rebecca told him in little more than a whisper.

'Why?' Luke asked in a voice almost as quiet as hers.

Rebecca glanced down at her shaking hands and gripped them together to still them. 'He has my inheritance. He has had it for five years. Had he not stolen it, I would never have been forced on my uncle's charity or been forced…' She broke off hastily, aware she had been about to mention his role in prompting her to desperately seek financial security. 'It is *my* money. My father left me five thousand pounds. It was to be my dowry when I married David.'

'You are not marrying David,' was the steely calm response to this information. 'And you have no need of a dowry.'

Rebecca turned her head then, sparkling aquamarine eyes clashing with chips of black onyx. 'No, I have no need of a dowry, for I have no intention of marrying. But I need the money my father left for my protection. It is mine and I intend having it to secure my future.'

'You have no intention of marrying?' he smoothly echoed

her words as his eyes steadily held hers. 'Is this my answer?
You've considered my proposal for a day or two and rejected
me?'

'It's been more than a day or two,' Rebecca couldn't help
but fling at him, recalling his prolonged absence. She now
understood why she had seen nothing of him. No doubt he had
spent a great deal of his time carousing in places such as this.
She had been correct in her assumption of his morals and of
the debauched scene she had witnessed at Ramsden Manor. In
all probability it was a regular occurrence and had been since
first he took up residence.

'Have you missed me, Rebecca? Been counting the days?'
he taunted her with soft satisfaction and she immediately
swung her flushing face away again, drifting honey curls catching his cheek.

'Not at all. I was merely hoping you would come by so that
I could advise you of my decision and finally settle matters
between us. I thought it best not to come to the Manor seeking
you, lest I intrude on one of your…at-homes,' she taunted him
with a honeyed-voice and bittersweet smile.

He caught at her face then and firm fingers kept her looking
at him as he said, 'It still rankles, does it? Even though I told
you there was nothing to it. Nothing at all for you to worry
about.'

She shook her head free of his clasp, breathing hard, her
turquoise eyes glittering shards of ice. 'I do not worry…I never
think of it,' she lied. 'I care not what debauchery you seek.
Just leave me alone. I'm going home now.' She half-rose from
the bed but he was immovable. In her desperation to be free
of him she slapped hard at his face while attempting to duck
beneath one of his braced arms.

He pulled back a little, allowing her to stand before catching
at her shoulders and partially lifting her backwards on to the
bed so she was now sprawled across it rather than perched on
the edge. Then he followed her down.

Her fists beat at his shoulders and were swinging for his face again when he restrained them, forcing them back either side of her head.

'This isn't the way to endear a new protector, Rebecca,' he softly mocked. 'Gently at first. I'll let you know soon enough when I want things rougher.'

She closed her eyes and moistened her lips, her wrists straining against the weight of his pinioning hands. 'I hate you. Why can't you just leave me be?' she choked on a stifled sob.

'Because I can't. And whether you come to Cornwall with the benefit of a wedding ring or not matters little to me. But come with me you will.'

Rebecca flung her head around and glared up at him. She twisted her head this way and that, trying to clear the trailing silky tendrils of hair tickling her face. 'I'm going nowhere with you. I wouldn't even go willingly to the end of this street with such as you.'

'Perhaps you're right,' he agreed, feigning thoughtfulness, as he easily curbed her attempts to throw him off. 'It's a long way to take you only to discover you're a disappointment and need to be returned. It's as well to find out now if you're likely to show talent and be useful,' he said, mock solemn. 'It would save us both inconvenience and you an amount of unnecessary travel.'

He moved one of his hands, still clasped to her wrist, towards her face and carefully removed the irritating strands of hair, the backs of his dark fingers deliberately, caressingly, trailing the creamy satin of her cheeks and jaw.

Rebecca swallowed the ache in her throat. This was too much! Why was everything of late always a disaster? Why couldn't she have found Simon simply? Or simply not found him? Why couldn't the landlord have been a sincere or helpful fellow? Or, if neither, merely thrown her straight back out on to the streets? Why was she always prey to devious rogues and scoundrels who meant her harm? Why had David died? she cried silently to herself. He had cared for her; loved her in a gentle, respectful way. He had never forced her on to a bed and pinned her there while he taunted her with hateful words and tormenting touches.

She sensed rather than saw his mouth nearing hers and jerked her head away, forcing her cheek into the yielding softness of the mattress, her breathing fast and erratic. If he kissed her she was lost, she knew that, and that self-awareness squeezed the first tear between her lashes.

'Let me kiss you, Rebecca,' he softly requested as his mouth tenderly teased her face and rested close to hers. He slowly tantalised the sensitive corner of her firmly pressed lips. 'Please,' he coaxed hoarsely.

'No,' the word burst, strangling, from her throat, as she vainly renewed her efforts to rise from the bed.

'Why not? I've kissed you before.'

Rebecca choked a despairing laugh. That's why, she wanted to scream at him. That's the whole point. Instead she said unsteadily, 'You don't really want to kiss me. It's not what you intend at all. You just told me that.'

She sensed him smile, heard it in his voice as he murmured against her skin, 'I'll stop whenever you say, I promise.'

'No,' Rebecca quickly denied him, panic harshening her voice. He knew very well, as did she, that within minutes she would be rendered mindless and her mortification would scale new heights.

In response, his parted lips trailed her throat, warm and fluid, yet never resting to actually kiss. Rebecca sensed the treacherous coiling in the pit of her stomach as the lean, abrasive side of his jaw slid against the smooth silk of hers and her eyelids drooped and her breathing became shallow. The warmth of his breath stirred the hair close to her ear as he slid his open mouth across a sensitive lobe and she shuddered and reflexively turned into him. His face buried into her neck, fanning moist heat against the vulnerable crease between neck and shoulder and she sighed, closing her eyes and unclamping her mouth.

Luke drew back a little to look at her, while the gnawing ache in his loins and the incredible tenderness and protection she evoked in him did battle. He rested his face into her spread, honey hair. Even in this stinking hole she held the fragrance of fresh air and lavender, and he wryly realised that she truly had nothing to fear from him. He wanted her with a desperation that surpassed anything he'd ever experienced in his adult life, yet the thought of taking her virginity here, on some whorehouse bed, made him feel nauseated.

He'd only frightened her in retaliation, because she had terrified him so much. At one time, and not so long ago, danger and thrill had been a daily part of life and he'd adapted to it, eventually relished it to such a degree he recalled those days with nostalgia. But the thought of her certain fate tonight, had he not seen her, left a residue of fear that even now soured his stomach and caused his heartbeat to erratically strengthen. And he might not have seen her. He could have chosen to sit at the opposite side of that card table.

She might have passed the doorway earlier or later when he wasn't there. He might even now have been oblivious to her presence, while he eased himself with that blonde whore in a room nearby. He probably would have laughed, as would others, on hearing a scream coming from a chamber, imagining it to be fun and frolicking within. His head bowed close to hers and his hands tightened jerkily on her wrists at the sheer torture of it. Rebecca gasped with the painful pressure and he soothed her with careful fingers, nuzzling with apologetic tenderness against her cheek.

'You may kiss me if you don't move your hands,' she whispered in defeat, unable to deny the yearning longer.

'What?' he demanded, a smile in his disbelief.

'Don't move your hands…you mustn't move your hands,' she stressed as she twisted towards him. Their faces were inches apart on the bed as she murmured, 'Please don't move your hands. Promise me you won't.'

Firm, dark fingers slid from her wrists and entwined with her pale, trembling ones, as he said huskily, 'I swear,' just before his mouth touched hers.

Rebecca closed her eyes and tilted her head as he moved her

on to her back and braced himself over her. She clamped her small, slender fingers purposefully around the considerable length of his as he carried their joined hands to bury in the silken softness of her hair.

He kissed her with slow, wooing sweetness and a hot urgent passion which made his fingers crush shakingly about hers, as he fought to limit his need. Clasped fists disentangled from luxuriant golden hair to mutually caress her body while skilful skimming knuckles deftly, covertly raised and disarranged her skirts.

Rebecca felt her own teasing fingers and her response to them and in feverish awareness pushed their coupled palms away across the covers. He controlled the sweep, taking them back up to her head, his thumbs free to soothe her face as the magical kiss protracted.

It was so slow and so deep their faces barely moved, fused together while his tongue made leisurely, probing strokes into her warm satin mouth, exploring and exciting. He could feel her small, intuitive movements jerking her hips up to meet his and discreetly shifted position. Reflexively her legs spread a little and a silken calf slid naturally over the black-suited, brawny length of one of his. Tiny panting sounds began breaking far in her throat, yet still she wouldn't relinquish his gripped fingers.

The erotic assault was calculated, unremitting, until she was squirming against him, her tongue tentatively unfurling to seek and copy his. He manoeuvred her subtly; dexterously rearranging hampering skirts so a solid, trousered knee could wedge unimpeded between hers. It slid unhurriedly up, opening her thighs.

He abruptly lifted her, while rearing back to kneel on the bed and settled her relentlessly hard against him, so she widely straddled the iron-muscled rigidity of his thigh.

He had anticipated her immediate alarm at this sudden change in position. As she frantically twisted her mouth and hands against his to escape, he seduced her expertly, inexorably, until she quietened and accepted it. As she relaxed back into him she moulded herself breast to groin against him, with an innate rotation of hips. He encouraged her to do it again with insistent, guiding hands, meeting her movement with increased pressure of his thigh while eroticising the kiss.

Their mouths clung now barely apart and his tongue probed with deliberate, measured thrusts between her hot swollen, lips. She ground against him faster and then, fearful of the wild, enslaving sensations controlling her, fought again to tear her mouth and her body from his. But he was inflexible, pinning her against him with one clamped hand against her buttocks and the other behind her head maintaining hard sensual contact.

After a heart-thundering moment, Rebecca surrendered with a sobbing sigh, grinding her hips harder and faster against the reciprocating rock of his body.

Luke sensed her tense and then arch and deliberately jammed against her, heightening abrasive friction until she convulsed and shuddered. As her back bowed further and she moaned into his mouth, he finally released her lips, and relaxed. Her head lolled instantly back exposing the rose-flushed ivory of her throat. His face followed, dropping forward, his steamy mouth resting against the column of satin skin as she shook and gasped and her fingernails dug savagely into his hands.

Boneless languor bathed Rebecca and Luke lowered her gently back down to the bed. But as he tried to immediately remove himself, her arms and legs tightened about him and she whimpered. He did too. He wasn't sure whether to laugh or cry. He rested his face against hers while desperately trying to avoid contact with any other part of her. He felt sure he might explode at any moment and the excruciating torment was too much. He gradually disengaged himself from her clinging grip and touched his mouth to hers before he pulled away and stood up.

He walked to the window and looked out, then leaned his feverish forehead against the cold glass. He walked to the door and stared at the wooden panels, then rested his head and fists against that too.

He turned back to the bed and gazed at her. She lay quiet

and sated, her golden head fallen to one side, with locks of hair coating her flushed face. In his demented desperation he wondered whether he had time to quickly find one of the tavern whores and relieve himself before reason reclaimed her drugged mind and body.

He watched her stir and turn on to her side, before resettling deeply into sensual torpor.

So this was love, he realised with an ironic little smile; this mix of tenderness and torture, elation and misery. There was a lot to be said for never having left Cornwall. God only knew why he had. He could have dealt with the whole Ramsden business from there if he had put a mind to it. But he hadn't; some irrevocable duty had brought him to Sussex and now he knew why. Destiny...fate, he'd never yet believed in them.

He walked back to the bed and squatted down on his heels close to her. A fond finger came out to touch her cheek and rouse her.

Rebecca smiled against the finger that lovingly outlined her lips but she didn't open her eyes. 'I like it when you kiss me,' she murmured artlessly.

'I know you do,' he said gently. 'You'll like it even more next time. When you let go of my hands.'

Drowsy, large-pupilled turquoise eyes looked wonderingly at him, then she smiled. The dark finger by her mouth stroked along the bruised scarlet of her lips and she playfully caught it, bit down on it and then soothed it with her tongue.

Luke closed his eyes and choked a pained laugh at the innocent teasing and the images it evoked. Christ, it wasn't fair. Where was that hard-bitten, selfish bastard when he needed him?

He slid his hands under her and tipped her forward into his arms and stood up, holding her turned into him like a child. She immediately coiled her arms about his neck and nestled against him.

'We'll be married on Sunday,' he told her in a tone that was neither request nor dogmatic, as he stooped to collect her velvet cloak from the bed on his way to the door.

He placed her with her back to the door, facing him, blatant self-mockery and raw tenderness mingling on his darkly handsome features. Large, lean fingers settled the blue velvet carefully about her, drawing the hood up over her head and tucking in the strands of hair around her sensually flushed face. She looked up at him with wide aquamarine eyes and his steady, amused gaze never left her trusting face as he withdrew the key from his pocket and unlocked the door. He finally moved away, pulling her with him so the door could open.

'Let's get you home,' he said with a caress of a smile. He scanned the empty corridor, grabbed at her hand, and then started along it.

He descended the stairs, keeping Rebecca shielded behind him, hoping to God that the silver-haired harlot didn't materialise out of the smoky atmosphere. The noise of gaming and revelry was becoming deafening: a raucous female chuckle was heard followed by uproarious male laughter and some lascivious banter.

'Found your brother then, my dearie,' came a lewdly insinuating voice from behind.

Rebecca made to swirl about, recognising it instantly to be Queenie Spencer, but Luke held her facing the exit as he turned to the woman.

Queenie goggled at him, wondering where the hell he had materialised from. 'Struth, but he was a big, handsome brute. Wealthy too, she reckoned, as her materialistic eye roved his impeccably styled black clothes. No doubt one of the Quality.

She wetted fleshy lips and smirked at him. 'Everything to your satisfaction then, your lordship?' she suggested with ferocious cunning and a meaningful nod at Rebecca's hooded profile.

Luke despised the woman openly with black diamond eyes and a curl to his mouth while he considered. He could ignore her, leave, and risk her causing an uproar and attracting the attention of every whore and patron within the place, or pay her. Not that the money bothered him in the slightest, it was the implication for Rebecca.

As another chorus of lusty laughing erupted, he wondered where Ross had got to, whether he had already left. As though in response to his silent call, his brother clattered down the stairs at that precise moment, a brandy bottle grasped in one hand and the silver-blonde in the other. Both spied him at the same time. Ross jovially called out his name, greeting him with a waving bottle and Molly narrowed spiteful eyes at Rebecca.

Rebecca heard Luke's name too. Sure she recognised Ross's voice, she made to turn and investigate. Luke slapped a fistful of notes into Queenie Spencer's humid palm, disgustedly shaking off the pudgy fingers that reflexively closed over his. He tightened his restrictive grip about Rebecca's shoulders and speedily ushered her outside.

With athletic ease, Luke swung into the saddle behind Rebecca and turned the black stallion's head towards the coast road. Rebecca settled back against him, instantly sliding her arms beneath his jacket seeking warmth and comfort. He drew her hood further forward on her golden hair as the wind whipped brine off the sea at their faces, then urged the restless animal into a trot.

Rebecca rested peacefully against him, closing her eyes as the evening's events ran through her mind in slow motion. Some made her shudder in recalled horror, others that she lingered over provoked trembling of a different sort, causing her body to heat. But there were niggling oddities that puzzled her.

'Were you really invited to Brighton Pavilion tonight?'

'Uh-huh,' he grunted on a smile. 'Are you impressed?' he asked softly against her velvet hood.

Rebecca considered for a moment. 'I suppose I should be. But I'm not sure. I know very little about the Prince Regent and his court.'

'Well, I know a little more,' he commented drily. 'That's why I decided to have a game of cards with Ross instead.'

'Am I supposed to believe you simply preferred the Bull and Mouth tavern and...*gambling*, to Brighton Pavilion and exalted company tonight?' Rebecca probed with more than a tinge of sour disbelief in her voice.

'I'm a country boy at heart, Rebecca. I'm happiest with simple pleasures. I've no need of such people.' He gave the top of her head a slow, indulgent smile. 'Besides, once we're married I won't be looking to go out and…gamble in the evenings. I shall be a model husband. And such society invitations will lessen. It's Lord Ramsden's eligible bachelor status which makes him sought after by scheming hostesses.' He added, mildly cynical, 'Not to mention the hundred or so thousand a year.'

Rebecca twisted to look at him. 'Am I a simple pleasure, then?' she asked, feeling illogically insulted, and apparently unmoved by his fortune.

'More hard than simple, I'd say, Rebecca,' he ironically remarked as glittering black eyes roved her beautifully solemn upturned face. But he managed a wry smile.

Rebecca returned him a contented one and again nestled back, reflecting once more on the thrilling evening's events.

'Jake Blacker seemed to know you,' Rebecca mentioned against the warmth of his chest, as her fingers began a tiptoeing, cautious exploration over hard ridges of muscle on his linen-covered torso. She hadn't been so casually close to him before and the desire to touch him, while he was otherwise occupied, was undeniable. His silence made her pull back a little and once more look up into his shadowy face.

She saw the flash of white in the dusk as he smiled. 'Lots of people know me, Rebecca.'

'But he seemed…disturbed by your name,' she persisted. 'Why?' She sensed him shrug and his hand slipped beneath her velvet cloak and a firm thumb caressed her midriff. She tried a different approach. 'Do you know him?'

'I've never seen him before,' he answered truthfully.

Rebecca relaxed back against him and as their fingers touched beneath her shielding cloak and spontaneously laced, she quivered with recalled ecstacy.

'Jake Blacker has a fearsome reputation,' she told him in a

voice muffled by his coat. 'He is a foul blackguard…a smuggler who runs the risk of hanging if caught. I hope Simon is not very involved with him. For all such criminals run that risk,' she whispered brokenly. 'And I suppose it is only fair they should pay for their crimes. Don't you think?'

'Absolutely,' he said but in an odd tone of voice that made her think he might be laughing. She immediately drew back to investigate. But he turned his head away, shielding his expression. His eyes were narrowed and intent when he looked back at her and then he bent his head to warm her wind-chilled lips with his.

'I'll find Simon for you. Don't worry,' he said soothingly against her mouth before he purposefully spurred the black stallion into a gallop so that any further questions were impossible.

Chapter Ten

Molly Parker slid a covert glance at Luke from the corner of one blue eye, trying to decide whether she could stomach yet another rebuff. Devil take him to hell! Why give him an opportunity to insult her for the third time?

But that bored, perfect profile turned to the leaded window of the taproom loosened her fine resolution, and tightened her fists around the mug of porter in front of her on the rough-hewn bar top. She glowered disgustedly at the bitter brown beer, wishing it a stiff French brandy instead of this cheap slop Bertram rationed his girls.

Why did this stranger, infuriatingly, have to be the most imposing, handsome man she could ever remember patronising the Bull and Mouth? She had worked in the place for nearly a year now and had entertained clients as diverse as an escaped French prisoner of war, fresh out of the sea in a last bid for freedom; to an octogenarian duke fresh out of his sick bed in a last bid for life.

This one was ridiculously wealthy too. Her heart thudded miserably as she remembered her last humiliation, when he had dismissed her and the pot of money laying in the centre of the card table, and walked away from both.

The French prisoner of war had been penniless...and sopping wet, having swum a good deal of the ocean between the rotting hulk of the penal ship where he had been incarcerated, off the Kent coast, and the pebbly shore of Brighton. But Bertram Spencer had welcomed him quite cordially, while bundling him upstairs into Molly's care. 'Général de Montfort' had been whispered about. So had promise of generous payment when he was reunited with his compatriots and country. Exhaustion and hunger had taken their toll on the wretch, providing Molly with one of her slackest evenings. A welcome night's rest always sweetened her attitude.

She had worked at this den of iniquity long enough to know when to play blind, deaf, and dumb. Thus she never saw kegs and chests come ashore and cram the Spencers' cellar. She never heard any hissing debate in the dead of night as to payments due and owed, and she never uttered a word about any of these oddities. Her reminiscence inevitably skewed to the decrepit yet lusty old duke. She shuddered, recalling his fetid breath and decaying loose-skinned body...and his energy... That foul memory did it for her. She slid off her bar stool and was adjusting her low-cut satin bodice and her coiffure when the taproom door opened.

Her teeth ground in frustration. Another blond stealing his attention! She watched Luke Trelawney's mouth curl sardonically. But he raised a languid hand and curtly beckoned, encouraging the newcomer to join him.

Simon Nash walked forward hesitantly, a searching glance about the low-beamed room settling briefly, interestedly, upon Molly as she fumbled behind her for her stool and reseated herself.

Her professional interest quickened. Gawd! Another welcome, attractive man new to this dive. She gratefully acknowledged his attention with flirtatiously lowered eyelashes and dimpling pink cheeks. She swivelled on her stool to face the bar and took a satisfied swig from her porter before recalling, with distaste, what she drank.

'You got my message,' Luke stated evenly but the contempt he felt for the man was obvious in his cursory gesture at the chair opposite him.

Simon quickly seated himself, fidgeting with straightening

the sleeves of his navy woollen jacket. He placed his hat on the table then removed it and arranged it carefully on the floor by his chair. Unsteady, work-roughened fingers raked a thick lock of sun-gilded hair back from his sea-beaten forehead. Anything to occupy himself and dodge those stone-cold eyes he knew judged and condemned him.

He gulped a steadying breath, blinked wide navy eyes, and summoned youthful brashness to his aid. 'I thought perhaps you got my message,' he boldly challenged the imposing man who was casually leaning into the carver chair, his powerful physique making its solid frame seem as insubstantial as matchwood.

Luke allowed a genuine smile to momentarily soften his mouth. So the lad was badly rattled and without the skill to adequately disguise it. But what championed his cause most, Luke wryly realised, was not his gaucheness, but his flaxen hair and blue eyes and an undeniable likeness to his beautiful older sister.

'*Your* message?' Luke queried, prepared to humour him for a while yet. 'You've been keen to seek me out?'

'Er…yes. I told Blacker I should like to meet with you,' Simon gruffly informed him. 'Blacker has told me that you and Rebecca are…er…very well acquainted. I knew it was my duty to introduce myself to you…in the circumstances.'

'Did you, now,' Luke remarked softly and smoothly, quelling an urge to reject sentimental indulgence in favour of gripping his prospective brother-in-law by the throat and demanding to know where he had hidden during more worrying circumstances affecting his sister. He steadily reined in his temper. 'Which circumstances?' he coolly invited through closing teeth.

'Those that made you leave messages at every local tavern that you wished to speak urgently with me,' Simon impulsively retorted, sensing he had a weak advantage but unsure why.

A humourless, thin smile cautioned Simon to quieten. He did so, swallowing further words with a visible jerking of his Adam's apple.

This was not going at all the way he had hoped. He had been cornered eventually by Blacker at Horsham and received, not the beating he had expected for his unpaid debts, but the first piece of good news in an age. A cut lip had been inflicted, almost as an afterthought, by Blacker before they parted quite amicably.

Simon was astute enough to realise the motive behind this leniency. Blacker's devious mind had already deduced what profit lay in a wealthy man becoming involved with the Nashes. And Simon couldn't deny he owed him a substantial amount. He couldn't deny either that he had been a naïve, gullible fool to ever have become hopelessly embroiled with scoundrels way out of his league. But that was another matter.

For the moment what monopolised his thoughts was that his reserved, homebody sister had ensnared a man such as this. If what he had heard whispered was true, Luke Trelawney was rich as Croesus, one of the landed gentry to boot, but most importantly…as dangerous as sin. Nobody, to Simon's knowledge, frightened Jake Blacker. Yet that felon had sweated merely rasping the name of the suavely dressed gentleman lounging opposite him.

Rebecca was extremely beautiful, no denying it, but completely out of social circulation and apparently keen to stay that way. She was also without the artifice debutantes and demireps alike employed in hooking a sophisticated man of the world. Or so he had thought.

And he doubted men came more worldly-wise or sophisticated than this impressive aristocrat. Blacker had grudgingly admitted he was a fine figure of a fellow, when Simon had pressed him for a description so he would recognise him. It had been nowhere near as generous as it could have been. Part of him wanted to laugh aloud with glee and relief. But he didn't dare.

He was desperate to know more about Luke: exactly how deep his interest was in Rebecca. Not that he was about to fight for her virtue. She was almost twenty-six now and way past her marriageable prime. If this urbane man's interest was less than honourable, Simon was realist enough to know it was only to be expected and still to be gratefully encouraged.

But he was happily prepared to be optimistic. 'Blacker tells me you introduced yourself as Rebecca's fiancé. He also tells me that the name of Trelawney and...' he lowered his voice to a conspiratorial hiss '...free trading...have long been linked. In fact, he seemed keen to tell me more, but unfortunately we were unexpectedly interrupted that night...' He flushed and fidgeted, running a finger between his collar and his sticky neck.

'By the Revenue men?' Luke remarked, all feigned sympathy, before complaining with the same spurious commiseration, 'They've no sense of timing.'

Oblivious to Luke's sarcasm, Simon glanced swiftly about. 'Is it true?'

'Rebecca and I are to be married. Your sister will be leaving Sussex and removing with me to Cornwall,' Luke tonelessly supplied.

Simon gulped at this information, his mind in a delightful spin. 'And the other...is that true?' he demanded, unsure whether he wanted to hear it confirmed or denied.

'Why so concerned?' Luke quizzed sardonically. 'Are you going play the outraged protector? Raise fraternal anxieties as to my morals...my suitability as a husband for Rebecca?' he taunted and had the satisfaction of seeing the immediate guilty flush crawling the younger man's cheeks.

'I thought not,' he stated smoothly. 'Now I think it's my turn. Perhaps you'd like to furnish me with a few answers. Where is Rebecca's inheritance? Why haven't you done all in your miserable power to provide for her since your parents' death? Why haven't you risked your inconsequential life protecting her from harm and men...perhaps such as me...during the past five years? And, finally, perhaps you'd like to give me one good reason why I shouldn't teach you a painful lesson in family duty.'

Simon scraped back his chair, about to impulsively jump to his feet and flee, but Luke had unwound from his in a lithe second. He inclined menacingly towards Simon across the rickety taproom table. 'Sit still...there's a good lad. We're still barely introduced. We've a long way to go yet,' he mocked with a lop-sided smile and eyes as cold and hard as gravel.

'I think we've enough now,' Rebecca remarked as she lifted the basket, weighing the fruit with her hand. 'Martha is going to be pleased with you, Lucy; no doubt a blackberry pie will be coming your way at supper time and jam later in the week.'

In pleased response, Lucy's hand dived back into the basket, stole one of the largest, ripest berries and carried it immediately to her mouth.

Rebecca followed her away from the hedgerow, seeking the rough track that meandered away from the woods towards the Summer House. They strolled in amicable silence, both absorbed with their own thoughts, and a quiet appreciation of the rustling, russett-leaved countryside.

Rebecca knew now was as good a time as was likely to present itself, to broach the subject of Lucy's imminent return to the village of Crosby and her family. 'I have some news for you, Lucy,' she introduced the subject lightly.

Lucy swished to face her and walked backwards with a smile. She tilted her head to one side so brunette curls trailed over one shoulder.

'Well, let me see,' the girl teased. 'Does it concern a local nobleman? Perhaps a very handsome certain gentleman?'

'In a way...' Rebecca admitted with a small laugh. There was certainly little that escaped this young lady's notice. She sobered; Lucy's premature return home at Christmas might not be at all welcome. Lucy could rarely be drawn into chatting about her family. Her stepfather she would barely acknowledge. Yet at Christmas Lucy must leave, for she and Luke were to be married.

The thought of her secret fiancé—for she had made Luke pledge not to announce their betrothal until Lucy had been told—made her stomach knot in that familiar, bone-melting way. He had been quite serious about marrying her on the

Sunday following her disastrous rendezvous with Jake Blacker and the vile Spencers at that horrible tavern in Brighton.

But there was no possible way Rebecca could abandon her pupils so selfishly. The parents of the day pupils were entitled to some notice of the school's closure and more specific arrangements were necessary for Lucy. It had taken all her powers of persuasion to make him see that she had certain responsibilities to take care of prior to becoming a married woman.

Dwelling on the method of her persuasion made her heartbeat so erratic it was a bittersweet ache.

Noting the sturdy wooden stile to one side of them, the last on their trek home, Rebecca diverted to it. She sat down, leaving some space for Lucy to join her, and placed her basket on the springy turf by her side. 'I believe you've already guessed that Lord Ramsden has asked me to marry him, Lucy.'

'Indeed, no,' Lucy cheekily denied in a tone that made her tutor blush. 'That's not at all what I suspected.'

Rebecca sensed her colour heightening and steeled herself to regain her composure. That this fifteen-year-old girl was more experienced and worldly than she was was undeniable and regrettable. But Rebecca quietly acknowledged now that she had gained more sophistication in the last month than in the last five years. And she was thankful for it.

She had too long cocooned herself in memories of happy times with her dear parents and David. Now it was time to emerge from that nostalgic haven as a woman. Relinquishing all that was safe and familiar, and trusting Luke wholly with her body and soul, after so short an acquaintance was daunting, she had to admit. But she loved him. And she clung to the belief that he loved her and would soon tell her so.

So Lucy would no longer shock or worry her with crude innuendo. 'We are to be married, Lucy. We have settled upon Christmas as the date. Mr Trelawney wanted us to wed sooner, but...'

'I'm sure he did...' came Lucy's amused muttering.

'But I have decided,' Rebecca continued calmly, giving no hint that she had heard the sly aside, 'that we shall marry at

Christmas. That way it gives your stepfather time to make alternative arrangements for your future. He might wish to place
you at another small academy or appoint a governess for you
at home.'

'You're sending me home?' Lucy choked, white-faced.
'You're sending me home…to him?' she repeated quietly now,
with resigned bitterness in her tone and her pinched, chalky
complexion.

Rebecca searched her face, confused. She had just been
thinking how mature the girl was…how perceptive in all adult
matters, yet something as simple as her tutor's marriage putting
an end to her time at the Summer House seemed never to have
entered her head. But the saucy miss had never believed her to
be preparing for marriage. Becoming mistress to the lord of
Ramsden Manor, while he remained in Brighton, need not have
disturbed Lucy one iota.

'Naturally, I shall have to return you to your family, Lucy,'
Rebecca gently confirmed. 'Mr Trelawney is determined to return to Cornwall and his estates there and I shall, of course, go
with him.'

'I could come,' Lucy immediately seized upon the possibility. 'I could go with you. You will need a maid if you are to
be a fine lady. I could be your maid. I know what to do. I had
a maid of my own when my dear papa was alive. Not one
shared between Mary, Mama and me because that bastard is
so mean to us all.'

'*Lucy!*' Rebecca cautioned in a tight voice. 'Please do not
speak in such a way. You do yourself no favours by using such
language. Or me,' she ruefully admitted. 'What will your
mother and stepfather think you have achieved here if you return home so coarse and ill-mannered?'

'He is a vile, lecherous bastard,' Lucy exploded, her face
crimsoning now with rage. 'And I've told him so. Why do you
think he hits me? Because I hate him creeping to my room at
night when Mama is indisposed or huge with child? Because I
hate his filthy hands on me?' A piercing laugh jerked out of
her. 'No. That I can stand. Sometimes I even encourage it. Do

you know why? Because then he leaves Mary be. No. It's my unruly tongue that earns me this!' She punched a screwed-up fist so swiftly and so savagely against her own face that she made herself flinch.

Rebecca instinctively reached out to enclose and comfort her in her distress while chilling, numbing shock drenched her. And shame, for Lucy had confirmed what she had partly suspected yet never had the courage to consciously confront. At that moment she detested Rupert Mayhew with a violence that shocked her.

Lucy roughly pushed Rebecca off. She gained her feet in an angry leap and was backing away from her tutor in a second. 'You marry your lover,' she hissed. 'And as soon as you like, for it makes no difference to me. I'm never going back there. Never.' She twisted angrily away and, gathering up her lemon muslin skirts, began running along the track in the direction of the Summer House.

'Is Lucy back?' Rebecca gasped at Martha before she was fully inside the kitchen door.

'Why, yes,' Martha told her, a worried crinkling about her eyes as she digested Rebecca's breathless agitation. 'Came in like a whirlwind she did, and stamped straight up them stairs to her room.'

Rebecca closed aquamarine eyes and sighed heavily, with relief at finding the girl home, and worry at the task that still lay in front of her: for there seemed no alternative to returning Lucy home.

Rebecca automatically tipped the basket of fruit into a colander and slowly poured a jug of cleansing water over the berries. She let plump fruit slide idly, soothingly, between her slender fingers.

Was it such an outrageous idea? Why could Lucy not accompany them to Cornwall? She could finish her year's tuition. Her piano playing might improve with perseverance. Would odious Rupert Mayhew care whether his stepdaughter gained her refinement fifteen miles away along the coast road or a hundred or so miles away in another county? He had made no effort to visit or enquire after Lucy's progress.

Implying that Lucy's prospects of finding an eligible husband might increase in Cornwall would be no small consideration to a man such as Mayhew, Rebecca decided, biting her lip and allowing herself a small smile as she recognised her first descent into sophistry. Perhaps she should parade Luke or Ross before him as examples of Cornish manhood, for she was well aware that no ambitious parent would object to such handsome, wealthy gentlemen. She enthusiastically warmed to the idea. Luke and Ross would be ideal allies in this. Both charming; and of good family she was sure, although she had to admit she had so far learned very little about the Trelawneys.

Luke had told her about his brother Tristan, at home in Cornwall, running the estates until his return. She knew he had a sister, Katherine, in her late teens. His mother was alive but, sadly, his father dead. These few tidbits of family information had been gleaned over the past few days, when he visited. But they never seemed to have a great deal of time to talk. The reason for that brought a simultaneous smile and sigh. And she knew she couldn't wholly blame Luke for their lack of conversation. It was a frightening new power she wielded over this strong, passionate man but its effect was addictive.

Rupert Mayhew, she briskly decided, dragging her feverish thoughts back to duty and Lucy's predicament, would probably welcome the idea. She was absolutely certain that he would not mind his stepdaughter's removal to Cornwall in the least.

But Luke was sure to, she realised with a wry grimace at that ridiculously overlooked consideration. She had an unshakable pessimism that her future husband might raise very great objections indeed.

'No!' Luke stated with an absolute finality that lost something when coupled with the tender look in his brown eyes.

'Come here,' he sighed out with mild authority, as Rebecca's chin came up in defiance. Long, lean fingers beckoned, as did his wryly charming smile. But Rebecca fought the temptation to go to him and jammed herself back against the sink. She was determined to make him hear her out.

'You've not listened to me properly,' she calmly began, still ignoring his outstretched, tanned hand. 'When I said I wanted to continue schooling Lucy after Christmas I didn't mean to imply that we had to postpone our marriage. Or that I would refuse to come with you to Cornwall and stay here in Brighton. That wasn't what I meant at all.'

'Oh, good,' Luke drily remarked, mock-relieved. 'Because there was never the slightest chance of any of that. I'm still not sure that waiting until Christmas is necessary. We should have been married yesterday as I planned. Travelling west now, while the weather is still fine, is far preferable…'

'Your motive has nothing to do with travelling in fine weather, and you know it,' Rebecca interjected, then she flushed. Dilating black pupils and heat stoking at the back of his eyes mesmerised her, for she knew too well what that intense look heralded.

'Indeed, it hasn't…much,' he admitted. 'But, nevertheless, it is a genuine consideration.' He strolled towards her and, taking one of her hands, led her through the kitchen and into her small parlour.

Luke gently pushed her down into the comfortable old fireside chair and then hunkered down beside her. 'Now…' he muttered on a drawn-out breath, as sepia-coloured eyes astutely watched her solemn profile, 'what's brought all of this about? Yesterday everything was settled between us: you would write to Mayhew and arrange for Lucy's return home…'

A dark finger trailed gently along an ivory cheekbone, urging her to face him. When she did not but continued to stare into the leaping flames in the hearth, he tilted her chin towards him.

'What is it, Rebecca?' he asked, concern hoarsening his voice as the tormenting possibility she would try to withdraw from their betrothal bedevilled him. He'd come to see her at the Summer House this evening, as he did every evening, with the excellent news that he had at last located Simon and found him well; yet now he felt the time was not right to impart any of it.

'Why won't you let me deal with Mayhew?' he probed gently. 'I can tell, from the way you've spoken of him in the past, that you've no liking for him. It's high time I introduced myself to my neighbours. And I suppose he could be classed as one. I'll ride over tomorrow and explain the situation to him.'

'No,' Rebecca cried, a cloud of silky-gold hair rippling about her shoulders as she twisted to face him. 'No, don't do that,' she wheedled with a disarming, wavering smile.

Immediate suspicion narrowed his eyes at her vehemence but she wasn't ready for explanations yet. The whole situation whirled chaotically in her head—whether to scour her mind for more plausible reasons why Lucy should accompany them to Cornwall than those already voiced; whether to simply tell Luke of Lucy's awful accusations; whether to vent her own suspicions as to the vile nature of the girl's stepfather.

What would Luke do? Feel similar outrage and want to help Lucy? Or take the view that the matter was none of his or his future wife's concern? Turquoise eyes soberly searched his hard, handsome face. He was a man, after all...one of strong passion as she knew.

Soft colour flowed into her face at those delicious yet fearsome memories; her wonderous yet incomplete knowledge of his sensuality. For there was more to love-making than she had tasted so far. The magical closeness of kissing and cuddling enchanted her, yet she knew this left him sometimes unbearably tense and frustrated, and prone to a disturbing self-mockery.

His slow smile made it obvious he'd a hint of the reason for her protracted silence and rosy complexion. 'What are you thinking?' he demanded, brilliant eyes half-concealed by long, lush lashes as they targeted her lips.

'I'm thinking I should like to know more about you and your family. About your background...' she told him speedily. 'And that it's very warm by the fire,' she lied, shielding her glowing cheeks with a cool hand. 'But I'm mostly thinking that we never talk enough…'

A low oath made her pause. He twisted about and was, within a second, sitting on the floor by her chair. One knee was raised and he idly rested a hand upon it, opening his broad palm to the warmth to be had from the ruddy embers.

'Talk to me now then, Rebecca. Tell me what's worrying you.' Brooding dark eyes abruptly relinquished the smouldering coals and burned into her exquisitely demure face. 'You have to trust me…and you won't, will you?' His mouth slanted while he waited for her reply, his eyes hungry for every nuance of telltale emotion.

'I barely know you, Luke.' As she saw his head jerk back in frustration, she quickly added, 'But…but I'm glad we're to be married.' She sighed, knowing those few feeble words in no way conveyed the depth of emotion this man aroused in her: the conflict of logic and love; the need for independence and support.

She put out a conciliatory hand to touch his sleeve. He seemed unaware of her gesture, so her slender fingers moved to tentatively stroke the abrasive side of his jaw, copying the caress she had received from him minutes before. She felt the flexing of lean muscle beneath her timid fingers as his teeth closed and he half-smiled into the fire.

'Well, don't do that, Rebecca. I thought you wanted conversation instead this evening.' Her fingers made to spring away but he caught them and held them firmly within his.

'So…what shall I tell you?' he quietly began, almost as though he spoke to himself. Her slender, pale fingers resting within his dark, broad palm, received loving attention as he divulged, 'I'm thirty-two years old and have spent the majority of those years in Cornwall. The countryside there is dangerous and rugged…but beautiful. The people…very similar. I've never felt the need to move anywhere more fashionable. Bath draws me but rarely now. I liked it better before it gained such popularity with the *haute ton*, but I still have a fondness for it because of happy memories.

'At one time, Tristan, Ross and I were sharing lodgings together as students. Tristan and I at college and Ross at Grammar School. We had some fine times,' he recalled with a smile that turned to such an infectious laugh it made Rebecca join him.

'It was probably simply nostalgia for those days which prompted me to buy a mansion there, for I rarely use it. I'm nearly always at Melrose. But I shan't pretend I've lived a quiet, uneventful existence on a remote countryside farm. I'm not going to insult your intelligence by claiming to have lived a blameless life; yet neither have I done anything deliberately evil to feel ashamed of. My adult years have been spent in the way of a fairly typical Cornish bachelor.

'As to my family, as you know, my father died some eleven years ago and left me Melrose, still unfinished after thirty years. Not that he didn't have the money to finish the building...he and my mother were always squabbling over how to do so.' He glanced at Rebecca and smiled. 'It was the breath of life to them to argue about paint colours or window symmetry or the style and pitch of the roof to the east wing addition.'

'Did I tell you how the estate came to be so named? It was taken from my mother's maiden name—Demelza Penrose. When she was seventeen and they began courting, they came upon a tumbledown house while out walking. He promised her that one day he would buy the whole of that dilapidated estate that spanned two miles along the Cornish coast and that they would marry and live there. For they both fell in love with it straight away. They could see the potential in its setting and acreage that other, more experienced landowners, could not.'

'A year later when she married into the Trelawney clan, they moved into that ramshackle cottage and lived in what was little better than a hovel. Yet they classed it as a wedding gift, each to the other. My father worked on it tirelessly, enlarging and improving it. And when his three sons were able and old enough, we helped him. Hence Ross's enthusiasm for carpentry,' he informed her with a smile. 'He really is rather good, actually.'

'What a lovely, romantic story. Your father must have thought the world of her,' Rebecca wistfully sighed.

'Indeed,' Luke confirmed with a faraway gaze. 'And she of him. His stipulation that the house should be willed to the eldest male son gave me more anxiety than she. But he had prepared well: she has an elegant dower house on the estate which was built with her blessing. It was a long-standing family tradition for he came from a landed family, but being the youngest son, he inherited very little.

'At the time of his death it was approaching being the finest house and grounds in the county. It now is. And it has been enlarged again and finished. My mother assures me that what I have done, with her guidance and advice, would have found favour with him. She tells me she loves its graceful elegance.

'She is now in her fifty-first year and still very beautiful. She was barely nineteen when I was born and still enjoys very rude health. She and my sister Katherine walk the clifftops close to Melrose most days. Even the rain rarely keeps them inside. The winds tend to since a couple of sheep were lost over the edge. Katherine is made in her image…just as beautiful and quite a problem with her eager gentleman callers. I hope Tristan is rationing her favours fairly while I'm away.

'What I told you a month ago about my ability to provide for you is completely true. My father left the majority of his estate and stockholding to me. I've considerably increased his bequest. My shipping interests have been especially profitable…' Noticing Rebecca's slight withdrawal and her increased colour as he obliquely referred to propositioning her as his mistress, he frowned. 'I never apologised for that, did I?' he rebuked himself.

'It doesn't matter…' Rebecca began in a thready voice.

'It does and I do regret it. I'm sorry. I badly misread the situation between you and your uncle. It was idiocy to jump to such a ridiculous conclusion about you. But then perhaps I should add,' he mentioned drily, 'if I have a failing, it's that I'm an incorrigible cynic. Apart from that, I'm not such a bad fellow. Sociable, generous…' He paused thoughtfully. 'But now I shall have to be less accommodating and find them all alternative housing. I've no intention of sharing you. It's high time I had some privacy. Don't worry. They'll all love you,' he reassured her with a tender smile.

'Will you?' was sighed unbidden and immediately regretted from Rebecca.

Chapter Eleven

'I'll send Gregory over to the Manor,' Martha asserted. 'He can bring her back with a flea in her ear. That miss is the most wilful, selfish minx…'

'Hush, Martha,' Rebecca began, but Martha was not to be quietened.

'It's time there was some plain speaking about that…that young woman,' Martha spat. 'She's run off again, that's what she's done and she knew you was going with his lordship to town. My guess is that she's done it on purpose. And it's about time that you had a day away, too. And off she goes bold as brass. Straight to that young carpenter, I'll lay a pound to a penny—'

'Enough, Martha,' Rebecca cut determinedly into her disjointed tirade, a hand held up, begging silence. But Martha's chins wobbled indignantly, readying for another attack.

'I believe you're right,' Rebecca placated her. 'She probably has gone looking for John. She was very upset yesterday and, I have to admit, I was expecting her to hide straight away… Oh, heavens, what is the time?' She sped through to the parlour and looked up at the ancient wooden wall clock. It was practically one o'clock in the afternoon and Luke was expected at any minute.

Martha stomped through into the parlour after her. The

kitchen door opened and Gregory shuffled in, feathery carrot tops quivering in his fists.

'Boots off!' Martha ordered with a grim cursory glower over her shoulder. Gregory was then ignored. 'Don't you go making his lordship start searching for her as soon as he gets here,' she warned Rebecca. 'You two need some time to yourselves. I reckon as he might have some pertickler reason for wanting to take you to Brighton and you might never know of it if'n you send him off on a fool's errand. We got Gregory for that,' she emphasised with a nod, shelving her crossed arms on her bosom.

There was intentional intrigue in Martha's tone. 'Such as?' Rebecca probed with a smile.

Martha tapped the side of her nose, wagged her head, and bustled back to the kitchen and her husband. The cosy kitchen, and its warm aroma of spiced buns, drew Rebecca too, but her mind was again with Lucy. Martha was probably right. It was likely that Lucy had done this today, of all days, out of spite, to ruin Rebecca's first proper outing with Luke.

Rebecca was to shut school early today and they were to lunch and shop in town, he had stated yesterday before departing. Rebecca had walked the lanes of Graveley with her young pupils, just before midday, delivering messages about her new circumstances and her school's closure.

She had taken a few precious minutes chatting to Kay Abbott over the parsonage gate, finally confiding her exciting news to her friend, and had received joyful congratulations. On her return from that pleasant interlude, Lucy was nowhere to be found and Rebecca had been gone barely an hour. She saw no harm in doing as Martha suggested and allowing Gregory to take the trap over to fetch her. It was a bright yet autumn-fresh day. A brisk walk across the meadow to the Manor might have tired Lucy and dispersed some of her mischief. Rebecca had the greatest sympathy for the girl's predicament and hadn't given up hope yet of persuading Luke to help her in some way.

She had been prepared to persevere with the subject last night before he left, but... A small, wistful smile slanted her full mouth, for the very last words she had spoken to him remained unanswered.

Why hadn't he answered her? Why had he said nothing when she had so needed his reassurance? Why had he looked at her in that smouldering, intense way that made her feel she was the centre of his universe and yet not confirmed what she longed to hear? Just one small word would have enchanted her. Had he simply said 'yes' she would have been in heaven. In desperate confusion at his silence, she had been about to compound her mistake: pretend it a joke, even apologise, for she knew that after such a short acquaintance as theirs, to speak of love too soon could be foolish and humiliating.

And so it had proved. But no further words were necessary...or possible. He had, within a moment, kissed her deeply, skilfully into silence. He had manipulated her body and mind in the way he knew best. And when the hour was late and he gazed down into her rosy, swollen-lipped face and told her of today's arrangements for their outing to Brighton, she surfaced just enough from her sybaritic languour to sigh and smile agreement.

'Look at you,' Martha clucked at Rebecca, spoiling her reverie. Spinning her about, she neatly rearranged the silken hair into a twisted golden coil that neatly trailed the blue velvet cloak she wore. Martha stood back and assessed her young mistress with a critical eye, nodding her satisfaction.

'Handsomest couple in the whole of Sussex,' she muttered to herself, before turning to Gregory and giving strict instructions regarding Lucy: the speed of the fetching and the strength of the lecture on the way home.

'I'm not sure that this is really proper,' Rebecca advised her fiancé with a mischievously demure raising of her delicate dusky eyebrows.

Luke leaned towards her in the carriage rocking its way carefully down the slope to the town of Brighton. Sartorially splendid black-coated forearms rested on equally elegant knees.

'I can't imagine you ever doing anything that wasn't proper,

Rebecca,' he gently mocked her as his eyes caressed the beautiful sight of her. With golden hair, creamy skin and turquoise eyes matching that soft velvet she wore, she looked radiant. The difficulty was keeping to his seat opposite her rather than joining her and taking up where they had left off last night.

Rebecca smiled through the window, well aware of his fixed attention and relaxing into a warm contentment because of it. 'I may be of somewhat advanced years, my lord, but I am still a spinster and we are not even officially betrothed. I really ought to have a chaperon when abroad with you,' she teased, knowing he hated it when she addressed him so formally.

'I believe you're probably more in need of one, Rebecca, when we're within doors...' He smiled at her immediate blush before remarking in an odd, sardonic voice, 'Besides, you will have one, when we reach Brighton, and the most appropriate one there is for an unmarried, orphaned woman.'

Rebecca gazed enquiringly at him. When he said nothing, but merely leaned back against the comfortable, cushioned interior of his travelling coach, surveying her through sleepy eyes, she shifted forward on her seat towards him. Turquoise eyes searched the hard, angular planes of his handsome face but he gave nothing away. The wonderful possibility entered her head and her soft lips parted to voice it, but she dismissed it. It couldn't be...not so soon...but he had promised he would...

She sighed out uncertainly, 'You've found Simon.' When he said nothing, but his sooty lashes momentarily touched his cheeks and his mouth thrust in something akin to agreement mingled with ironic regret, she flung herself across the carriage. Silken, lavender-scented hair clouded his face, velvety arms twined about his neck and soft lips found a hard, dark cheek.

'I knew there had to be some advantage in unearthing him,' he muttered hoarsely as muscular arms immediately entrapped her against him.

The sudden violent rocking of the carriage made two pairs of eyes widen, then roll. The groom and driver grinned knowingly at each other; the driver's tongue poked into his cheek and his thick, straggly eyebrows disappeared beneath a similar fringe. He started to tunelessly hum, then shrilly whistle, anticipating his diplomatic duty to drown out any embarrassing noises that might, any moment, issue forth from within.

'Simon!' Rebecca exclaimed as soon as she was within the doorway and spied his bowed sun-streaked blond head. Simon sprang up from the chair by the roaring fire, immediately stepping a pace towards her. But the mix of anger and relief sharpening his sister's voice made him hesitate. Neither moved or seemed capable of breathing for a moment; they gazed at each other as though frozen in a tableau. Simon's blue eyes shifted to the man standing a little behind Rebecca, his chiselled features set in an impenetrable look.

'Simon!' Rebecca breathed again as her eyes closed and she allowed the wonder of his presence to douse her fury a little. Within a second she had propelled herself the length of the room towards him and enveloped him in a hug. 'It's so good to see you…so good,' she murmured into his rough woollen shoulder, a betraying shake in her voice and dew glistening on her lashes.

'It's good to see you, Rebecca,' Simon gruffly responded. As he sensed the watery sting in his nose and his arms shaking about her, he realised just how sincerely he meant it. Overwhelming shame swamped him so abruptly that he dipped his head to rest atop hers, attempting to conceal glossy navy eyes from the tall, silent man, so closely watching their reunion.

'I'll see if lunch is ready. I'll be but a moment,' Luke said quietly from the doorway before quitting the room.

Rebecca gazed out of the window upon the busy Brighton street scene. This hotel was situated in the most exclusive area of the town and their beautifully furnished private room on the first floor had an excellent view of the fabric warehouses, beyond which could be glimpsed a sparkling grey ribbon of sea. Her attention was momentarily arrested by two young ladies alighting on to the cobbles from a smart phaeton. They giggled together and waved to the dandy driving their transport before hastening into an emporium displaying exotic silks, satins and laces.

'Why didn't you write then, if you didn't want to visit?' Rebecca demanded of her brother, as she swung back towards him, watching him now, as he gazed morosely into the fire. 'Can't you imagine how worried I've been? Not knowing what dangerous scrapes you might have been in? Don't you realise what terrible rumours there have been about treacherous villains in the area?'

In response, Simon sighed and threaded ten nervous fingers through his thick blond hair. He seemed about to reply but the door opened at that precise moment. He fell back in his chair, thankful for the distraction.

Luke approached them and sat in the gilt-framed wine brocade chair by the window. Firm, tanned fingers, briefly, imperceptibly, sought Rebecca's in a touch that was both reassuring and affectionate.

The hotel manager then glided in, silently traversing the luxurious carpet. There followed a stream of phlegmatic servants dressed in darkest black and crispest white. The long mahogany table set against a creamy watered-silk wall had its sleek surface decked with a delectable array of cold meats, fish dishes, pastries, pickles and salads within what seemed to Rebecca little more than a minute. The staff filed out in the same mute orderly way, the manager the last to go, after he had set out wine and crystal glasses to his absolute satisfaction. He bowed low into the room before pulling the door closed behind him, without having uttered a word.

Sure she had not seen so much food on one table since her sister Elizabeth's wedding breakfast, Rebecca was drawn slowly to it to investigate.

'Are more people to arrive and lunch with us?' she enquired quite seriously of Luke as her eyes roamed the sumptuous spread. It had arrived and been deposited so quickly, yet was beautifully prepared and arranged on the highly glossed table, with fine silverware fanned for use and lace-edged linen intricately folded by snowy porcelain plates. A magnificent swan, carved from glistening ice, shimmered centrally, and was encircled by slivers of smoked salmon, trout and other seafood delicacies. A warm finger stretched out to touch the glossy sculpture, and Rebecca gasped as it immediately slid down the bird's gracefully arched neck.

Luke watched her indulgently, before admitting, 'I hope you are both hungry, for there is just us to do justice to it.'

Simon couldn't remember when last he had feasted so well. On arrival at this place his stomach had been gurgling from neglect. The last proper meal he'd eaten had been that other bought for him by this man at the Bull and Mouth two days ago, while they discussed financial matters. His blue eyes lifted from his plate to watch the extraordinarily attractive couple seated close by him as they chatted and laughed intimately while eating. They had both done their utmost to include him in their conversation. Simon smiled to himself; but one couldn't help but feel intrusive: their eyes rarely left one another. It was a real love match, he suddenly realised, quite surprised, for he knew very few of those between couples, engaged or already wed. A delicious morsel of sweet pastry found its leisurely way to his mouth; he chewed and considered.

This relaxed, cosy atmosphere couldn't last. The matter of the missing five thousand pounds was sure to soon raise its ugly head. When it did, he hoped he would perform well and sound convincing. If not…he gave no further thought to the consequences of upsetting such a powerful, enigmatic man.

Perhaps he should be the one to introduce the topic; that way he might be able to control the way the discussion went and still be able to relax and enjoy to the full this pleasant afternoon with Rebecca. His crystal goblet of ruby wine once more touched his lips and a warm glow of alcohol hit his stomach and fired his courage.

'I know I have been despicable, witholding your inheritance, Rebecca,' he catapulted into their brief lapse in conversation, wincing as two pairs of eyes immediately fixed on him.

'Yes, you have, Simon,' Rebecca quietly confirmed, glad that her brother had had the decency to mention her inheritance and that she hadn't been the one forced to broach the subject. 'Have you any of my money left?' she directly asked him, pushing her plate away from her a little, her tasty lunch forgotten.

Simon's eyes shifted momentarily to Luke before seeking his plate. 'Very little, I'm afraid,' he carefully answered. 'But I'm confident I've just enough of it left to invest and recoup all that money of yours that I've lost,' he quickly added.

Rebecca continued, frowning at him, 'Surely not another harebrained scheme to get rich quick, Simon,' she chided. 'For the moment, I'll settle for what is to hand. It's better than nothing at all. If you intend to get proper employment, perhaps back with Gillows, then you can repay me in the future. For I should have all of what Papa left me. It was my due and my dowry,' she stressed with a minimal sideways glance at Luke's unreadable face.

'Yes, I know,' Simon agreed, unperturbed. 'But I've no wish to pay you back in instalments. I should like things sooner set to rights between us. I've behaved unforgivably and want to make amends as quickly as I can.' Another discreet sliding look took in Luke's bland expression: his lowered eyes examining the silverware with which his long, dark fingers casually toyed.

'What money of yours I had left, I have invested,' Simon said, relieved it was only half a lie. He dwelt on the banker's draft that had yesterday found its way into his account, astounding the bank manager. But the money certainly had been invested for Rebecca.

'Simon, no!' Rebecca rebuked in disbelief. 'Don't you dare... You've not squandered even that residue on some hopeless venture?'

'I'm assured it's a certain winner,' he stressed quickly and truthfully. 'A reputable company was looking for a few select backers to import spices and fruit and the return, I'm told, is guaranteed and phenomenal. I'm very fortunate to get this chance. There's also a possibility...if I satisfy certain requirements...that they might employ me.'

'It's illegal importing, isn't it?' Rebecca accused him in a tight voice. 'You're again involved with criminals…smugglers, aren't you?'

'No…I swear, I'm not,' Simon emphasised, then hesitated and qualified the assurance. 'To the best of my knowledge, the company is reputable and the proprietor an honest business-man,' he avowed, avoiding looking Luke's way at all. He thus missed long dark lashes screening sepia-coloured eyes and the very ironic smile twisting a narrow mouth.

'Please believe me, Rebecca. I swear to you that I regret what I have done over the past five years. When the money came to me from Papa's will it seemed like a godsend. I believed I would be able to escape that interminably boring job he had arranged for me at Gillows and make a career at sea, as I had always wanted. He should never have forced me into that apprenticeship. He knew I hated being imprisoned in-doors… I was slowly suffocating.'

'He did what he thought best, Simon,' Rebecca righteously defended her father. 'He wanted to secure your future with a worthy profession. He did it for you.'

'He did it for him,' Simon snapped. 'Because he was always so financially useless he wanted me schooled to take over the accounts, to try to recoup some of the losses he had made since Grandfather Nash died. *He* would have taken me to sea. Grand-father always promised me my own ship, but Father lost them all…every one.'

He repeated with quiet wistfulness, 'So, when my bequest came, I thought I would at last get my way; purchase a small vessel… But Father misjudged my potential,' he mocked him-self with a bitter laugh. 'Commercially, I am just as useless as he was. I not only lost all my inheritance but all yours, too. Almost all of yours, too,' he hastily corrected himself. 'It made me panic and listen to unsound advice. One night in Hastings when I was losing at cards to Blacker, he hinted he knew how I could make a tidy sum for very little outlay. You can guess the rest. He fleeced me of any profit by telling me that my booty had been lost at sea in bad weather or seized by the Revenue men. Strangely, his never was,' he admitted with a self-deprecatory grimace. 'I guessed his plan, but how could I go to the magistrates with such a tale? Blacker knew that, of course. He pretended sympathy; lent me money at an extortionate rate. You can imagine just how deeply embroiled I was. I have been running the length of the south coast...back and forth...trying to keep one step ahead of him and those batmen he employs.'

Rebecca went to her brother. She leaned over his shoulders, enclosing him in a comforting, forgiving embrace, her lips brushing the top of his head.

'Well, what's done is done and no use crying over spilled milk,' she unconsciously quoted one of Martha's favourite sayings. 'If Luke thinks this business proposition quite proper, I will not object to you using my money.' She smiled over the top of Simon's head at her fiancé. 'Do you know of this company, Luke? Tell Luke who they are, Simon. He may know of their reputation and be able to advise you as to their past successes or failures.'

'I know of them. They are very successful,' Luke economically supplied, giving Simon no chance to speak. 'I would have no objection to my money being invested in this venture,' he reassured, with a warm smile for her; it cooled to sardonic humour as it included her brother. 'Now...' he said, with abrupt finality, as he approached Rebecca and proprietorially drew her arm through his, 'if you have eaten enough, it's time we did some shopping. It's past three o'clock already,' he mentioned with a cursory glance at his gold pocket watch.

'Are you to come shopping with us?' Luke addressed Simon with an odd inflection to his voice which made the younger man hastily shake his head.

'No...no, I believe I might stay here and do further justice to some of this delicious food,' Simon excused himself.

Rebecca gazed at the burgundy-shot silk draped in intricate folds across the counter. Her fingertips slid across the fabric reverently, back and forth, loving the luxurious feel of it. She glanced up enquiringly at Luke.

'I like you in blue,' he said softly, intimately. 'But I dare say any shade would suit you.'

The hovering draper must have heard his quiet compliment for he hoisted on to the counter bolt after bolt of blue materials, from winter-weight midnight velvet to cobwebby cornflower muslin. With a flourish he swirled a little off each roll to display its quality and hue.

As the counter became crowded with jostling ladies, all apparently keen to see the sumptuous display of fabrics, Rebecca pressed possessively closer to Luke. Many of these over-perfumed, under-dressed women, she realised, with a new stomach-churning pang she recognised as jealousy, only really intended gaining the attention of the tall handsome man by her side. She began to feel hot, bothered and indignant at their blatant, inviting stares and sly proximity. A tall brunette's hard dark eyes slid from avariciously stealing across Luke's powerful physique to challenge and poison Rebecca.

'Perhaps a quieter shop might suit. It's like a common meeting-place in here,' Rebecca pointedly said, with a freezing look at the provocative, impenitent woman.

'Well, what are you buying? Everything?' a familiar voice called across the throng.

As a groaning oath escaped Luke, Rebecca spun round with a ready smile, welcoming Ross through the hostile females. He approached with a rather plain young woman dangling on his arm.

'Nothing personal, Ross, but we were just leaving,' Luke good-naturedly rebuffed his younger brother.

Ross quickly introduced them to Miss Arabella Stone, who smiled coyly and retained a limpet-like grip on his arm. 'We'll walk outside with you,' Ross immediately decided, seizing the opportunity for other company. The diffident young lady with him had been summarily foisted on him by her scheming mother earlier that afternoon. He had been looking to return her for the past hour or more, but the elusive woman was nowhere to be found.

* * *

Strolling towards the sea-front in amicable silence, Rebecca suddenly half-turned and waved to a woman in a pretty pink bonnet on the opposite side of the street. She was promenading with an elderly lady and they both raised gloved hands and beamed and hesitated. Luke tightened his hand over Rebecca's, resting in the crook of his arm, rightly anticipating she might want to rush off to greet them more lengthily.

'I'm keeping you to myself today,' he wryly excused his possessiveness. 'Who was that?' he mildly enquired

Rebecca looked up at him. 'Kay Abbott, the vicar's wife, with her mother. You have met Kay. She was at the Summer House on the day you…' She trailed into silence, unable to say, *Came to proposition me*, and unable to think of any other purpose to his visit.

'Ah yes, I remember now,' Luke said with a smile at the sea to the side of him. An affectionate thumb brushed satiny skin on the hand resting through his arm. 'Nice woman,' he economically summed Kay up.

'She is my best friend. Is that all you have to say?' Rebecca teased in a horrified voice. 'I told Kay today about our betrothal and that I would soon be leaving Brighton. I shall miss her so when I leave here,' she sighed wistfully.

Large fingers comfortingly enclosed smaller ones. 'She can visit us. You needn't lose touch.'

Rebecca laced her fingers into his, fascinated by the mingling of light and dark, large and small. 'Lunch was wonderful. It must have cost a fortune. But there was far too much. You should have invited Ross to dine with us,' she brightly suggested, quite disturbed by the waste of such splendid fare.

'I want today for us, Rebecca. I just manage to free us from your brother and we get saddled with mine. I want some privacy so I can talk to you.' As though an idea had just occurred to him he said, 'Actually, tempting Ross with a free lunch and as much as he can drink might just distract him enough…' He slowed his pace and made to turn but Rebecca pulled him on.

'You can't do that,' she hissed, horrified. 'You can't send him back now. He'll know it's simply to be rid of him.'

'Good…' Luke mildly began but the rest of his conversation was cut short.

'Let's go down to the shore,' Ross called from behind, having speeded up to join them with Miss Arabella Stone still an unwanted appendage.

Diverting to the beach, Ross suddenly unthreaded Arabella's arm from his and placed her close to Rebecca. 'I'm sure you two ladies must have things to discuss: fashions and bonnets and such,' he suggested in desperation. 'Luke and I need some bracing ocean air.' He unceremoniously dragged Luke ahead with him towards a wide wooden groyne that ran down to the sea. Luke grimaced his exasperation and apology at Rebecca before the two men picked their way past small battered boats, nets and pots and walked towards the smooth silvery water.

Arabella wrinkled her pert, freckled nose. 'Awful smell,' she said as a briny whiff of tar and seaweed stirred their hair. 'That's Lord Ramsden, isn't it?' Arabella queried immediately when Luke and Ross were out of earshot. Her grey eyes narrowed on the men some way ahead of them now.

'Yes,' Rebecca said, uncertain what else to add, yet sensing Arabella's steady, piercing gaze on her. There was probing interest in her eyes and voice and Rebecca knew that she was being proved correct in fearing fashionable young ladies of good families would target Luke. Just as those shameless women had so recently tried to do in the fabric emporium!

'Mama says he's terribly rich and such a good catch. And he and his brother are so handsome. But nobody seems to know much else about them.'

Rebecca choked a melancholy laugh and murmured, 'Exactly.' She stared ahead as Luke and Ross leaped from the wooden groyne on to the shingle and strolled to the sea. She studied her fiancé: his tall athletic figure and long dark hair whipping about his beautiful face. He suddenly threw back his head and laughed at something Ross said before he looked back to where Rebecca and Arabella stood on the promenade. Even at that distance Rebecca could sense his eyes exclusively on her, and when his hand raised and he beckoned, she instinctively obeyed and walked forward.

'You're not going on to the beach, are you?' Arabella gasped disbelievingly.

'Yes…come on,' Rebecca encouraged the younger woman. 'We can stay on this wooden jetty. Your gown won't get dirty,' she reassured Arabella.

'Mama will kill me if she discovers I have behaved in such a hoydenish manner. This dress…' she swirled the lilac skirt of her walking dress out from her legs '…cost a fortune.' She grinned. 'But never mind. I believe she is still with Mrs Pettifer taking refreshment at Dilly's Tearoom. She will never know. I haven't seen her in an age. They gossip for ever when they get together,' she confided as she followed Rebecca along the wide wooden slats, taking great care to avoid touching the fishing nets.

Luke started to stroll to meet them. Realising he was about to lose his companion and again be encumbered with Miss Stone, Ross intercepted him and started skylarking. He shoved Luke close to the water's edge, into the frothy tide. He then backed off, whistling, and casually skimming flat pebbles across the glinting waves. Luke walked out of the surf, shaking brine from his calf leather shoes, but laughing. He swiped out at Ross, then abruptly grabbed him, throwing him further into the sea, so foam sprayed up his brother's immaculately clad legs.

'Oh, my goodness,' Arabella breathed, horrified, before she giggled. 'I hope Mama does not see this…or ever hear of it. Such outrageous behaviour would have her fainting dead away.' She turned excited grey eyes on Rebecca as though they were conspiring in a marvellous plot.

Rebecca couldn't believe it either…but she watched fascinated as two expensively dressed handsome men frolicked quite unselfconsciously, and uncaring of being observed or ostracised. As Ross lunged at Luke and Luke dodged, evading him, Rebecca glimpsed two young boys playing naturally on a Cornish beach. She relaxed into the wonderful moment, mesmerised by their antics and the quiet realisation she had never loved Luke more.

'Arabella!' The screech came from behind them and Arabella's shining eyes and dimpled cheeks were replaced by a disappointed grimace. She lifted a hand to greet her mother even before she turned and spied the woman.

Ross walked back nonchalantly towards them and vaulted on to the wooden walkway. He politely offered Arabella his arm and began sedately escorting her back to her mother, a picture of masculine sophistication despite his damp trousers.

Rebecca gave Luke a worried smile as he approached. 'I hope Ross is not in trouble.'

'Ross is always in trouble,' he said, breathing hard from exertion. His dark skin was tinged a healthy pink, his black hair streaking his face in thick, glossy strands. He loosened his perfectly folded cravat and said, 'I could do with a swim.'

'You're surely not going to...' Rebecca pleaded and threatened.

He laughed. 'No. We could take a boat out fishing. The sea's calm.'

'That's a joke,' she whispered.

'No,' he answered her with a smile. 'Have you ever been sea fishing?'

She shook her head. 'I wouldn't dare. I can't swim. Simon loves fishing. He loves eveything about the sea...'

Rebecca searched her mind, desperate to think of something to say to distract him from any other bizarre ideas. But his rugged yet awesomely attractive appearance dominated her mind and she could think of no conversation at all. She could only look at him. For there was something undeniably appealing in the contrast of expensive finery and careless dishevelment; and the way he was so at ease with both.

'You look like a gypsy ruffian who has done well for himself,' she softly said. She had intended keeping it as a cherished secret description but it somehow escaped.

He looked up at her from the pebbly beach. 'Do I, now?' he

challenged, dark eyes gleaming and the start of a smile pulling one corner of his mouth.

'Indeed,' she chided. 'And not at all a suitable fiancé, I'm afraid. I might have to rethink....' Her words were cut off as he vaulted back on to the wooden jetty and swung her up into his arms in one swift fluid movement.

He walked down the landing stage towards the sea. 'Would you like to learn to swim, Rebecca?' he asked with deliberate insinuation.

'Put me down...someone will see,' she half-laughed and squealed, outraged, as her fists beat against his arms. 'Please put me down,' she wheedled, her mouth close to his face. 'Mrs Stone will faint dead away; poor Arabella told me such a scandalous sight would give her an attack.'

'Arabella and her mother have gone,' Luke said, with a cursory glance over his shoulder to the promenade, 'and there's no one else about apart from Ross. He won't care if I throw you in.'

Rebecca tensed uncertainly in his arms. 'Luke? You won't...you wouldn't dare...would you?'

Sensing her genuine fright, he tipped her comfortingly into him and murmured against her face, 'Returning home dry must be worth at least a kiss.'

She struggled in his arms. Realising she was instinctively nestling further into him, she abruptly gave up. 'I don't find this at all amusing. Put me down,' she ordered primly but with a betraying smile in her voice. Her mouth was temptingly close to an earlobe and in mischief and frustration she nipped at it with her small teeth. Remorseful in case it hurt, a lingering flick of her tongue soothed his warm, salty skin.

He immediately removed his arm from beneath her legs but still held her close so that she slid slowly down his long, hard body. 'That was a very nice alternative to a kiss, Rebecca,' he softly praised and tutored her. A long dark finger emphasised his pleasure by stroking her warming face and an intimate smile increased her colour and her confusion.

'I thought I was saddled with her for the rest of the day,'

Ross exclaimed as he reached them. He exhaled a deep, satisfied sigh at having at last jettisoned Miss Stone. 'Where her mother's been hiding herself all afternoon, I've no idea.'

The problems of searching for someone determined to remain concealed jogged his memory of something important. 'Oh, I nearly forgot. I meant to look out for you earlier today. I have some news.

'Before I left the Manor this afternoon, Miles bade me give you a message that John was nowhere to be found. John…the young carpenter,' he explained when Luke looked mystified. 'Oh, and he thinks that young Miss Mayhew from the school may be with him. Apparently Gregory Turner and Miles searched for some while; all the outbuildings have been investigated. They couldn't find hide nor hair of either of them. Do you think they might have eloped?' he suggested quite cheerfully.

Chapter Twelve

'I thought I told you never to come here,' grated an icy irate voice.

Jake Blacker twisted about and a snake-quick flick of his tongue wet his dry lips. 'You don't think I would have come unless the circumstances were exceptional, do you?' he flung back.

A thunderous look received this impertinence, making Blacker wince and avoid those feral eyes that raked him from head to toe. 'If you need to contact me, you use the crypt as postbox, as always,' snarled the small, squat man, glaring up from his inferior height into Blacker's face.

Blacker bit down on his lip and his temper. 'No one saw me; I've tethered my horse out of sight. Besides, I've a notion that the authorities are wise to the churchyard's use: any proper investigation will reveal it.'

Mayhew allowed a ghost of a smile as he dismissed Blacker's fears. 'Those dragoons will soon tire of staking out a desolate graveyard in favour of a jug in the snug of the Red Lion. But forgive me if I don't offer you a seat or a drink,' he sneered. 'I'm sure the only reason prompting you to risk my good reputation...and therefore your life...' he smoothly interjected '...is desperation to pay me what is long overdue.'

His sarcasm and contempt weakened Blacker's nerve. 'I cannot extract one penny from that wastrel who owes me so much,' he whined. 'Paying you my share of that last consignment of brandy is presently impossible. Chipping in on the gold shipment bound for Calais this week is quite beyond my means.'

'Indeed? Is that so?' Mayhew spuriously commiserated as he stalked closer. 'Who is this man you cannot seem to deal with? Shall I have to do it for you? Do you want that favour added to what you owe me?'

Blacker gave a bitter, jeering laugh. 'It might not be quite so easy as you, or even I thought. This youth suddenly has a very dangerous champion.'

Mayhew swung back towards him, intrigued. 'A knight in shining armour?' he mocked. 'You are a dolt, Blacker. Where is this unassailable reputation you boast of? Where are these thugs you brag do your every bidding? The Falconers gang in Kent, where I lately was, have batmen who are mine for the asking. Give me this young puppy's name and I will settle it. But you will pay. Indeed, you will pay.'

'Simon Nash,' Blacker immediately supplied.

'Nash...Nash?' Mayhew rolled the name off his tongue, scouring his mind for the reason it sounded familiar.

'And the man who gives his protection to that family is...Luke Trelawney,' Blacker added, maliciously satisfied by Mayhew's stunned expression.

Then Mayhew's ugly features faced the ceiling and he howled, 'Luke Trelawney? Of course,' he scoffed. 'Why didn't I think of that? Luke Trelawney has come from Cornwall to champion some ne'er-do-well milksop.'

'This ne'er-do-well milksop has an extremely beautiful sister,' Blacker hissed. 'She is one of the most beautiful women I have ever seen. And now Trelawney's seen her. They are betrothed.'

'Not Rebecca Nash, surely?' Mayhew dismissed, reflecting on that beautiful face and body, yet prim and proper attitude. But for his blasted wife's ailing health following her confinement, and a month of pressing business matters that had taken him from Bournemouth to Kent, he would have visited the delectable Miss Nash at the Summer House school. After all, he had the pretext of checking on the unlikely progress of that hoyden of a stepdaughter.

'The same,' Blacker righteously confirmed.

'Trelawney is involved with that virtuous schoolmarm?' Mayhew stated, amazed. 'Trelawney?' he repeated with an incredulous snort, ruminating on the last voluptuous beauty he had seen draped about the man in Penzance. The memory of that full-bodied, dark-haired wench made him sweat. 'You're mistaken. It must be an imposter. He rarely leaves Cornwall; or ventures further east than Bath.'

'It's Trelawney and his brother Ross. They're at Ramsden Manor. Luke Trelawney inherited the Ramsden estate, by some quirk of lineage.'

Mayhew stood stock still. It could not be true! Yet while he had been away he had heard noised abroad that Robin Ramsden had his estate entailed on some distant relative from the west country. He had not been bothered enough to probe further. Knowing Robin for a philanderer, he had not been surprised at gossip of his sordid death, or that the new owner of the estate would, at first, choose to keep to himself until rumours quietened.

Trelawney! How he hated the name and the man. Luke Trelawney had forced him from successful free-trading in Devon and Somerset, to seek new pastures and coastlines. Four years ago, having fled Somerset and the Revenue virtually penniless, he had covered his tracks sufficiently to make a new identity and life. And he had been lucky and done remarkably well for himself in duping a wealthy widow into believing him a personable, trustworthy fellow. Now she knew differently, it hardly mattered. They were married and he had gained this beautiful house and substantial funds in the bank. She and her two brats were a minor hitch.

He was sure Trelawney knew nothing of his whereabouts, his new name or his business with these local smugglers. It was ironic. It was fate. Fate had decreed his revenge could now be taken on the unsuspecting enemy. And perhaps very sweetly, he grinned to himself, as Rebecca Nash dominated his mind.

'Trelawney is now Lord Ramsden and is betrothed to Rebecca Nash?' he asked, almost lyrically.

Jake Blacker nodded curtly. 'And Simon Nash is now quite brazen about what he owes me. I've not had the opportunity to warn the pipsqueak of all I know of his prospective brother-in-law. He continually avoids me.'

'Well, we shall have to do something about that,' Mayhew purred. He hated Luke Trelawney with a vengeance. For it was only luck and cunning that had put him in this genteel house rather than in gaol…or on a gibbet. He resented Trelawney's wealth, his good looks and his sexual conquests. He always had the most attractive women fawning over him.

Whether Trelawney intended Rebecca Nash to be his wife or mistress, her chastity was sure to be of vital importance. His thin smile turned to a lusty laugh.

'I do believe that the virtuous governess and I are overdue for a talk. My stepdaughter's progress is suddenly of immense concern to me. There is a way you can repay me, Blacker, and perhaps keep your purse in your pocket. Assist me in a little…conversation with Miss Nash tonight at Devil's Cove. I warrant Trelawney might pay handsomely…even beg…to get that blonde angel back intact.'

It was impossible! How could he have found out so soon?

Rebecca stared, flabbergasted, at the stooped, elderly man propping ancient joints against the kitchen doorframe at the Summer House.

'And master says as ter be as quick as yer can fer it's terrible important that he speaks to yer,' Bert Morris impassively advised through the clay pipe clenched between stained teeth.

Re-reading the note in her hand, Rebecca tried to extract some inkling of the writer's mood and purpose. The only detectable tenor was the urgency apparent in the phrasing of two brief lines of scrawled script which summoned her immediately to Crosby.

Bert Morris stuffed horny hands into fraying pockets and stood morosely, waiting. When Rebecca simply continued staring at him in astonishment and consternation, he gave a backward nod of his bedraggled head. 'Sent the coach and pair fer yer,' he said proudly, drawing Rebecca's attention to the smart carriage, so different from the last creaky contraption they had shared.

Could Rupert Mayhew have so soon found out that his step-daughter was missing? Rebecca had known herself for barely five hours, and it was only the last two of those which had given her real cause for concern.

After Ross's staggering news in Brighton about the absent couple, they had all returned immediately to the Ramsden estate so that Luke and Ross could join the search for them. Although unbearably restless, Rebecca had obeyed Luke's ruling that she stay at home and wait for news, recognising the sense in it: for there was little she could do as dusk approached. She had never forgotten coming so terrifyingly close to the smugglers trekking through the woods some weeks ago.

How on earth could the news have travelled fourteen miles to the girl's stepfather so speedily? She just could not imagine. Or could she…? Of course! Rebecca gave a little blow of annoyance at her stupid lack of comprehension. Lucy might not have run away at all, but rather taken it upon herself to return home at once. Perhaps she had, after all, become resigned to her fate and decided to hasten to it rather than fearfully anticipate it. Rebecca could understand that; she was wont to rush to meet the inevitable herself. Her memory skittered over the day she had walked the meadow to the Manor in trepidation of confronting Luke with his proposition, yet unable not to.

Oh, Heavens! Rebecca threw back her head in despair at another excruciating possibility. Had John gone with her to Crosby? Perhaps to speak to her stepfather of his intentions? Rebecca dare not even imagine how the young carpenter would be received by the vile man who had harboured such lofty ambitions for his stepdaughter some six weeks previously.

'Is Miss Lucy back with her parents?' Rebecca immediately interrogated the dour-faced man before her, yet dreading his answer.

'Dun't know,' the man laconically advised with a chomp on

his pipe that sent foul smoke wafting Rebecca's way. 'Been in stables most of day. Jest been arst ta come and git yer. Best be gittin back, too. Light be going pretty quick. Best ta travel wi' some light,' he announced before taking the pipe from his mouth, inspecting it, then knocking smouldering ash on to the ground.

'Who is it?' Martha demanded over Rebecca's shoulder. 'Not them peddlers back again, I hope. I told them…'

'It's Bert Morris, Martha,' Rebecca quickly told her. 'He's come from Lucy's stepfather.'

Martha instinctively covered her mouth with a hand, unconsciously betraying her horror at this awful turn of events.

'I shall have to go and speak with Mr Mayhew,' Rebecca defeatedly sighed. Despite her antipathy for the man it was her duty to go and face the music. If Lucy and John had been too indiscreet…or intimate…or both…and Rupert Mayhew had discovered it, God help them all!

'I will probably not be more than a few hours. I'm sure Mr Mayhew will provide me with transport home later this evening,' she quaveringly reassured the woman, noting Martha's unusual pallor. Privately, she had little confidence in what she uttered. Mr Mayhew, she was certain, would oblige her with nothing other than blistering accusations, if her alarming suspicions proved correct.

'Luke will be back soon, I'm sure.' Another unlikely prospect, she dejectedly realised, for he had been sent on a fool's errand, after all. The last place he would think to search for Lucy and John would be her parents' home.

As the coach swayed to an uneven tilted halt fifty yards into the densely wooded track that wound to the main coast road, Rebecca didn't bother investigating the shadowy dusk, so lost was she in her own hectic thoughts. When the coach door jerked abruptly open, and Jake Blacker leapt in, slammed the door, and rapped for the driver to resume the journey, Rebecca barely had sense enough to breathe, let alone act.

'Mr Blacker!' she finally burst out in a mingling of fright and outrage.

'Indeed it is, Miss Nash,' he jeeringly greeted her before proceeding to settle himself comfortably into the cracked leather squabs.

'Well, don't just sit there like that!' Rebecca exploded after two stunned minutes, on realising he apparently meant her no bodily harm, but intended to snooze. 'What on earth do you think you're about?' she demanded as he did no more than stir enough to flex his legs. Perhaps the odious man simply thought he could hitch a ride to Brighton or one of the surrounding villages.

Unable to stifle a hysterical laugh from jerking out of her at the farce of it, Rebecca closed her tired eyes and a shaking hand pressed to her mouth.

This should have been one of the happiest days of her life. Her first outing with Luke had started so promisingly. The long-awaited meeting with Simon had brought wonderful release; their lunch had been exquisite; and loving and trusting Luke had become more natural with every contented moment. She had felt so joyful on the beach…so carefree. But that happiness had been cruelly curtailed. This marvellous day was changing into blackest nightmare.

She breathed slowly and deeply, composing herself. Fear and fury were the enemies of common sense, she knew. Sparking aquamarine eyes fixed on Jake Blacker with a resolution that made him curl a lip in a travesty of a smile.

'I am on my way to see a Mr Mayhew in the village of Crosby,' she detailed icily. 'And I would be grateful if you would remove yourself from this carriage and find your own transport.'

'Why should I? This is my transport, too.' Slitted eyes slithered over her body as he mocked her. 'By lucky chance, Mr Mayhew also has business this evening with me. It was at his suggestion that we now travel together,' he quite truthfully informed her, his tone tinged with sly amusement.

This news was so startling and enfeebling that for a long

moment Rebecca merely gaped at him. Then the chill started to creep and crawl over her skin. She wound her black-fringed shawl more tightly about her, feeling frozen to the marrow, yet knowing that very little of the cold was attributable to the ill-fitting coach windows. She wished now she had taken the time to fetch her heavy cloak before leaving, for she sorely needed its soft comforting warmth.

Something was not right. Something was not right at all. Despite her coldness, her golden hair clung to her neck in damp tendrils and beads of moisture stuck wispy curls to her forehead. Warm perspiration trickled down her back despite the shivering of her body and her icy hands. She tried to force her numb brain to logically sort and process information but it constantly rebounded from this monumental task to simply focus on escape.

Turquoise eyes spontaneously flicked to the coach door before she shot a glance back at Blacker and noted his grin. He was well aware of her thoughts of bolting and seemed entertained by them. 'I've seen a man nigh on cut in half by coach wheels when he tried that,' he recounted with morbid relish. He rapped imperiously on the coachwork and roughly commanded Bert Morris, 'Get going, man…faster.' But his glacier-blue eyes never left Rebecca as he silently challenged her to defy him.

'They won't do you no harm.' The young man emphasised his reassurance by nodding his large moon face at Rebecca. He lurched away from the boulder he leaned on, the flare in his hand throwing disjointed wobbling shadows on to the rocky wall.

Rebecca shrank back into a sitting position on smooth stone as his gigantic frame lumbered closer to her. One shapeless mass of a hand was gripping the flaming torch and the other huge paw, she breathlessly noted, was clenched by his side. Her heartbeat seemed to fail completely as he crouched down close by her. 'Here…throw these at 'em. They'll leave you be,' he knowledgeably said, but with a blank expression. He raised his fist then abruptly spreadeagled fat fingers. Pebbles scattered around

Rebecca's skirts and she jerked her trembling legs closer to her body, simultaneously wrapping her shawl and skirt yet tighter.

The dank odour of the cave made her stomach churn, but it was the squealing, inquisitive vermin that occasionally emerged, streaking from behind boulders lining the rocky prison, that really nauseated her. She did as the giant said and unsteady fingers launched pebbles into corners shrouded in blackness. The scurrying and squeaking increased and a flash of long whiskers, teeth and string-like tail helped her aim increase and improve. When finished with her missiles, her arms hugged quickly about her shins and her forehead sank forward to rest on her knees. Despair and fury made tears tingle hotly at the back of her eyes but she was determined not to break down.

She had been delivered to this isolated beach spot by Blacker what now seemed like several hours ago, though Rebecca realised that it could have been less than one. A permeating salty stench mingling with boat oil, seaweed and rotting fish clung to her nostrils, so that every breath heightened the dreadful sickness swamping her.

She had no chance of escape: not only had she this monstrous simpleton to get past, but the evil-looking ruffians standing guard outside this coastal dungeon and along the clifftop. The prospect of risking an encounter with any of those leering thugs made her throat clench and her heart achingly pulsate.

When Blacker had forced her roughly down the shifting shingle path to this desolate place, she recalled passing some four or five shadowy figures. From their sibilant hissing with Blacker, she gleaned that each one of them wanted the task of guarding her. But that popular job had been entrusted to 'Clarkie', as this mountainous half-wit was called, until Blacker returned. She also overheard the dire consequences threatened by Jake Blacker should any man lay a finger on her person. Her teeth ground together as she prayed that every one of them would heed his warning. The idea that she would gladly set eyes upon Jake Blacker again was totally illogical yet, compared to those batmen outside, he seemed ridiculously welcome.

From where her head rested upon her clasped hands, she

glanced assessingly up through her lashes at Clarkie. Although he was oafish he seemed relatively inoffensive, even showing her some kindness: once Blacker had left she had easily persuaded him to unbind her hands. But Rebecca was sure he would do all in his immense power to prevent her escaping.

'Is Mr Blacker coming back soon?' she asked Clarkie with an amity she was far from feeling. She was desperate to draw some information from him as to why she was being held prisoner. A hysterical bubble of laughter choked in her throat. Rupert Mayhew might be upset at his daughter's behaviour, and hold Rebecca responsible for it, but this was taking retribution to ridiculous extremes.

Rebecca's forced smile faded: Clarkie was avoiding looking her way at all. Grasping at what reason her exhausted mind retained, she realised that her abduction and imprisonment might have little, perhaps nothing, to do with Lucy. His daughter *was* an uncontrollable hoyden and Rebecca had failed to improve her, but Rupert Mayhew would need to be insane to risk punishing Rebecca so harshly. But Mayhew was involved, for she had caught his name mentioned in gruff asides, several times, by the men outside. And Jake Blacker had spoken of him in the coach.

Blacker would divulge nothing, and the longer she pleaded with him to tell her the purpose of it all and her fate, the more evil pleasure he seemed to gain from keeping her in ignorance. The only connection she could make out was Simon. Simon knew Blacker and owed him money. But why Rupert Mayhew, an apparently respectable businessman, was embroiled in it all, was beyond her fright-limited powers of deduction. And why holding her would aid them was even more of a mystery—they must know she had no money.

An exasperated sigh warmed her clasped, cold fingers and Rebecca determinedly tried to catch her guard's eye. 'Do you know if Jake Blacker is returning soon?' Rebecca repeated, mounting frustration sharpening her voice.

'Ain't to say nothing,' Clarkie dolefully said, wagging his head.

'Is there a blanket about this draughty hole somewhere?' Rebecca demanded through chattering teeth. She was freezing and her shawl did little to ward off the November sea breeze. Merely the whoosh of tide rushing in over shingle induced uncontrollable shivering in her.

Clarkie shambled towards her, awkwardly removing his tar- and sweat-stained jacket. He clumsily draped the enormous tattered woolen garment about her quivering shoulders. The reek from it made Rebecca's stomach heave but she gave him a grateful smile. 'What's in those barrels?' she asked, desperate to get him talking on any subject: it might perhaps lead to another.

'French brandy,' he briefly informed her but with a shy, rather sweet smile.

The thought of a warming drink consumed Rebecca's mind and would not be shaken off. She had drunk brandy once or twice on special occasions with her papa, and a drop when she had been ill once with a severe chill. She reminisced on the fiery warmth and sense of relaxed well-being it had instilled. Rising from her cramped position on the smooth bed of rock, she gingerly flexed stiff limbs before approaching the barrels ranged against the cave wall and tapping the one closest. It thudded dully. 'Have you a cup? I should like some,' she said with the most charming smile she could muster.

'Can't drink that,' Clarkie warned harshly. 'It'll kill you. Kill you down dead,' he stressed agitatedly. 'It be made specially too strong to drink so's we get more in each of them barrels. We got to mix it up with water afore we sell it. Men been found dead as can be on the beach from opening up them barrels and drinking it,' he gruffly explained.

Rebecca trudged away, but couldn't face huddling down again on the stone-cold seat. 'Why am I here?' she pleaded. He avoided her eyes and stared out into blackness in the direction of the moon-silvered sea.

'Nobody tells Clarkie nothing. Clarkie's dunderhead.'

'You shouldn't believe what others say about you, Clarkie,' Rebecca said gently, with a butterfly touch for a beefy hand. 'You have fine qualities. You are a better man than those ruffians outside and Jake Blacker. All wish me harm. Yet you have been kind to me. You have kept me warm with your coat, you warned me not to drink that deadly alcohol and you untied my sore wrists.'

'Exactly why he is a dunderhead, Miss Nash,' a deceitfully smooth voice stated from the shadowy cavern entrance. 'And why he will later pay for his disobedience...as will you for leading him to it.'

Rebecca's heart leapt, lodging in her throat, as she twisted immediately about and squinted into blackness. Rupert Mayhew stepped into the flare of yellow light, only his face illuminated near Clarkie's gross middle, making him seem disembodied and miniature.

'But enough of this unpleasantness,' he chided himself, bestowing a reptilian smile on Rebecca. 'How very nice it is to meet with you again, my dear. I had hoped to renew our acquaintance sooner, and under more agreeable circumstances, but 'twas not to be.' He gazed smilingly around the cave interior as though it held some happy memories for him. 'I hear from my acquaintance Blacker that you have a rather foolish brother. I also hear that you have acquired an extremely dangerous lover. Quite unexpected...nay, astonishing...Miss Nash, I must say. You must tell me all about it while we await his arrival at my house.'

'This is quite outrageous, Mr Mayhew,' Rebecca bit out through her chattering teeth, the bizarre reference to Luke passing unnoticed in her wrath. Far from feeling terrorized by this repugnant little man, as she had anticipated she would, she was incensed. For two pins she would have flown across the dark void that separated them and slapped that smirk from his ugly face. Her small fingers curled so tightly that savage fingernails scored her palms. But she steeled herself against such folly: she was going to need every ounce of composure and logic.

'I imagine that your stepdaughter, Lucy, must have told you by now,' she enigmatically mentioned with admirable self-assurance.

'Told me? Told me what?' he demanded, uncertain whether to dismiss it or show curiosity. 'Why would my stepdaughter tell me anything? And how? I've not seen her. I've received no letters…'

Rebecca swiftly masked her expression of heartfelt relief. So Lucy was safe…at least from him…and he knew nothing of her elopement, if indeed that was what she and John had attempted. She threw her captor a disdainful look.

'Why, told you that you are the most repulsive man I have ever had the misfortune to meet, Mr Mayhew,' she clearly announced. So much for logic and composure, she regretfully acknowledged, as Mayhew's stunted body recommenced stalking very purposefully her way, fists curling at its sides. As he drew level with Clarkie, the giant began clumsily gesturing and grunting for clemency on Rebecca's behalf. Mayhew contemptuously shoved double-handed at the barrel-like figure.

'Don't you dare touch her,' threatened a hoarse, familiar voice.

'Simon?' Rebecca croaked. Her throat was so parchment dry with fear she could barely articulate her mingled query and relief. She dodged Mayhew and fled to the cavern entrance where her brother was detained, with his arms pinioned behind him by Jake Blacker.

'Ran the pipsqueak to ground at last,' Blacker sneered as he cuffed the side of Simon's head. Blacker's pale eyes shifted to Rebecca, lingering on her dishevelled yet still beautifully appealing person. 'Well, here's one of the Nash family I've a softer spot for. Or should I perhaps say a harder one…?' He roared at his own lewd banter, restraining Simon as he fought to physically remonstrate with him.

'You keep your lecherous hands to yourself,' Mayhew hissed menacingly. 'And make sure that those pillaging louts outside do likewise. Do you think that Trelawney will pay for spoiled goods?'

Simon managed to extricate an arm from his captor's painful grip and grabbed Rebecca close, desperate to comfort her.

'I'm sorry,' he whispered into her soft hair. 'I'm so sorry.'

Rebecca gazed anxiously up into his strained shadowy face.

Her shaking white finger soothed a graze close to his ear, from Blacker's knuckles.

'What is this all about? Is it the money you owe Blacker? Why is Mayhew involved?' she whispered urgently.

Simon shook his head, signalling ignorance and defeat. 'I've never seen that ugly dwarf before. And I never believed Blacker would stoop to this…imprisoning you to force my hand.' His voice cracked and he bit at his lip to steady it. Rebecca felt prickles frosting her as she realised just how close to disaster they must be: Simon was very near to breaking down.

'What a touching little scene,' Mayhew mocked. 'Well, make the most of it, for it will surely be your last unless I have what money is due me.'

'Due to you?' both Simon and Rebecca uttered, astonished.

'Naturally,' he scoffed. 'Obviously whatever money you owe Blacker the dolt has already pledged. Partly on this consignment of brandy we see all around us, but more importantly on one of gold soon due to cross the channel to Napoleon to pay his mercenaries. Because of Blacker's outstanding debts I am now becoming embarrassed for funds myself. And needs must when the devil drives,' he grated.

'You will never get away with this,' Rebecca vibrantly challenged him. 'Abduction and imprisonment are serious offences, Mr Mayhew. You will be arrested and tried…imprisoned.'

Mayhew howled, head back, in genuine, raucous laughter. 'Indeed, I shall, if caught,' he agreed, wiping a mirthful tear away with a stubby finger. 'Well, it is to be expected, I am afraid, my dear Miss Nash. There has been a noose with my name on it for some twenty years or more. Abduction and imprisonment? Small fry compared to smuggling and murder…oh, and treason. For the crown takes a rather dim view of my providing our old foe Napoleon with the wherewithal to pay his rag-tag troops; or returning to him prisoners of war so they may rejoin the fray. Buonaparte paid up rather well for a Général de Montfort. But it is all purely business, of course. I have no political allegiances, and no love for the *monsieurs*. The *mesdemoiselles*, of course, well, that is a different story,' he lasciviously chuckled. 'The

French mademoiselle…yes… Which brings me in mind of another matter.' He addressed Blacker. 'Where is my nemesis? Has Trelawney had my message?'

'I left it with a doddering old cove named Miles at Ramsden Manor. Neither Trelawney nor his brother were at home. A young couple had gone missing from the estate and they were searching the locality for them.'

Mayhew swore beneath his breath and Rebecca held hers, the mention of Lucy and Luke vying for priority in her whirling, incoherent thoughts.

'Well, let's hope for the sake of *these* young people that he arrives at my house at the appointed hour and is amenable to my plans.'

'Why do they mention Luke so often? It is almost as though he is implicated other than by his relationship with me,' Rebecca whispered to Simon before noting her brother's odd expression.

'Blacker told me once that the Trelawneys and smuggling had long been linked,' Simon reluctantly sighed out. 'I believe these two miscreants have known of him far longer than you or I.'

Rebecca felt as though she had received a physical blow. She clung to Simon while struggling for breath. It couldn't be true. Luke involved with smuggling? Luke a criminal? Never! But her frantic mind raced back over the past weeks and pounced on the evening she had sought Simon at the Bull and Mouth tavern in Brighton. Blacker had recognised the name of Trelawney, if not the man, and Luke's reputation had greatly worried him. And then, on their ride home, when she had quizzed him about it all, he had seemed oddly amused and had evaded answering her. Pieces of a puzzle which had niggled at the back of her mind seemed to suddenly converge and, harrowingly, fit. There were the tubmen she had seen trekking through Graveley woods. In the direction of Westbrook! Surely not to the Manor? No, it must be coincidence. They were in the area because of Blacker being once more local. But there *was* something menacing about Luke…a ruthlessness he screened with urbane manners. She couldn't deny that, for she had glimpsed it; had sensed it as long ago as when he had first propositioned her.

'Ah, I see Miss Nash looks concerned that I know her lover's history. And I'll wager better than she does herself,' Mayhew perceptively guessed, gratified by this new discovery and how he might use it to wreak further damage on the man he feared and hated. Making this lovely woman despise his old enemy might be the sweetest revenge of all.

'Why, let me enlighten you a little, Miss Nash. Luke Trelawney and I are old acquaintances. Very old. I knew of his father, Jago Trelawney, of course, before I knew him. In fact, I like to take credit for hastening that man's death. For he wouldn't see sense,' he impassively recounted. 'Then, when his son Luke took over the family business, we never saw eye to eye. There was enough sea and trade for both of us to make a good living. But he wanted more…too much…' His yellow eyes gleamed demonically and Rebecca realised that the man was insane. 'He did his level best to ruin me. And nearly succeeded,' he softly admitted, nodding, with a faraway look in his feral eyes. 'But I have come back to haunt him for I'll warrant that after the skirmish at Lizard Point, he honestly believed me dead. And it certainly suited me to disappear from Devon…and the Revenue.' He gave Rebecca a twisted smile. 'He is a perilous man, my dear, not at all a seemly husband for such a sweet innocent as you. One of his Cornish trollops would prove a far better consort. That lush brunette he keeps in Penzance especially, for I swear the lovely Wenna considers them already wed…in all but name. No doubt she will be keen to make your acquaintance and seek you out if you remove there. She has a fiery temper, as I recall.'

'I will listen to no more of this,' Rebecca choked breathlessly across his speech, her body stone-cold yet her heart afire with a dreadful, caustic fear. 'You are an evil man. You are lying to poison my mind against my fiancé and ruin our lives. By your own admission you hate him. I will listen to no more of your malice.'

'I swear on the life of my sweet baby son that all I have just told you is the truth. If I have ever loved at all, I love him,' Mayhew said, in a voice made husky with sincerity.

'Pay him no heed,' Simon gruffly ordered Rebecca, frightened by the intensity with which she was now quivering in his arms and the glossy wideness of her eyes. 'He is a madman too full of bitter grudges to know night from day, let alone truth from falsehood.'

A careless shrug and expletive met Simon's insult. Then without another word, Rupert Mayhew curtly indicated by flapping his hands that they should all move outside. He shoved at Clarkie, wordlessly gesturing he should go in front and light the way back to the clifftop.

Luke had been more tolerant and philosophical than he would have believed himself capable: certainly more than the terrified pair had expected. He might even have been a little amused, had it not been for the fact that his day with Rebecca had been so rudely shortened. And he had so much planned for today...so much to finally tell her on what he had chosen as his perfect day.

The young runaways had been apprehended at the King's Head at Guildford, as Ross had guessed, on their way north to marry at Gretna Green.

On arrival back at the Manor, famished and thirsty after setting such a cracking pace home, they had all rested in the hallway. As Miles greeted them and limped over, Luke gave the butler an immediate order for refreshments and Miles immediately gave him...the greatest shock of his life.

Luke stared at the note. He raised sightless eyes to the sheepish young couple huddled close together on hall chairs. Black eyes dropped to the paper again, stark white against his unsteady dark fingers. His grip tightened, making the paper quiver and the black script dance out of focus. He felt blood leeching from his face and that well-remembered raw fear torturing him, as it had once before at the Bull and Mouth tavern.

A mere scribbled note, yet, insignificant as it seemed, the seconds taken reading it were the most harrowing moments in his life. Even the time his mother had run to the shore to find him and tell him his father was critically injured had never wounded him with such aching force. And now the source of that day's pain had unbelievably…impossibly…brought him this, too. The raging mix of despair, fury, guilt and dread burned indelibly into his soul and he knew the taste and feel of it would remain with him until he died.

He sprang out of his velvet-seated chair and paced aimlessly to the stairs, half-aware of Ross's anxious hazel eyes on him and the young couple warily tracking his every move.

Ross walked over and prised the folded paper from his rigid fingers, digesting the few lines within a second. He gazed at the side of his brother's face, noting his back teeth grinding, mis-aligning his jaw, and the tic by his rigid, compressed mouth.

Luke swung back to regard Lucy, strode to her chair and hunkered down by her in one swift fluid movement. The frightened young woman tried to pull back close to John for protection. Luke firmly took her chin in gentle fingers. 'Now think hard, Lucy,' he stressed hoarsely. 'What I am going to ask is very, *very* important and I'm hoping you can help me. If you have an inkling of anything at all that may help you must tell me, even if you feel it is of little significance or that you are betraying members of your family. You *must* tell me…I *must* know it.' He paused before asking huskily, 'If your stepfather wanted to hide something away from home…something very valuable to him, where would he put it?'

Chapter Thirteen

An odd stillness, interspersed only by the sucking and rushing of sea on stones, at first made no impression. Rebecca felt so exhausted and so emotionally drained that sinking on to the shingle to weep and sleep beckoned.

Nearing the clifftop, Blacker suddenly grunted in exasperation and shouted to Mayhew.

'What now?' Mayhew gutturally hissed and then froze as moonbeams picked out a flash of gleaming steel in his comrade's hand.

'Where are the others? Where are my men?' Blacker demanded and warned in one breath, shifting his knife from hand to hand.

'Fool, I told you they were not to be trusted. Where are they? Throwing dice, I'll wager. Or playing cards. You leave them for a moment and they skive off to their own devices.' His muted tirade was interrupted by Blacker cupping his mouth with his hands and emitting a low, melancholy hooting. The plaintive sound induced a violent shivering in Rebecca and she nestled into her brother.

Blacker prodded urgently at Simon and Rebecca, wildly gesturing at them to scramble the last few paces to the craggy clifftop, before again issuing that eerie call. The silence thereafter seemed impenetrable as they all listened and waited: even the ocean music seemed to have diminished.

'I don't think they'll hear you in the Red Lion,' mentioned a sardonic voice that made Rebecca's heart leap and pump frantically.

'Well, this one might, but I doubt he'll be a lot of use,' Ross added to Luke's comment as he strolled out of a thicket, shoving a stocky, balding ruffian in front of him, a blade at his throat. The fist gripping the knife raised suddenly and the heel of it came down savagely on the back of the man's head, knocking him out cold.

Luke's black-clothed figure detached itself from the rock he was resting back against, and he walked into the pool of yellow light thrown by Clarkie's flare. 'Come here, Rebecca,' he ordered softly, his dark eyes engulfing, seducing her across the flickering patches of dark and light. But the fleeting chance of escape was lost as love and suspicion warred within her, making her hesitate and cling to Simon.

'I think not, Trelawney,' Mayhew grunted, striding to Rebecca's side. One cruel, stubby hand wound into her long, silken hair and yanked it back, exposing her creamy throat to the night air and the gleaming blade in his fist. 'She's wary of the smuggling fraternity, my old friend. Something in your history, perhaps, that frightens her?' he scoffed, while the silky steel caressed tormentingly up and down her moon-pearled skin.

'Shouldn't you be dead, Merrill?' Luke rasped bitterly, his black eyes fixed unwaveringly on Rebecca.

'Tut...tut. You shall confuse everyone, Trelawney. My name is now Mayhew...Rupert Mayhew. Ronald Merrill is certainly dead and buried...or drowned, should I say? At Lizard Point...remember that night?' he taunted him. 'And I hear that yours is now Lord Ramsden of Westbrook. Who would have thought such nobility of a man so closely linked with free-trading? But then you always were unpredictable,' he allowed, grudging admiration quietening his voice. 'Tell me, how did you find out about Devil's Cove?' he interrogated, with a backward nod of his head indicating the tide-lashed rocks below.

'Your stepdaughter told me, Merrill. She told me lots of

things. Things that make me ever more determined to see you
hang from a gibbett and die very slowly.'

'Not a sensible comment, Trelawney,' Merrill snapped as the
knife tracing Rebecca's throat stilled and the flat of it pressed
down making her jerk and gasp. 'I knew that little bitch was
spying on me. And I never could teach the slut to guard her
tongue.'

'And you'll get no more chances,' Luke vehemently told him.

'I've no need of any,' Mayhew sneered. 'After tonight, I shall
be long gone from the area. That drab I married has no money
left and the house is mortgaged to the hilt. Why stay? I believe
I would have been gone a year sooner but for the promise of a
son, and the ambition Lucy might whore her way into some rich
roué's affections. She showed some potential...' he said with
chilling gravity. 'But we need never again meet. I will leave you
in peace if you accord me the same favour. Tangling with you
was never wise,' he reluctantly admitted with a grimace. 'The
continent beckons, I think. All I require from you is money to
send me on my way, then you get your bed warmed by this
blonde lovely.' He grunted a sly laugh. 'I suppose you didn't
bring your buxom Cornish doxy with you to Sussex, Trelawney?
Pity,' he answered himself after a long second of singing silence
in which turquoise and black eyes fused. 'For I'll wager that
dark-haired beauty knew a trick or two to keep a man happy.
Forgoing the cash and swapping Miss Purity here for that wench
might even have appealed...'

'Where are my men? Have you killed them?' Blacker suddenly cut across Mayhew's lecherous musings.

'Dead drunk only, I imagine,' Ross interjected quietly. 'By
the time they've run through the money I gave them, though,
they possibly might have poisoned themselves. Such loyalty you
two inspire,' he sarcastically sneered. 'I wonder why that is?'
He stirred the body of the unconcious man at his feet with a
disdainful boot. 'One only prepared to stay here on duty.'

Mayhew glared his contempt at Blacker at this news, mouth-
ing an obscenity. But he politely said to Luke, 'So glad to hear
you're being generous with your money. One thousand of your

pounds will buy you back sweet Miss Nash. Oh, she is untouched.' He slid his free hand tormentingly, insolently inside Clarkie's jacket that Rebecca still wore, pulling it wide to expose his intention as he roughly clutched at a softly rounded breast, making her shudder and try to break free. 'Almost untouched…for the present…'

'Merrill…' Luke harshly warned him, fear and rage in his voice as he stepped two paces closer.

'But I have a crew who have seen nothing of a woman for a month or more,' Mayhew racked him further, as the silver steel recommenced its lethal fondling along Rebecca's neck. 'I'm sure this little angel would make a very welcome addition on their next channel crossing. See how she quakes at the thought?' he taunted Luke. 'No doubt afeared she'll never find her sea legs. Not to worry, my dear, you'll never need them, you'll be spending the voyage flat on your back.'

'Let her go now, right this minute, and you can have more money than even you can run through in a lifetime, and that racing sloop you coveted,' Luke desperately offered and then realised his mistake. In his panic to get Rebecca safely free of the blade, he was firing the man's insatiable greed and malevolence. He could sense Ross breathing fast and shallow by his side, impatiently waiting for the signal to go. But they were too far away from the weapon at Rebecca's throat. He didn't dare risk it until they were closer and he was sure Simon perceived what he had to do.

'Well, well, who would have thought it?' Mayhew derided softly. 'That I would eventually hold within my grasp Luke Trelawney's downfall. You'd pay me anything…give me anything, wouldn't you?' His spiteful fingers again grabbed intimately inside Clarkie's coat making Rebecca jerk then freeze in his arms with her eyes tight shut against the nausea rolling in her stomach. 'Well, I'll take your money, Trelawney, and your sloop and you can beg me on your knees to stop pleasuring her…see how she likes it?'

The patch of light haloing Luke wobbled and Mayhew ground

out at Clarkie, 'Hold the flare still, you damned fool.' But Clarkie lowered the torch and speared it into the sandy ground.

'What are you about?' Mayhew hissed anxiously at the simpleton, as Clarkie lumbered closer with swaying head, scrunched-up face and a weird moaning wringing from his throat. 'Get the horse and cart now, you dullard, or you'll get it,' Mayhew screamed at him, gesturing wildly at the old farm vehicle tethered nearby. But his threats and rage did nothing to halt the giant's inexorable progress towards him.

Clarkie's hand closed over the blade at Rebecca's throat and an animal growl of physical pain and rage erupted. He shoved the dimunitive man back from Rebecca with such force that Mayhew actually ran backwards several yards before he sat down heavily in the darkness.

The abrupt removal of Mayhew's support had Rebecca sinking quite gracefully to the ground. Simon was on his knees beside her before he was roughly pulled away and Luke lifted her in his arms. Across her swimming head she heard Luke's guttural threats and commands to Simon, before he kissed her hard and swift, removing what little breath she had left. His dark hands were at her face, in her hair, reassuring, trembling touches for them both and then he tipped her into Simon's waiting embrace and was gone.

Running with her in his arms, Simon swiftly deposited her in the waiting cart. He jumped up to the driver's seat, croaked urgent encouragement at the old cart horse, and they began rattling away along the coast road. As Rebecca pulled herself to a sitting position on the splintery boards, she realised that they were escaping pandemonium. Blacker and Ross were locked in combat, each gripping blades and looking for deadly openings to use them, and Mayhew was now on his feet and running towards the battling men.

Rebecca watched in horror and fascination as Luke raced towards his brother. She gasped aloud as the smuggler Ross had previously knocked out scrambled up from the gritty ground. He lunged at Luke and they scrapped for little more than a few seconds before the batman once again hit gravel and Luke was sprinting to Ross's aid. Ross swiped his dagger in a vicious arc in front of him, making his two assailants back off a few paces.

He lobbed a weapon over Blacker's head and moonlight glanced off the lengthy blade as Luke's hand arrested it mid-flight. The expression on Ross's face fascinated her. He was smiling…no, laughing…as though he were thoroughly enjoying himself. He gestured a warning to Luke of more opposition, and Rebecca twisted about too, as the cart rumbled further away from danger. A rabble of about four men was running up the hill having exited a dimly lit building. As they got closer, Rebecca recognised them. They were Blacker's men and, no doubt, now fired with Dutch courage purchased at the Red Lion tavern.

Simon yelped and whipped the old cart horse into some speed and rounded the wooded bend in the track. Under the canopy of trees both moonlight and the affray were lost from sight. After about a minute of frantic driving, Simon pulled up sharp and clambered quickly into the back with Rebecca. He took her ashen, chilled face between his palms, feeling the chattering of her teeth through her cheeks and the incessant quivering of her whole body.

'I have to go back and help them, Rebecca. I know Luke bade me deliver you to the Manor and I know he'll probably want to kill me as much as those ruffians for not obeying him. But I have to go back. They are badly outnumbered, even if the giant rallies enough to aid them; his hand was nigh on cut in half.'

Rebecca merely nodded her acceptance and understanding, incapable of speech.

'If you keep heading along this road, and as fast as this old nag will go, you will eventually come to Brighton. After that you know the way. You can drive that old trap of yours as good as I can. This will give you no problem.' He embraced her hard against him, and then he had vaulted over the cart edge and was sprinting back towards Devil's Cove.

Rebecca clambered on to the seat and groped about for the reins with clammy hands. She wanted to stay; to go back to the two men she loved. But she knew she was close to hysteria or fainting. She would be a perilous hindrance, not any help. The old cart horse swayed its head about and looked at her and for some reason, in filtering moonlight, she recognised the animal and remembered its name. It was old Bessy, the mare who had delivered her and Lucy to the Summer House what seemed now aeons ago.

'Come along, Bessy old girl,' Rebecca quaveringly encouraged. 'I'm sure you know this road, even if I don't. I'm trusting you.'

The old mare whinnied softly and the merest flick of the reins had her breaking into a reasonably steady trot.

The last dying embers collapsed into the grate, sparking a dull orangey glow from flaking coals. Rebecca rested her head back into the fireside chair in her parlour and again allowed exhaustion to overtake her. But the old wooden clock behind her on the wall chimed two o'clock, defeating her and making weary eyelids flutter up.

She had been back at the Summer House for two hours; arriving at midnight, she had found Martha and Gregory still waiting for her, frantic with worry. She had felt incapable of furnishing lengthy explanations: she was still too close to hysteria herself to cope with it in others. But with the promise that all would be explained in the morning and assurances that she was absolutely fine, they had eventually left her to desperately needed solitude and rest.

She had decided not to go to the Manor despite having heard Luke's explicit instructions to Simon that that was where she was to be taken. As the chill night air cleared her shock a little, she had realised that the Turners, already worried, would wait up to see her safely home. With immediate peril at bay, the quiet solitude of the journey freed her mind. All Rupert Mayhew's malicious talk of Luke's Cornish past monopolised her thoughts...and so she went to her own home.

She now felt so emotionally drained that the thought of Luke and her brother and perhaps Ross lying injured or dead at that isolated coastal spot evoked no more than a whimper and a tightening in her already sandpapered throat. She had wept all the tears she possessed, she was sure, and after two hours of utter desolation only an aching emptiness remained.

But even that raw listlessness would not prevent her again torturing herself with what Mayhew had revealed of Luke's life in Cornwall. All had been divulged in spite and anger, but there was truth in it. In a strange way, as Mayhew had spouted his venom and Luke had denied nothing, Rebecca realised she never expected him to, for part of her already knew. And it was not the thought of her fiancé being a criminal that seared into her soul, but the thought of him being with another woman…kissing and touching someone else in the way he did her. Smiling and joking with her in that intimate way she believed was uniquely theirs. And to her shame, she realised she hated and envied that beautiful, faceless mistress with a passion that ground her teeth and made her shudder, weeping, in her chair. And she hated him, too, for bringing her so low.

Her thoughts returned to yesterday evening when she had obliquely asked him if he would love her. He had said nothing and now she knew why. There was a woman he already loved and, by Mayhew's reckoning, she classed him as her property. They were practically wed…in all but name, Mayhew had said.

She had been a naïve fool trusting in him, believing in his implausible explanations. Everything had pointed to him being a dangerous philanderer…and a liar, too. Besides the scandalous incident with the bawds at Ramsden Manor, he had been at the Spencers' tavern where harlots strolled about in their petticoats and where rooms were provided for men to pay to do business with them. Because she so wanted to believe him a fine gentleman, she had accepted he gambled rather than whored. She had been a total ingenue and there was no excuse for such self-delusion in a spinster of nearly twenty-six.

He had been ruthlessly tricking her. She was sure now that he never truly intended them to be man and wife and his suggestion that they marry in Brighton had merely been a sham. He probably knew very well she would object to such a rushed affair, but might be seduced into travelling to Cornwall as a besotted fiancée. The tears started again as she bleakly wondered just how many *chères amies* he intended collecting. They flowed freely as she realised, despite it all, she still loved him and so wanted him to come safely back to her.

What little warmth was to be had from the parlour fire finally expired and the chill surrounding her feet seeped upwards. She wearily stood and made her way to the kitchen, taking comfort from the residual warmth in the cooking stove before she climbed the stairs to her bedroom.

The familiar redolence of dried lavender calmed her and she instinctively breathed deeply of its soothing fragrance. Removing her shawl and her shoes, she kneeled on her thick mattress, her arms self-comforting, as she simply pitched forward into the luxury of its yielding comfort. She gathered the soft, plump quilt about herself and rolled into it, holding it high and tight about her, and within a few minutes was deep in dreamless sleep.

Long dusky eyelashes swept against her warm feathery nest then weightily drooped closed. They brushed abruptly up again. It had been a sound…and there it was again. Rebecca shoved back on her elbows and strained to listen. A faint, recognisable click made her heart leap up and hammer into her throat. It was her parlour door closing, in the same quiet, careful way she shut it herself, when not wanting to disturb Lucy at night.

She scrambled from the bed, perching on the very edge of it, still woozy and befuddled from deep sleep. A trembling hand cleared tumbling golden hair from her face while the other tried to straighten her crumpled clothes. Her frantic mind attempted to weigh up possibilities. It might be Simon or Luke…or Mayhew or Blacker. Despite the viciousness in the way the Trelawneys fought, there were overwhelming odds against they and her brother being victorious at Devil's Cove. That horrifying fact made her spring from the bed and seek the wall close to the door. She hugged its cold hardness and listened again: soft footfalls in the kitchen below her bedroom were quite audible, despite the distorting, pulsing blood in her ears.

If Luke and Simon were injured…or dead…then Blacker or Mayhew would come for her and God only knew what awaited her at their hands. Her terrified mind tormented itself with Mayhew's threats to put her aboard one of his smuggling boats, yet it was the thought of Luke or Simon or even Ross laying dead that made her stuff a fist into her mouth to stifle a sob. She silently sped to the window. Scudding clouds had freed the moon and its silver glow illuminated the smooth marble top of her washstand…and her small scissors. She tiptoed back to the door and stood quaking just behind it, the cold metal gripped in one of her hands.

Her bedroom door slowly, silently swung inwards towards her and a flickering candle glow danced high upon the ceiling. A wavering male figure was traced gigantically on her wall. He had halted just out of sight behind the door, as though he too were waiting, taunting her with his presence. It was the sort of fiendish cat-and-mouse game Mayhew would revel in, she was sure. Unable to bear the suspense longer, Rebecca emerged with a sobbing cry, and lashed out wildly with her weapon, just as the man turned to go.

There was a thud and a curse as the intruder dropped the candle, plunging the room into moon-dappled darkness and then her hands were imprisoned and she was roughly pulled against a broad, black-clad torso. The familiar lemon-fresh scent and powerful feel of him was so marvellous that Rebecca's small hands fought to freedom just to clutch voraciously at him in undeniable love and stupendous relief.

An innate sensuality in the way she clung and wound herself about him forced a groaning, throaty laugh from Luke. 'I believe you missed me, Rebecca,' he murmured. One of his dark hands threaded into her hair, guiding her shadowy face towards his. And then he was urgently, deeply kissing her, as his unsteady fingers circled her neck and smoothed up and down, seeking damage.

'Are you hurt?' he broke the kiss to gasp against her mouth. 'Did they hurt you at all?' She shook her head against his face, her open mouth sweeping with unintentional allure close to his. Thumbs at her jaw tilted her face back to his and he groaned thankfulness and relief into her mouth before the kiss rekindled.

Despite the wonder of his presence and his gently erotic kiss, the spectre of Simon's fate and Ross's, and every other suspicion and fear cramming her mind tonight, began to roil and surface again. The temptation to shove them down, submerge them beneath this anodyne bliss that enveloped and subdued her whenever Luke touched her, was so enticing. But Simon's fate was paramount. And so was her pride.

Her clinging mouth and body tore from his with such abrupt force that she fell back a few paces into the room and sat upon her bed. 'Where is Simon? And your brother? What happened to those felons...Mayhew and Blacker? And what about Clarkie? Poor brave Clarkie.' She barely paused before exclaiming, 'Lucy!' She had completely forgotten about her pupil's plight in all of this. It was difficult to reconcile that so many disasters had occurred within the space of not yet one day. 'Where is Lucy? Is she safe?' she tremulously demanded.

'Hush...' Luke soothed her, immediately reaching to gather her close again. Rebecca swiftly stood up, evading him, wrapping her arms tight about herself, instilling warmth and courage. She would never again be a mindless fool she fervently vowed, avoiding eye contact with the man who could bring her to it, oh, so easily. But she needed to know the outcome of this terrible night and to extract that information in a calm, sensible way.

Luke's dark eyes narrowed on her, his intelligent gaze steady and assessing. 'Lucy is very safe and in Judith's care at the Manor,' he quietly informed her. 'She and John were en route for Scotland, hoping to wed. They hadn't travelled very far when we caught up with them.' His eyes shifted to the crumpled quilt as he said huskily, 'I thought I'd chosen the wrong room. I didn't expect you to be behind the door, armed and dangerous.' His eyes caressed her dishevelled appearance. 'I'm sorry if I disturbed you. I tried to be as quiet as I could, I guessed you might be asleep. As for your brother, he went to the Manor...as you were expected to,' he grimly reminded her. 'As to how he is...he looks a bit of a mess...'

'Is he badly hurt?' Rebecca whispered, trepidation widening her eyes to glossy stars.

'Split lip…black eye. Oh, that was me, when I discovered you weren't at the Manor where I had specifically ordered him to safely deliver you…on pain of death. So, all things considered, he got off very lightly. Apart from that, he and Ross suffered a few scratches. I think Simon might need the physician to stitch a wound in his arm but it can wait till daylight. They both seem in excellent spirits…mine, actually,' he sardonically reflected. 'The first place they headed when we got back to the Manor was the liquor store. They're no doubt still outdoing each other with tales of their past heroics…fuelled by my brandy decanter… Come here,' he tacked on the end, extending long fingers towards her.

'And you?' Rebecca quickly sidetracked. 'Are you hurt?'

'A few minor scrapes…oh, and a pair of scissors stabbed in my arm…apart from that I'm fine.'

'Oh, I'm sorry,' Rebecca breathed and rushed forward a few paces as though to investigate what damage she had wreaked. She pulled up sharp. If she was to maintain her self-possession, keeping her distance was vital.

'Don't stop,' he softly prompted. 'You were doing just fine. Come here.'

Rebecca turned and walked away, her heart thumping as she put the bed between them. Her fingers ran along the smooth marble top of the washstand. 'And Mayhew and Blacker?' she asked in a gulp. 'What of them?'

'Mayhew's dead and Blacker wounded and delivered to the local magistrate with two of his batmen who didn't make good their escape. The magistrate wasn't too happy about being woken in the early hours. The Revenue will also have some questions for them, I've no doubt.'

'For you, too, *I*'ve no doubt,' Rebecca bitterly observed and then immediately regretted the unguarded comment. She was determined to retain her caution and composure.

The ensuing, pulsating silence between them seemed interminable. 'Well, come here,' Luke eventually said wryly. 'I can't

tell you if you stay over there. Let me hold you and I'll explain.
I wish now I had told you sooner. I didn't want you to hear
fragments of it that way. I know I've been a bit reticent about
a lot of things: the danger in my past, our family's link to smuggling…and the Ramsdens. I've been foolishly waiting for the
perfect moment. I thought I had it this afternoon. Everything
was going so well. I can't remember a day I've enjoyed more…'

'A *night*, perhaps…?' Rebecca scathingly snapped.

'Come here and I'll explain that too,' he gently said, but on
a grunt of rueful laughter.

'You have explained before,' Rebecca spat at him, infuriated
by his mild amusement and unruffled manner when she was so
desolate. She gathered her golden hair away from her face in
icy, nervous hands, twisting it neatly over her shoulder. 'You
explained about other things that troubled me and so very persuasively that I actually questioned what I had seen with my
own eyes and began to believe ludicrous stories. What was I to
you?' burst furiously, unstoppably, from her. 'Some cargo to
carry off home? Some quaint rustic novelty for you to toy with
until you grew bored? What would have become of me, I wonder, when that day came, and I was far from home and friends
who truly cared for me? Ross told me you were very generous
to your discarded mistresses. He told me you would happily
return me to Sussex…secure my future and reputation…I think
that was how he put it.'

'Ross knows nothing of my affairs.'

Rebecca choked an hysterical laugh. 'What does that mean?
Was I to be sent back, then without your financial help? Is that
how you conduct your *miserly affairs*?'

Luke threw his head back, frowning regret at his thoughtless
phrasing at the silver-flecked ceiling. 'Rebecca, my patience with
this is near ending. Mayhew…Merrill, as I knew him, is a criminal of the worst sort…thief, rapist, murderer, traitor, inveterate
liar. The list is endless and I've no intention of expounding it
all now.' With a muttered curse and a few strides he was round
the bed and reaching for her.

Rebecca jerked away, crashing into the washstand, slapping

out furiously at his outstretched hands. 'Don't you dare touch me. Don't…you…dare,' she choked, silent tears slowly dropping from her eyes. 'I believed you…I trusted you…but no more.' She feebly tried to disguise her distress and regain her composure with conversation. 'You didn't say how Clarkie is,' she pushed out through the tears blocking her throat. 'Will his hand heal?'

The silence between them seemed interminable. Just as Rebecca gave up hope of a reply, he told her quietly, 'Clarkie is dead. He was a very courageous man…he deliberately gave his life ensuring that Mayhew lost his. I envy him, too. Mayhew was mine. I wanted to kill him and was about to. For some reason he wouldn't let me. He ran at Mayhew and his weight took them both over the cliff. Without him close to you tonight…' He sighed deeply into silence and bowed and shook his head.

'You're overwrought, Rebecca,' he said soothingly. 'And understandably so. We'll talk about all of this in the morning. We both need to sleep before we say any more.'

'And don't you dare patronise me either,' she raged at him. 'I might have been a childish idiot thus far, but not any more. I have nothing to discuss with you in the morning, Mr Trelawney. Or at any other time. If you would just tell Simon I should like to see him directly he rises, I would be grateful. If you would now quit my bedroom and my house, I would be more grateful still.'

Moonbeams filtered across his perfect features, highlighting his expression. There was a chilling hardness intermingled with the humour about his eyes and mouth. 'You don't want to see me any more, Rebecca?' he softly enquired. 'Are you sure?'

'More positive than I have ever been about anything,' she tremulously asserted.

'Well, I think you're probably right,' he dulcetly concurred. 'I told you once before that I will not apologise or beg forgiveness without just cause. You refuse to have faith in me; without trust and loyalty, there can be no marriage. Whatever I say…whatever I tell you about my past life, my behaviour here, there, wherever…it all meets with your suspicion. You want to believe the worst in me, don't you? Why is that? Is it safer that way?' he perceptively suggested. 'Are you frightened of what we're getting closer to? I want a wife…children. What do you want from me, Rebecca, apart from the Summer House and a goodnight kiss? I trust you. I believe everything you tell me. Yet you'd rather listen to that malicious pervert Mayhew than me.'

He paused for a long moment before saying, 'Which prompts me to ask why you felt you couldn't tell me about him abusing Lucy. You knew, didn't you? It's why you wanted her to accompany us to Cornwall. Why was it she could confide in me yet you couldn't?'

'Why would you care?' Rebecca threw recklessly up into his dark face. 'You're a lecher, too, aren't you?'

He smiled slowly and she knew she had backed herself both physically and verbally into a corner.

'If that's what you insist I am, Rebecca. Anything to please you.'

Rebecca sensed ice stinging her face and body. She had lost all advantage, all control, and was way out of her depth and floundering. She hadn't anticipated this. She had expected he might be forced on the defensive, not that this showdown might require her apologies.

Rebecca glanced fearfully up at him. She hadn't seen him move yet he seemed closer, mere inches away now and towering over her. The moon escaped the cloud once more, brightening the room. She threw her silver-gilt head back and met his eyes squarely, implying a courage she was far from feeling.

'You're no better than those villains at Devil's Cove, are you? And masquerading here as a gentleman has all been too much for you, hasn't it? I can understand now why you never intended staying. Maintaining the sham must have been so arduous…quite beyond you,' she uttered scathingly, starting to slide away from him. As a dark hand propped idly against the marble top of the washstand, she shifted in the opposite direction. As his other casually leaned for support too, trapping her between rigid muscular arms, she became quite still.

'I take it with that little character assessment you're terminating our betrothal,' he drily observed.

Rebecca managed a brief nod of her head, not deigning to bestow on him speech.

'Well, I'd rather we didn't finish on bad terms,' he said.

'There is no other way for us, I fear,' she breathlessly rejected his conciliation.

'Surely a kiss then before parting, Rebecca?' he lazily suggested, not bothering to hide his amusement or confidence.

The knowledge that he was still laughing at her and she was still utterly despondent made her swing a hand up at his face with all the bitter pain of humiliation and betrayal and loss. The blow knocked his head sideways but, that apart, his stance remained unflinching. He turned back slowly to look at her, then straightened, and his hands removed from the marble top to cool her flushed face. His thumbs brushed her pearl-satin skin as dark eyes travelled her features and settled on her mouth. Her lids lowered as his face neared hers with tormenting leisure. He kissed her with thorough expertise, imprisoning her between the washstand at her back and his strong immovable body.

For one whole minute she fought him, standing frigidly, until the heat moistening her mouth and her loins spread and betrayed her, tenderly filling her breasts and liquifying her limbs. She sobbed in anguished surrender to it, rested into him and allowed him to swing her up in his arms. His mouth was still fused to hers in a kiss of calculated seduction as he carried her to the bed, lowered her gently and followed her down.

By the time their slick mouths slowly unsealed, Rebecca's breathing was shallow and erratic. Luke raised himself on his elbows to look at her and she followed him up, as though magnetised, eyes closed and slender throat arching temptingly towards him. His hands supported her head, long fingers digging deep into the silky mass of hair as he gently, abruptly made her look at him.

'Do you realise how terrified I was today, Rebecca, when I

found out Mayhew had you?' he demanded hoarsely. 'I have lived most of my adult life in danger but, today, when Miles gave me that scrap of paper and I thought I might have lost you…' His husky voice cracked and Rebecca gazed up wide-eyed at his first loss of control. He sat up properly, pulling her with him so she half-straddled his lap and their faces were inches apart.

'Don't do this to me, Rebecca. I told you yesterday that I've lived the life of a typical Cornish bachelor…I'm neither saint nor sinner. Just a man. And if I've been drawn into smuggling because of my heritage, you shall have to blame those damnable Ramsdens you revere. For they started it all.'

The shock and disbelief in Rebecca's face made him give her a lop-sided smile. 'It's true,' he said with mild emphasis. He settled her more comfortably against him, his chin resting atop her golden head as he recounted the story.

'When my great-grandmother Charlotte Ramsden eloped to Cornwall with my great-grandfather Jago Trelawney her family were outraged. They believed it was he who had seduced her. But he was simply a respectable, but devilishly handsome—oh, it runs in the family—' he interrupted himself to tease her 'young man in Brighton visiting a relative. But Charlotte saw him in town and the rest, as they say, is history.

'Family folklore has it that, in fact, it was she who seduced him and when he left for Cornwall, she followed him home. But he loved her and they were happy despite being quite poor and living frugally. Coming from a well-to-do family, Charlotte was used to pretty things. So she bought some French lace from an itinerant smuggler…then French perfume and brandy. She had a good business brain and realised that if her fisherman husband crossed the channel for her, luxuries would be cheaper still and she could have more of them. He did anything to please her…another family tradition, perhaps,' he reflected with dry self-mockery.

'Anyway, that was the founding of one of Cornwall's greatest smuggling dynasties. One hundred years later my father was the finish of it. The free-trading Trelawneys died with him.

'He and Merrill were bitter adversaries, although in the same trade. My father smuggled and made a fortune from it but there were things he would never do: take payment from the homeless *émigrés* escaping the French revolution who pleaded for passage to England, or betray his country in any way. Merrill had no such qualms. He would do anything for money and only for money and, if payment was not forthcoming, he would kill without compunction.

'A French aristocrat and his family fleeing persecution were unlucky enough to be brought over by Merrill. They had nothing apart from the clothes they stood in. When he realised that they couldn't pay him, he killed the count and raped his wife and daughter. My father happened to be on the same stretch of beach that night, unloading. So was I.

'I was eighteen then and in the family business although, even at that time, I preferred our Bristol shipping office. There was always a legitimate side to Trelawney shipping, more as a screen than an enterprise, but only I saw its potential. Tristan and Ross…especially Ross,' he grunted on a rueful laugh, 'always preferred the excitement of night runs and skirmishes with the Revenue. Well, to be honest, they were quite exhilirating times and useful, for we all learned to fight young and well.'

He sobered and sighed. 'My father and I came upon the distraught French women and the count's body just as Merrill was setting off again. A vicious fight broke out between the Merrill camp and the Trelawneys. My father sustained a serious back injury inflicted by Merrill's dagger, for the cowardly bastard had knifed him from behind. But he seemed to recover.

'While he was out of action, recuperating, I had started to put more emphasis on legitimate transactions and expanded our fleet at Bristol. He began to see that there was colossal profit to be made. But that same injury killed him three years later. Almost to the day.

'Finding Merrill and killing him was always a priority. I thought I had done so four years ago, at Lizard Point in Cornwall when the Trelawneys and the Revenue ran his motley crew to ground. I have some fast cutters I allow the Revenue to use against the smugglers. I have been getting personally involved in a lot of skirmishing…more than I need to. But old habits die hard, I suppose, and then there's Ross to keep entertained and on the straight and narrow. Sometimes I worry that a smuggling life might seduce him back. He continually craves for adventure. Perhaps it's in his blood.'

Rebecca felt his warm breath on her neck a moment before the moist heat of his lips touched behind a sensitive ear, making her lids droop and her head sway.

'I'm not going to pretend that I'm morally outraged by the principle of free-trading; but for the most part it is operated by vicious thugs, and commercially I lose. Legitimate trade always suffers when smuggling is rife. It is impossible to compete with contraband prices and I was always determined to be a wealthy shipping magnate…and I am.'

He raised a caressing hand from her hip to touch her golden hair. Taking a thick, silky strand, he smoothed it between his long fingers and thumb before they threaded up close to her scalp, turning her to face him. His hard narrow mouth rested close to hers as he softly enquired, 'Do you believe me, Rebecca, or still suspect me a villain?'

Interminable silence throbbed between them. Tell me about your mistresses too, she wanted to scream at him. Tell me you don't love this dark-haired woman who believes you wed. She merely murmured, 'I'm not sure.'

'Well, I'm sure you know what an incorrigible reprobate would do with you next.'

Rebecca swallowed and moistened her lips, unwittingly drawing glittering eyes to her glistening mouth.

'So who am I, Rebecca? Your fiancé or a marauding Cornish smuggler?' was breathed warmly, softly against her chilled face.

'You're the man I was betrothed to,' she finally said.

Chapter Fourteen

'Good to see you again, Simon,' Mr Johnson greeted the blond man before turning his attention to Rebecca. He cordially extended a large hand and solicitously found her a chair.

Simon watched the gallantry with a jaundiced eye. Not so long ago he had been plain 'Mr Nash', and not nearly so welcome as he appeared to be now his account was bursting with almost six thousand pounds.

'Miss Nash, you are aware that your brother is today to transfer your inheritance into your own account and henceforth you may use those funds as you choose?' the bank manager asked.

Rebecca smiled vaguely. 'Yes, I am aware of that,' she confirmed. She simply wanted these niceties over and to be back out into the refreshing seaside air, for her interminable headache seemed worse today. Worse than it had for the past week. It had come upon her when she had cried herself to sleep the night Luke had slammed out of her life for ever. She hadn't had a day free of it since. She pushed those hurtful, humiliating memories aside and concentrated on Mr Johnson's droning advice.

'...at compound rates of seven per centum,' his voice penetrated her mind. She smiled and nodded, adopting an expression of what she hoped passed for intelligent interest befitting a spinster of twenty-six as he advised on stocks, bonds and other investments. For she was, indeed, now twenty-six, she sadly realised. Three days ago, she was miserably sure, was the date she became a confirmed old maid.

'But I'm sure your brother will advise you on such matters...' Mr Johnson's nasal speech cut into her melancholy.

Rebecca noticed with a small, wry smile that Simon had the grace to blush at the unhappy inference that he be her trusty financial adviser.

Mr Johnson pushed papers across his desk towards her. 'Just sign these please, my dear, so all the formalities are taken care of.' As Rebecca finished with the documents, he convivially remarked, 'A young lady of such independent means will doubtless want her own property. Perhaps even two. For renting one in the season could bring you a nice income. And you must make your money work for you, you know. I have heard your grandfather made excellent profits as a landlord. I could put you in touch with a property agent I know...'

'Thank you but, at present, I am not ready for such commitments. I need some time to think...'

'Of course...' He gave an apologetic smile. 'No doubt you'll want to wait and see who your new landlord is. He may be kind enough to sell you the Summer House, for I know from what your brother has told me, you have a particular fondness for that little building.'

'True, but as the ownership of Ramsden Manor is still so uncertain, Rebecca will not want to wait for ever,' Simon interceded, quite swayed towards the bank manager's idea that Rebecca should find a new home and a business venture to boot.

'Oh, the matter of the Ramsden estate is finalised. I hear from my acquaintance, Willoughby, that the matter is now settled. But I know no more.'

'The Trelawneys are soon moving out?' Rebecca demanded in one shaky breath.

'Packing up to go even as we speak, so I have heard. Now, if I can be of any help to you, Miss Nash, with investments or advice, please do not hesitate to come and see me.' The encouragement was sincere: female clients were a rarity. One of such stunning good looks was definitely a sight for sore eyes in his dusty office. She had quite brightened his day; a pity he seemed to have dampened hers. The pretty lass had been in better spirits on first meeting twenty minutes ago.

'Well, that's now done and out of the way.' Simon sighed his satisfaction as they gained the cobbled street and the warmth of a pale November sun. 'Let's go to Dilly's teashop for a brew and a bite to eat before I take you home. Oh, I have some news for you,' he mentioned in passing, as he took Rebecca's arm and they strolled on.

Rebecca lifted her cup absently to her mouth, then replaced it untasted. 'Did you know that Luke and Ross were readying to leave for Cornwall?'

'No,' Simon admitted. 'They've said nothing to me. But then I've not seen a lot of Luke recently, and Ross and I…well…' he grimaced uneasily.

'You mean when you two get together you're both usually too in your cups to discuss anything sensible,' Rebecca mildly censured him.

'He is grand company…' Simon excused his excesses with a boyish smile.

'What news have you for me?' Rebecca asked, before sipping her tea and gazing through the teashop window. She watched an urchin flower seller accosting strollers and children playing hopscotch in patches of autumn sun.

Three months ago this would have been one of the happiest, most fulfilling days of her life. After five anxiety-ridden years, struggling to earn enough to live, her future was finally secure. She had enough money of her own to live free from worry for the rest of her days. She could even afford small luxuries, yet she felt empty and depressed.

'I shall be leaving the area soon, Rebecca.' Simon cautiously broke the news of his departure. 'I have employment,' he proudly finished. 'Luke has offered me a position at his Bristol shipping office. If all goes well, I might get aboard a vessel.'

Rebecca stared at him, stunned by the fact that he was going away again and who was responsible for her loss. 'Luke has given you work? Why?'

'He said he might some while ago and he has proved true to his word.'

'I thought you were promised a chance of employment with the investment company you used....' Rebecca's words tailed off. When would she grow up? When would she stop being such a credulous idiot? Her fingers tightened about her cup as her brain sifted information and found answers. She watched the hopscotch games as she said bitterly, 'It was his company you invested with. Was it his money, too? Was nothing left of my inheritance?'

'No,' Simon quietly admitted. 'I didn't have a penny, so he loaned me two thousand pounds and I made a ridiculous profit on it. I've paid him back,' he quickly affirmed. 'Every penny I borrowed has been returned. His only stipulation... command...was that your money was to be repaid, and that I should let you think that the scheme was my idea.'

'I see...' Rebecca breathed, knowing she didn't really see at all why Luke would go to such lengths to help her or why, having done so, he would try to hide such generosity.

Probably her independent means ensured she would never be a financial burden once she was discarded. She closed her eyes and ground her teeth. It was probably nothing of the sort. He was kind and generous and the honest gentleman she had always wanted to believe him. All that he had recounted about his fight against smuggling on the last fateful night she had seen him had been confirmed to her the very next day...and by her own brother. Luke had been right. Luke was always right, she wistfully acknowledged. Had she done as he said and slept before making accusations, by the following day she would have had the validation she required.

For Luke, Ross and Simon had been summoned back by the magistrate to give evidence and information of the circumstances of the affray at Devil's Cove. The Revenue men were there too, Simon had told her. He had also told her in what high esteem Luke Trelawney was held by those men and how grateful they were for his loan of vessels to aid in ridding the south coast of treacherous free-traders.

She was so ready to believe him mean-spirited because accepting she had lost him through pride and jealousy was anathema. She shook trailing curls of honey hair back from her face and gazed through the window at the laughing children, desperately rallying and summoning back those very failings. He was still a philanderer. He had no excuses that night for the women he kept. No denial or sweet words of explanation there.

'You won't tell him we've spoken of this, will you, Rebecca?' Simon broke into her self-torment. 'He was adamant you shouldn't know of his part in reinstating your inheritance. If he found out I had betrayed his trust…I don't want to jeopardise my opportunity with Trelawney Shipping. I'll never get another as good…'

'I shan't say anything, Simon,' Rebecca cut in. 'In all probability I shall never again see Luke; even a chance meeting is unlikely if they are soon to return to Cornwall.' The truth in this statement made her voice brittle and a sheen enhance the brilliance of her aqua-coloured eyes.

'It's just a tiff,' Simon dismissed lightly, quite genuinely bewildered by his sister's distress. 'Ross knows nothing of any rift between you and Luke or that your betrothal is over.'

'I would rather you didn't discuss this with anyone, Simon,' Rebecca emphasised in a hiss, white with shock. 'It was never an official betrothal. If Luke has said nothing, probably he too feels it concerns no one else.' Or probably it bothers him little, she sadly thought.

She was aware of Simon's dark blue eyes scanning her face. Lowering his voice, he said, 'It wasn't anything to do with what that fiend Mayhew told you…about…'

Simon halted and cleared his throat. Discussing another man's mistresses with a female relative was almost as embarrassing and unheard of as discussing one's own. But he was her brother: she had no mother to advise her and he guessed that their self-centred older sister Elizabeth had never bothered to put her straight on such matters. A surge of affection softened him. He did owe her so very much. He wanted to see her happy and settled. A subtle tack was required.

'You know very little of what goes on in the world, Rebecca,' he began gently. 'You have shut yourself away for too long in Graveley…with just the Turners and the vicar and his wife as adult company. Because you have no experience of…umm… society and…er, men and the way they go on…'

Rebecca raised limpid turquoise eyes to her brother's kindly blue gaze. 'If you are trying to say that Luke has mistresses and I shouldn't let that bother me for it's commonly accepted behaviour…' Her voice faded away.

Simon blushed to the roots of his blond hair but he managed to stutter, 'I'm sure he loves you, Rebecca, no matter what he does…or who else he… Dammit, Rebecca,' he groaned, 'you're not supposed to even acknowledge such…things, even if you do hear about them.'

A pained laugh escaped Rebecca. 'I have a splitting headache, Simon,' she cut into his confusion with the quite truthful complaint. 'Would you take me home?'

'I've packed up the rest of Lucy's things,' Martha told Rebecca as she walked in through the kitchen door, removed her bonnet and discarded it on a kitchen chair. 'Gregory can take the trunk over in the morning, if you like.'

Rebecca gave the woman a grateful smile and thought of Lucy, back at home now with her mother. Simon had returned Lucy home the day after the fracas at Devil's Cove, and she knew by the time they arrived late that afternoon, the woman would already have had a visit from the authorities regarding her dead husband and his nefarious activities. Rebecca could only guess how poor Mrs Mayhew must be feeling. She only hoped that the removal of that odious man from her life was accepted with the same quiet contentment that Lucy had received the news of her stepfather's death. Rebecca had an instinct that Rupert Mayhew would have treated all the women in his life in the same appalling manner.

'Has your headache cleared?' Martha interrupted Rebecca's thoughts.

'A bit better, thank you, Martha,' Rebecca lied. If she told the truth, Martha would fuss the evening through, trying to ply her with potions, instead of returning to her cottage with Gregory.

'I heard today from Mr Johnson at the bank that the Trelawneys are packing up to leave. Do you know if that's true, Martha? Have you heard?'

Martha removed her apron and carefully folded it. 'I believe it is, Miss Becky.' She raised her grey eyes to study Rebecca's tense features. 'If he won't come to you, you should go and see him,' she prompted. 'Perhaps it can't be put right…but you won't want him going away thinking bad of you, now will you?' She sighed and shook her greying head. 'Supper's in the oven,' she added, then hesitated at the kitchen door as though about to say more, but with a sad grimace was gone.

Rebecca swallowed, then swallowed again, trying to clear the blockage forming in her throat. She would not cry. She would not cry again, she threatened herself and abruptly stood up. She walked through into her parlour and then aimlessly back to the kitchen. It was so quiet and lonely now Lucy had gone. Simon now used the Summer House as lodgings, but she rarely saw him. He only used her home to sleep and eat, she wryly realised. She sat at the table and looked about her kitchen, pondering on what Mr Johnson had said about the possibility of buying the Summer House from the new landlord. Or purchasing a larger property in town, perhaps to rent. A shaky hand went to her face. She couldn't concentrate on anything.

With a cloth protecting her hands, she withdrew the earthenware dish from the oven and looked at the tempting chicken and vegetable hotpot. She put it on to the draining board to cool for she knew she would never eat it. Her stomach rolled, but with nausea, not hunger. She automatically covered the meal with the cloth in case Simon wanted it when he arrived home.

Her eyes shut tight against the abrupt sting of tears. Her golden head sank forward and with every ounce of her being she willed Luke to come to her. Even the haunting mortification of their parting could not diminish her desperate need to see him.

Her body flamed at the memory of their final hour together when he had tantalised her inch by squirming inch with sweet seduction and ruthless passion into such fevered surrender that she had actually pleaded for release, not once but twice before he finished with her. For she had tasted the ecstasy of fulfilment on a tavern bed; and he had promised her, when his hands were at liberty, it would be rapturous. But it was such bitter pleasure. Those long, hard fingers had merely been instruments of torture, as had his cruel mouth. He had not once kissed her. Even when she desperately sought to intercept his mouth with her own before it could recommence plundering her body, he would not allow it. Leisurely, punishing torment would ensue until she clung and writhed and raised herself against him.

That was when he would deliberately break contact with her raw, aroused body and stroke her face or her hair until some of her aching need died and her shame and pride renewed and she would fight to spring from the bed. And he would start again.

As dawnlight flushed the sky and he straddled her once more she had finally found the will to lash out but not to stop the tears. His pitiless mouth teasingly lowered, just touching hers when she no longer cared. Firm fingers slid against her wet face forcing her to look at him as he tauntingly enquired, 'Is that enough to remember your Cornish smuggler by?' before he left her with the sound of the door crashing closed, echoing in her ears.

Rebecca gazed through the kitchen window at the fading light. If she was going she ought to go now to return before dusk. And she knew she would go. Just as two months ago she had had to go and apologise for her immaturity, so she had to go now, before he went away, and do so again. For she was still lacking in worldliness, as Simon had so rightly judged earlier today.

Martha was right, too. She couldn't bear the thought of him returning to Cornwall and thinking ill of her. Her insults that night made her head bow now with shame. He was also due her thanks. For without him she would be still penniless and perhaps even dead or worse by Mayhew's hand. She owed him so much, and so wanted to see him, just once more; her pride was a small price to pay.

The grass felt damp against her legs as she hoisted her silver-grey skirts and nimbly climbed the last stile. The countryside was so different to the last time she had walked this meadow, with thundering heart, to speak to him. Then the weather had still been warm and sultry, the grass still short and dry from a long hot summer. But it was mild weather for this time of year, she impressed upon herself, her thoughts cleaving to any topic rather than the coming encounter.

She shook her skirts to straighten them as she gained the parkland that abutted the driveway to the Manor and began calmly walking across it. In the distance she glimpsed John, recognising him by his fair head. The sight of that young man made her wonder whether he and Lucy would again see each other now she was back home. John was leading that coal-black stallion Luke rode. So Luke was at home. Her pace didn't falter. Her eyes closed and she threw back her head a little, instilling courage. Her hands impulsively tidied stray locks of honey hair and she smoothed her skirts. She approached the corner of the mellow brick house and rounded the corner to the great door. And froze.

It couldn't be happening to her. Not again. The scene that greeted her removed her heartbeat and her courage. But it was too late to quietly withdraw, she realised, panic-stricken, for he had raised his head away from the woman he embraced, and seen her.

Their eyes locked across the brunette's glossy head. His expression terrified her. He looked pleased…almost triumphant. He put the woman away from him and walked towards her.

'I'm sorry,' Rebecca murmured, admirably controlling her voice and her spontaneous need to flee. 'I…I didn't mean to intrude. I have simply come to bid you farewell. Goodbye,' she managed before twisting swiftly away and heading back towards her meadow.

A dark hand on her arm halted her and turned her about. The overwhelming urge to lash out at him was just curbed. Aware of the young woman curiously watching them, she simply jerked her arm free of his grasp.

It was impossible not to stare. She was very pretty, Rebecca realised. Very pretty and very young, nothing like she would have imagined from Mayhew's lewd description. This woman—girl, for she looked still to be in her teens—had a fresh beauty, not the voluptuous appeal that had tormented her. Somehow that made it all so much worse. And Luke did love her. She had witnessed not a quick affectionate hug for a friend but a close leisurely embrace for someone cherished.

'I'm glad you've come over, Rebecca,' Luke soothed her, taking her arm to draw her forward. 'I'd like you to meet my sister.'

Wide, disbelieving turquoise eyes immediately sought his face, making his mouth twist in bitterness. Rebecca glanced back at the pretty girl, remembering the last time she had been at Ramsden Manor and strange young women were explained away as someone's 'sisters'.

As though recalling the same incident, a grunt of hard laughter choked in his throat and he stared off into the distance. 'Shall I find my mother to confirm her identity?' he sardonically suggested and so quietly that only Rebecca heard.

'Katherine,' he called, beckoning to the young woman. She approached straight away with a friendly smile.

'Katherine, this is Rebecca Nash, a very dear friend.' Initially Rebecca's eyes searched his for sarcasm at this introduction. Then, as though the French translation occurred to them both at the same time, Rebecca blushed and looked at the gravel drive and he pivoted on his heel with a savage curse. 'Where are the others?' he bit out to his sister with steely control. 'I should like to introduce them all to Rebecca.'

Katherine was distracted from answering.

'My lord,' Miles huffed out, as he hobbled down the stone

steps. 'Mr Willoughby wants to speak with you... Hello, Miss Rebecca,' he broke off to greet Rebecca immediately he laid eyes on her. 'I haven't seen you for a while. Why haven't you been by to see us? Judith was only saying the other day, Where's that Miss Becky been? My lord, he says it's urgent you inspect these documents,' Miles's meandering discourse turned on his master.

'Tell him to wait,' Luke enunciated carefully through closed teeth.

Undeterred by his master's odd moods, which he was now quite coming to terms with—for over the past week Miles had experienced everything from blackest rage to saddest despair— he ignored this mild testiness and continued about his business. 'And young Mr Trelawney says he wants to speak to you about which mount is best for Miss Katherine. The grey mare or the...'

A low string of oaths trailed in Luke's wake as he stalked off a few paces, hands thrust deep in his pockets, as though to steady his temper.

Miles was unperturbed and smilingly took Rebecca's hand, patting it affectionately in pleasure at seeing her after all these weeks.

Luke watched them for a moment before approaching again. 'Come inside the house. I'll apologise now for it's like a lunatic asylum in there,' he said tightly. 'But Katherine will keep you company until I have dealt with Willoughby. Please,' he urged softly as she hung back. 'I'm very glad you've come to talk to me.'

'Rebecca and I will be fine, Luke,' his sister said with a smile. 'I shall find Mama...oh, and Sara and Jago.'

The names washed meaninglessly over Rebecca as Katherine linked arms with her as though she had known her for years and lead her to the steps of the Manor. But Rebecca's eyes were fixed on Luke's tall athletic figure as he took the front steps two at a time, his tense speed denoting great exasperation.

Entering the familiar cool hallway was like walking into mild chaos and explained Luke's odd apology for the state of his house. There were packing cases lining the walls and large documents strewn around on hall tables. There were several men of business perusing the paperwork.

As she took two paces into the house a young boy of about five careered into her. Rebecca automatically steadied the child on his feet.

He grinned mischievously at her as Katherine swung him up into her arms and planted a kiss on his forehead. He struggled to be put down again and she complied, ruffling his jet-black hair.

'That's young Jago, named after his grandfather and his great-great grandfather,' Katherine helpfully supplied as the young boy dashed down the stone steps. 'He's my nephew, Tristan's son. Tristan couldn't come. He's looking after Melrose. But his wife, Sara, is here. There she is,' Katherine said, indicating a petite brunette who was ascending the stairs, carrying an armful of colourful gowns. 'She came along with us to keep Jago happy. He does so love his two uncles. I'll introduce you to Sara later. I wonder where Mama is...' She gazed searchingly around the strewn hallway. 'She's probably gone to lie down in a darkened room,' Katherine giggled, surveying the disorder. 'I think it's all been too much.' She turned amused, hazel eyes on Rebecca and at that moment her likeness to Ross was quite undeniable.

'As you might have guessed, Luke wasn't expecting us. Do you know, in all the time he has been in Sussex he has sent us only two proper letters,' she complained. 'The rest were all business missives for Tristan about the mines and shipping and boring suchlike. No gossip. But we knew there must be something vital keeping him away from Melrose. He likes to think he's indispensable. So we decided to come and investigate, and make it a surprise. And here we all are on the very day he is packing up to move out. I don't think he's very pleased about the timing of our surprise.' Katherine grimaced.

'I'm sure you all meant well.' Rebecca managed to edge a few words into the chatty monologue, before her eyes once more anxiously sought Luke's face. Katherine was right: he didn't look pleased at all, she realised, biting her lip. He probably wasn't very pleased about the timing of her surprise either. She must have considerably worsened his temper by turning up unexpectedly at such an inopportune moment. He obviously had important business matters as well as his family to deal with.

Because he was such a gentleman he had tried to make her feel welcome; but it must be inconvenient and embarrassing for him to have her around right now. No wonder he looked so irritated.

It was impossible to detach her hungry eyes from his lean profile. The angular planes of his jaw looked sooty and she realised he was unshaven. He looked a little haggard too, probably lacking in sleep, she guessed. She discreetly watched him listening, head bowed, to a middle-aged fair-haired man who was indicating something on a large, unwieldy document, while trying to position the flapping chart against the wall for support. Luke shifted position at that precise moment and looked up straight at her.

The noise and bustle in the hallway seemed to recede and Rebecca was aware of nothing for a long moment but the intense dark eyes trained on her with such relentless force that she felt her knees weaken.

'You have lovely hair…and eyes.' The compliment finally penetrated through her trance and Rebecca tore her eyes away.

'Thank you,' she said graciously to Katherine, frantically wondering how she could extricate herself and slip away. She was sure it was what Luke really wanted, despite his well-mannered insistence she stay.

'Ross said you were very beautiful,' Katherine added, making Rebecca wonder why Ross would have bothered mentioning her at all.

'Oh, look, here's Ross now,' Katherine said, spying her brother exiting the library into the crowded hall with a glass in one hand and a large piece of cake in the other.

Catching sight of Rebecca, Ross immediately walked over. 'Hello, Rebecca; nice to see you,' he said with a genuine warmth. He looked about for Luke then back at her and seemed about to say something, but decided against it.

'You didn't say Simon was still here,' Katherine chided Ross.

Rebecca had already noticed her brother and was staring, amazed, as he too emerged from the library with a slice of cake in his hand. 'This is Ross's friend, Simon,' Katherine said in a low, excited breath. 'I met him earlier today. Isn't he so handsome?' she quietly squealed.

'Note the family likeness,' Ross drily hinted with a private grin at Rebecca. When his sister looked mystified, he relented. 'Simon is Rebecca's brother.'

Katherine looked from one to the other of them. At Rebecca's wry confirmation, Katherine blushed, mortified, and actually punched Ross slyly on the arm. 'Why didn't you say?' she hissed, with her head down, before another crafty thump made him spill his drink and a quarrel start.

'You young people…you do love a rumpus,' Judith scolded, unsuccessfully suppressing a smile. 'Hello, Miss Becky…now why haven't you been by before to see us?' She proffered the tray she held laden with slices of madeira cake, treacle biscuits and glasses of pale wine.

'I planned to,' Rebecca told her quite loudly over the warring siblings, shaking her head to decline anything from the tray. 'There have been so many unexpected turns of event…'

'It's all been so exciting, hasn't it?' Judith said with shining eyes. 'What with smugglers…and fighting…and the Revenue. And I'm so pleased that young Simon's back from his travels. It's so nice to have a houseful like this.' She chuckled. 'Just like the old days. We used to have some wonderful times years ago. I've catered for hundreds in my time,' she impressed upon Rebecca, before turning to offer her refreshments elsewhere. Her foot kicked against a wooden toy boat discarded on the marble tiles and it skidded noisily away. She gave a little screech as her tray tilted.

A firm hand drew Rebecca backwards, out of the chaos just as she heard Katherine demand, 'What smugglers? Ross, you haven't… If Mama finds out you've been involved…'

The last Rebecca saw as Luke wordlessly lead her away was Simon steadying Judith's tray while helping himself to a glass of wine. As they passed the men of business, Luke bid them terse farewells. But his pace didn't slacken until he reached his study door.

'I'm sorry,' he quietly said. 'The whole place is bedlam.' He leaned against the door, head tilted back, and sighed as he turned the key in the lock behind him.

Rebecca's eyes immediately latched on to the movement.

'To keep them out, Rebecca, not you within,' he drily reassured her before he pushed away from the door.

'Sit down, Rebecca,' he quietly, politely invited her. As he seated himself behind his desk, she took the wing-chair she had used the last time she sat before him in trepidation. He looked at her and started to speak but a child's cry cut across the words. It escalated to a scream, then changed to laughter.

Luke swiped a hand about his shadowy, angular chin, stifling a muttered imprecation and Rebecca knew he was about to apologise again for his family.

A rush of tenderness swamped her. She had never seen him so vulnerable…so tense. It made her want to rush around the desk and hold him, comfort him. She felt warm blood suffuse her face at the very idea. His reaction to such a show of affection might wound her battered pride yet further. He had made it quite clear that their relationship was over when he had taunted her with having something to remember him by. Memories of what he had done to her before his callous abandonment shattered her fragile self-possession completely. Another rush of blood stung her face and she could bear no more.

'I'm sorry, I've arrived at a bad time,' she tremulously said, hastily standing up. He stood too, as though to prevent her leaving.

'*They*'ve come at a bad time, Rebecca. Not you. I was hoping you would come over once you found out I was moving out.' He allowed self-mockery to twist his mouth. 'For if you hadn't…I would have given in later today and come to you, and I didn't want that.'

His words and wry expression confused her. But she was aware he wouldn't yet let her leave. She searched for conversation to mask her wavering courage and her desolation. For he really *was* leaving. The evidence was scattered about his hallway and now he had confirmed it to her. 'I like Katherine very much…Ross, too. You're very lucky to have your family about you. Sometimes I long for those days when Simon, Elizabeth and I were all at home together as a family, arguing and fighting,' she wistfully told him.

'Arguing and fighting, Rebecca? You?' he softly mocked.

Rebecca blushed but defended her tomboy days. 'Of course. Elizabeth and I would run Mama ragged with our constant bickering. She was always saying she would box our ears if we didn't stop. I hit Elizabeth once with my hairbrush when she stole my favourite doll. I suppose I was about twelve then,' she said, a reflective little smile curving her soft mouth. 'Mama was furious…she thought I'd knocked one of her teeth out.'

Aware of his amused interest and unnervingly steady attention, she fell awkwardly silent. He seemed in no hurry to say anything, so to lighten the expectant tension, she continued, 'And Simon and I were always squabbling over who won games. One day, when he accused me of cheating, I punched him and threw the chessboard at him.' This time she had nothing further to add to break the quiet. She stood before him, unsure why on earth she had just confided those private, precious memories.

'Did he hit you back?' Luke eventually asked, not quite so amused.

A sweet, nostalgic smile met his anxiety. 'No. Simon used to indulge me; and I did cheat sometimes,' she softly admitted. 'But he nearly always let me win…even when I didn't deserve to.'

'Strange…you have the same effect on me, Rebecca…' he slowly, sardonically, said.

Rebecca raised searching eyes to his. There was no sign of vulnerability now.

Chapter Fifteen

'What have you come to say to me, Rebecca?' Luke asked with such quiet determination that even an excited shriek from his nephew echoing around the hallway didn't elicit any change in his expression.

Clammy hands gripped together behind her back. She had come to take her leave and she would. She had come to apologise and thank him too, and she would do so, she exhorted herself.

'Shall we sit down again?' he suggested with a wry smile.

Rebecca gratefully sank into the chair, relieving legs that felt too weak to support her. 'Simon and I were in town...at the bank. I learned that you are moving out and came to say good-bye,' she said quickly. 'I didn't want you to leave and...'

'And...?' he tonelessly prompted.

'And think I was ill mannered enough not to...to... I—I didn't want us to part on bad terms,' she stammered.

'I thought there was no other way for us, Rebecca? Wasn't that what you told me?' he remorselessly reminded her.

Remembering the words she had tossed at him in her bedroom a week ago made her colour rise and her eyelids lower. She banished the mortifying memories and hastened on. 'I also...I owe you an apology. I said some unforgivable things. I insulted you, and I am very sorry. I was wrong to suspect you...accuse you of consorting with smugglers or with…people who are none of my concern.'

'Which people?' he relentlessly probed.

She tossed her golden head back then and glared at him. She would not mention his mistresses. She would not give him the satisfaction of glimpsing her distress or jealousy. But she hadn't yet finished. She still owed him thanks and she would complete what she had come to do. 'I also wish to thank you for the return of my inheritance.' She froze. She had completely forgotten that Simon had charged her never to speak of it, that it might affect his future employment with Luke's shipping company.

Wide turquoise eyes darted anxiously to his face. 'I guessed you had helped Simon return my money…that he invested in your company,' she breathlessly added. 'And I am extremely grateful.'

'When did you guess? Before or after he told you?'

Rebecca winced at the heavy irony, then again at his next curt words.

'I don't want your gratitude, Rebecca…or your indebtedness…or your sense of duty.'

His eyes roved her beautiful wan face. It was time to give in. He'd gained nothing by staying away: the strain of it was nearly killing him. Now she was before him in all her delicate golden glory he wasn't sure how he had managed it. This absurd situation was as much his fault as hers. His pride, her jealousy…her distrust, her immaturity…well, almost as much his fault, he wryly thought.

But then it was her artless innocence that had endeared him in the first place. He should have told her that he loved her weeks ago. Had he spoken sooner, he was certain their estrangement would never have come about. For it was all she had ever desired. Just the words—not possessions, material tokens of his honourable intentions. He'd waited, wanting perfection for her and ended up giving her nothing. And damn Merrill to eternal hellfire, for his malicious, lecherous tongue.

She now wouldn't rest easy until it was all brought into the open. Yet there had been no reason for her to know. The irony of it: none of those women had been of any real consequence, yet the fact that she knew they existed, and her knowledge was incomplete, was devastating her.

'Which people?' he gently demanded.

Rebecca ignored his persistent question. 'Simon didn't tell me, I swear. I…I'm glad he is to work for you in Bristol,' she added for good measure.

'If I don't employ Simon, it's likely he'll end up in gaol,' he casually imparted to her.

'What do you mean?' Rebecca gasped, her complexion chalky.

'Blacker let the Revenue know your brother was an associate of his and had been runnning contraband. The only way to appease them was to imply Simon had been spying on free-trading along the south coast at my behest. Were I to withdraw that…?' The subtle message drifted between them.

'Which people, Rebecca?' he very deliberately repeated, leaning across the desk towards her, hands lightly clasped in front of him. His warm gaze on her chilled face was obdurate and determined to exact an answer.

She moistened parched lips. 'Your mistresses,' spilled out, but so weakly she prayed he wouldn't expect her to repeat the hateful words.

'My mistresses? Women I consorted with before I even knew you? Why would they concern you?'

His enquiry was so mildly curious, she felt foolish. 'They don't,' she choked, rising immediately. She was reaching for the handle when she remembered the door was locked. And the key was removed. 'I want to be home before dusk…'

'Come, tell me why they trouble you,' he insisted. 'Should I worry that you were once engaged to a man you loved? It is in the past.'

'David is dead,' Rebecca whispered. 'He is gone from me forever. I will never see him again.'

'And neither will I see again any of the women I kept in Cornwall…except by unlucky chance. Do you believe me?'

'No,' she flung back at once, twisting about. 'Mayhew swore your current mistress considers you already married to her...in all but name.'

'Perhaps she did stupidly believe that,' Luke allowed quietly. 'But she wisely never said as much to me. I choose who is to become my wife and it would never have been a courtesan for whom I felt a passing fondness. I've never before met anyone I've wanted to marry. I've never asked anyone...even in jest. I've never before loved anyone. I've more cause for jealousy, Rebecca. I know you cared deeply for David and that's not easy to bear.' After a brief pause he asked huskily, 'Do you believe me?'

'Yes.' The word was immediate and whispered. Turquoise eyes limpidly attached to a steady dark gaze. She allowed herself the luxury of staring. Even when she saw him acknowledge her avid attention by relaxing back into his chair with a private smile, she still couldn't look away.

If only...ran wistfully through her head. Her inexperience had made her imagination run riot. Emotions she had never previously tasted had overwhelmed her: jealousy, passion; she knew nothing of them and could control neither. He could control both. She knew now what caused that self-mocking look that accompanied his goodnight kisses and gentle caresses. She knew why he shook and gripped the chair they sat in or the wall they rested against when she clung, reluctant ever to let him go.

He looked like that now, his jaw tense, his mouth twisted and his eyes sleepy: more so than ever. And he had deliberately shown her how easily he could change the tenor of his love-making and her pleasure; that her fulfilment was his to withhold as well as bestow. He was honest; he had never lied to her.

Yet she had lied to him on several occasions; had done so minutes before when asked why his mistresses bothered her. He wouldn't lie to her now if she asked. But she didn't want to know...she didn't... 'Since in Brighton, have you...?' she burst out.

'No one,' he said, without allowing her to finish or his expression to alter.

The next thought stopped her heart beating and she panicked and chased it out. But when it sneaked back she allowed it to rest, for living without him in Brighton, torturing herself daily with what she had needlessly thrown away, would be impossible.

It had been good enough for Charlotte Ramsden to selflessly follow the man she loved and Rebecca knew she could find the humility to do likewise. Jago Trelawney had married Charlotte, it was true. Her own chance of such happiness was now destroyed and there was no one but herself to blame. She had childishly terminated their betrothal and he had wisely pointed out the sense in it.

But while she breathed she wanted to be by him wherever he was, wherever that took her and in any way he would have her. She was sure he still wanted her. She recognised desire in those jet-fringed velvet eyes that ceaselessly caressed her.

'When you go home to Cornwall, may I come with you?' The shy plea hung, pulsating, in the quiet room. Just two months ago she had come here, stood by this door and despised him for propositioning her. Now she was back, voicing the exact proposal she had deemed an insult. She was begging him not to abandon her. 'I will be no trouble to you, I swear. I am a woman of independent means.' Her fragile pride made her stumble over her coaxing, 'If I…if we…don't suit, I will have money enough to travel to Brighton or Bristol where Simon is or—'

'You're not going to Cornwall,' he cut into her persuasion in a harsh, strangled voice. He wasn't sure whether to laugh or wail at the farce of it. But he felt racked, not only by what he'd brought her to, but his physical state. Unremitting sexual frustration coupled with the recent savage fighting and the heady exhaustion from lack of sleep had taken their toll on his mind and body. Lack of sleep, laughably, because he lay restless the night through in a waking dream of Rebecca…and what she was now sweetly willing to put at his disposal.

In her quiet, graceful way she was offering herself to him because she loved him. He knew that now for certain. Just as he knew that she was close to tears at what she thought was his rejection. But her dignity wouldn't allow her to weep or plead or attempt seduction. Wenna would have tried all three. He wondered how his brief note had been received. No doubt the banker's draft and deeds to the house in Penzance had sweetened her temper. He watched Rebecca reach for the door again, forgetting in her distress that he still had the key. She would simply try to remove herself; failing that, talk about trivialities until she could escape. And she did.

She had to get away now. She had to get away from this house, from the people chatting in the hallway, without breaking down. She was desperate for home and solitude. She retreated into conversation. 'So the matter of the Ramsden Estate is now settled,' she blurted out brightly. 'Who is to live here?'

'Newlyweds.'

'Are they from Sussex...local people?' she said distractedly, trying the doorhandle again just in case by some miracle it came open in her hand.

'She is...very local and he is new to the area.'

The information washed over her. She didn't really care who had this house, all she cared at present was how to speedily remove herself from it. She stared at the mahogany panels, feeling the hot burn of tears at the back of her eyes. 'May I have the key now?' she said in a rush. The sound of his footsteps behind made her move politely aside so he could reach the lock.

'Don't you want to know any more about these people?' he asked softly.

A swift hand slipped inconspicuously across her damp face. 'Not really. I shall move away to town so it will not affect me who lives here.'

'Well, I'll tell you about them anyway,' he said in such a deep, honeyed voice more betraying tears sprang to her eyes.

'The man's a bit of an arrogant fool,' he quietly began. 'He's not even told his beloved fiancée just how much she means to him. That the prospect of a future without her would make his life meaningless. Or that he's willing to live anywhere with her. In a hovel or a palace...anywhere so long as they are together. He's been waiting for the perfect moment to tell her all this and, of course, there never is one. He never believed he would remain long here in Sussex. While still arrogant, he thought he could take this beautiful, enchanting woman away from everything that was dear to her, treat her as though she was a precious trophy. But in his defence,' he added hoarsely, 'he always loved her...from the very first moment he saw her dripping wet in a woodland pond.'

Rebecca half-turned towards him, pain and uncertainty shadowing her delicate alabaster features. She suspected him of cruelly joking, he realised.

'Do you know what made him decide to settle here, Rebecca? Apart from the need to please his adored fiancée? It was the Summer House. That small unobtrusive building. He couldn't take it with him and couldn't leave it behind. And where else would his children play?'

She faced him fully then, wide wet turquoise eyes flying to his face.

He raised a slow, dark finger and the back of it wiped the tears from her cheeks with feather lightness. 'And he wants the manor restored...made splendid again, a fitting wedding gift for her...for them both. A gift each to the other to live in till the end of their days. Then for their children and their children's children. Renovation is about to start, so they'll have to live elsewhere for a short while. Perhaps the Summer House. What do you think she'll say, Rebecca, when this arrogant fool finally tells her all this? Will she forgive him? Still want him?'

'I think she'll say she loves him so much she would have followed him home...humbled herself just to be near him,' Rebecca solemnly murmured, her eyes fused to his.

The dark hand caressing her cheek sank, spear-fingered, into her silken honey hair and he cradled her against his shoulder. 'God, I love you. I love you so much it's like insanity,' he choked. 'I'm sorry. I should have told you sooner. I wanted everything to be perfect. It was idiocy, just pride. I wanted to give you something valuable too.'

He drew her backwards with him to the desk and sat right back in his chair, settling her on the seat in front of him, so that his muscular thighs enclosed her slender, soft ones. He slid open a drawer and withdrew two small elegant boxes and a folded paper.

'Open them,' he said hoarsely.

Unsteady white fingers raised the first lid. An exquisite ring nestled against snowy velvet: an aquamarine gem surrounded by diamonds sparked rainbow lights at her. She had never seen a jewel so awesomely lovely and she told him so. She raised the lid of the other box: a plain gold band gleamed softly.

His fingers unfolded the paper. 'A marriage licence. I've had it for weeks. I wanted to give you your betrothal ring on our day out in Brighton. I thought, as soon as we got rid of Simon and found a quiet spot. Then Ross and his young lady arrived. I was so desperate to get you alone and tell you I loved you, and talk to you about things, I probably would have hired a fishing boat and taken you to sea just for privacy and peace and quiet.' He dropped his head forward so their glossy black and honey-gold hair mingled. 'I can't wait any longer for you, Rebecca. I swear I can't.'

She swivelled against his body to look at him, aware, as he winced, of his tension and the heat radiating from him. 'I don't want to wait either. I didn't want to last time...' She flushed, and her dusky lashes screened her eyes. 'You could have stayed. I wanted you to stay,' she whispered.

'I know...and God knows, I nearly did,' he huskily told her, kissing her forehead. 'Seducing you was always easy. I could have done that two months ago. Sexually, you were made for me. You respond and fit against me as though it's the most natural place in the world for you to be.' He soothed her heating face with cool fingers. 'Don't be shy,' he said softly. 'It's right it should be that way. But I want all of you, every part. I want your heart and soul. You believed you hated me that night. You might have truly hated me if I'd stayed. For I wasn't thinking straight. I was still insane...jittery from fear of losing you and from fighting. Mostly, I was furious because you wouldn't trust me. I wanted to punish you. As ever, I ended up punishing me more,' he wryly admitted. 'I had sense enough not to want your first time to be that way.'

Long, strong arms wound her back hard against his rigid, throbbing body. She relaxed against his shoulder, her eyes closing while she dwelled on that leisurely teasing punishment. But it made her fidget and her breathing shallow.

'Which time will be that way?' she artlessly demanded.

Immediate laughter burst from him, shaking her in his arms. He kissed her neck through lavender-scented hair. 'See what I mean? You were made for me,' he growled. 'When I left you that night,' he reflected aloud, 'I rode off in a daze, unaware of where I was headed, and found myself by that woodland pool. In my lunacy, it seemed somehow fitting. It started here, I thought, so it might as well end here too. I just walked into it, at dawnlight, to cool off.' He nuzzled her neck as he continued, 'More absurd still, when I got back here and walked in dripping, Miles gave me a towel and a newspaper and didn't say a word. I'm sure he thinks I'm an escaped bedlamite.'

'Miles is a very good man. All the staff here are fine people.'

'And they love you too, Rebecca. You have that effect on people. Ross adores you. Clarkie loved you,' he said distantly. 'How long were you with him? An hour? Two? Yet he gave his life for you on that short acquaintance. I shall have to ensure that his family are cared for. I just wish he had lived so I could have properly shown him my eternal gratitude.'

They sat in blissful silence for a moment, Rebecca wrapped back against his torso with her arms covering his.

'What of Melrose?' she tentatively posed. 'What of your businesses in Cornwall? Are you truly intending to stay here permanently?'

'Yes. Tristan can take control of the mines. He has done so while I have been away and deserves as much. The shipping is my concern and operates from Bristol. I can get there as well from here as from Cornwall, when I need to. As to Melrose, it was never really mine. It belonged to my parents and I always felt that. It is a beautiful estate and we shall visit. I shall show it all to you. The cliffs, the coves, the beaches…the smuggling haunts of my youth…all of it.

'But I am a Ramsden as well as a Trelawney, and I've never

felt that more than I do now. I never needed to come here and oversee the sale of this estate. But come I did. It was my destiny. Time for one of the Cornish Ramsdens to come home. Time for the Ramsden line to have new life breathed into it…babies, nurseries…a fresh dynasty…my dynasty. I'm sure the first Jago Trelawney and Charlotte Ramsden would have approved. Aren't you?'

She nodded slowly, her face softly grazed by his unshaven jaw. 'Today when in town I reflected on my destiny. This morning I was resigned to remaining an old maid, for I was sure you no longer wanted to marry me. I am twenty-six now,' she hesitantly, regretfully told him.

He turned her face to his, suppressing humour as he read genuine concern. 'Twenty-six? It's high time you were married Rebecca,' he solemnly warned. 'Where is it exactly that your best friend lives? Close by?'

'Kay Abbott?' Rebecca queried, surprised. 'In Graveley at the vicarage. A few minute's walk from the Summer House. Why?'

'Is her husband—Adam, isn't it?—is he at home, do you think?'

'I imagine so. Yes, I saw him heading home on horseback earlier.'

'Good,' Luke said and abruptly stood up, lifting her with him.

An inkling of his intention penetrated her blissful languour. 'Surely, arrangements have to be made? He may be busy or unwilling…' she breathed.

'Is his church roof leaking?'

'Why, yes…' She broke off, noting his humour at her gravity.

'I'm sure he won't be too busy to accept the gratuitous loan of my builders to work on his church.'

'Well, what of your family? Your mother? I've not yet met your mother,' she anxiously reminded him, looking at the door.

'This is about *us*, Rebecca, not them. I've no real desire for pomp. Just for you. I want you…right now. If they become involved…' he tailed off. 'We can celebrate properly later in the week. Give them a reception. Can't we?'

She nodded, her eyes sparkling twin jewels that rivalled her glittering betrothal ring. Luke removed the aquamarine from its velvet nest and slipped it on to her slender finger. The other box was snapped closed and with the licence put into his pocket.

Rebecca looked down at her silver-grey skirts, creased from sitting so close to him and an anxious hand went to the trailing tendrils of honey hair about her face and neck. 'I look a mess,' she wailed.

'You look beautiful. You always look beautiful.'

She smiled up at his extraordinarily handsome face, the blue-black stubble shading his lean, angular jaw, making his appearance more piratical than usual. 'So do you,' she shyly whispered.

'Why, thank you, Rebecca,' he said with gracious sincerity, dipping to kiss her, as though no woman had ever before complimented him on his outstanding good looks.

He took her hand and lead her to the door and opened it with the key.

'Are you ready, Lady Ramsden?' he asked her softly with a wicked smile.

'Yes, Mr Trelawney,' she breathed.

'Say nothing,' he charged her with gentle warning, as they walked the corridor side by side. 'I'm just hoping Mother is still reclining with her smelling salts above stairs. Dammit! I've not shaved,' he muttered, wiping a testing hand across his face.

He held her elbow lightly as they traversed the hallway. The scene looked the same, Rebecca realised. Her life was perfection yet nothing in the littered hallway had changed. Ross and Katherine were still bickering. Simon was sipping from a glass of wine, one elbow propped idly against the wall as he indulgently watched them. Young Jago was crouched on the marble-flagged floor, skidding his boat against its smooth surface. Miles and Judith were bending over packing cases and discussing their contents as they moved items from one box to the other.

They walked quietly on and as Rebecca glanced again at Ross she saw he was watching them. Watching them intently. And then a slow smile just tipped his mouth and, unobtrusively, he moved his crystal goblet, toasting her, before he returned to his conversation with his sister.

They lightly descended the stone steps of the Manor and it wasn't until they reached the parkland that Luke's hand moved from her elbow to her waist and he pulled her close. Rebecca's arms immediately enclosed him in a loving hug, stretching to clasp together around his broad torso. He lifted her hard against him, kissing her and then in sheer joy spun them both about so her hair streamed out like a shining golden banner behind her and then they were walking on, in the direction of the Summer House.

*   *   *   *   *

HARLEQUIN Presents

The world's bestselling romance series...
The series that brings you your favorite authors,
month after month:

Helen Bianchin...Emma Darcy
Lynne Graham...Penny Jordan
Miranda Lee...Sandra Marton
Anne Mather...Carole Mortimer
Susan Napier...Michelle Reid

and many more uniquely talented authors!

Wealthy, powerful, gorgeous men...
Women who have feelings just like your own...
The stories you love, set in exotic, glamorous locations...

HARLEQUIN Presents

Seduction and passion guaranteed!

HARLEQUIN®
INTRIGUE

WE'LL LEAVE YOU BREATHLESS!

If you've been looking for thrilling tales of
contemporary passion and sensuous love stories
with taut, edge-of-the-seat suspense—then
you'll love Harlequin Intrigue!

Every month, you'll meet four new heroes
who are guaranteed to make your spine tingle
and your pulse pound. With them you'll enter
into the exciting world of Harlequin Intrigue—
where your life is on the line
and so is your heart!

THAT'S INTRIGUE—
ROMANTIC SUSPENSE
AT ITS BEST!

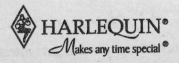

HARLEQUIN®

Makes any time special ®

Harlequin® Historical

From rugged lawmen and valiant knights to defiant heiresses and spirited frontierswomen, Harlequin Historicals will capture your imagination with their dramatic scope, passion and adventure.

Harlequin Historicals...
they're too good to miss!

HHDIR1